3–

MEMORIES OF MISTLETOE

WINTERVILLE

CARRIE ELKS

MEMORIES OF MISTLETOE by Carrie Elks

2109221

Edited by Rose David

Proofread by Proofreading by Mich

Cover Designed by The Pretty Little Design Company

1

"This place is a craphole. Did you and Dad really live here?"

Mason Parker glanced over his shoulder at his seventeen-year-old brother. Ty's nose wrinkled as he looked around the old cabin. Mason reminded himself—for what felt like the hundredth time since he'd picked Ty up yesterday morning—that his kid brother had every right to be annoyed about being here.

Even if he was already getting on his last nerve.

"Yes we lived here," Mason said, his voice low. "It wasn't so worn down then." And the floor wasn't strewn with paper and crockery and what looked suspiciously like animal crap.

"You should have gotten a cleaning service," Ty said, shaking his head. "This is gonna take you months to sort out."

"Us," Mason corrected him. "Months for *us* to clean it up. Anyway, it won't take months, just a few days." And wasn't that part of the plan? Put Ty to work so he didn't get so easily distracted by gangs and girls and cars, and anything else that took his attention away from his studies.

"I'm not cleaning this up." In the gloom of the cabin, Ty looked older than his seventeen years, mostly thanks to the square jaw they'd both inherited from their dad. He had his mom's coloring, though. His hair was a dirty blond, a sharp contrast to Mason's dark brown crop, and right now it was falling over his furrowed brow.

"If you want somewhere to eat and sleep, you will." Mason took a deep breath and looked around the cabin. It was much smaller than he remembered. But he also hadn't been here for over twenty years. The last time he'd stepped foot onto this wooden floor he'd been about half the height he was now.

It was watertight, that was one good thing. Whatever had come in and made all of this mess had entered through the front door. It was swinging open when they'd arrived. Maybe it had been open ever since he and his dad had left in a hurry, turning their back on this cabin and on Winterville for what he'd thought was for good.

He was wrong. But then he'd been wrong about a lot of things lately. Not that he wanted to think about that right now.

"This place got a bathroom?" Ty asked. "Or should I pee on the floor?"

"Through there." Mason inclined his head at a door to their left. There were four doors in total leading out of the main room. Two bedrooms, a bathroom, and a closet. This room was the living, eating, and cooking area. It was simple, but it worked.

Or at least, he hoped it would.

Running his thumb over his beard, he took in the state of the place. The damage really was cosmetic. Sure, they'd need new furniture once they cleaned it up, and some of the kitchen appliances would need updating, but he could handle that. And in the meantime they had sleeping bags and blow up mattresses.

Ty's face had a tinge of green when he walked back out of the bathroom. "It's disgusting." His arm brushed Mason's as he walked past him. "I'll do it outside."

"While you're out there, get the cleaning stuff out of the truck," Mason suggested. "You can start with the bathroom."

But Ty had already gone. Mason checked his watch. It was almost three. They'd been driving since eight that morning. He was dog tired, and not just from concentrating on the road, but from dealing with Ty's tantrums as they drove higher into the mountains and further away from civilization.

This had been the first place he'd thought of when his stepmother had called, telling him that either he take his brother or she'd surrender him to the foster system. Mason wasn't sure if she'd really follow through with that threat, but he wasn't about to take the chance.

He'd had enough experience with the foster system as a kid to know that he'd never willingly let a family member into its clutches. Not even when the family member was a bratty teenager who thought he knew everything.

Footsteps clattered back up the front steps. "Okay, I get it," Ty said. The bravado he'd usually worn like a suit of armor had vanished. "If I don't behave, I'll have to live here. Can we go back to Baltimore now? To Mom's?"

"You know you can't go back there, kid." Mason's chest felt tight. He could remember feeling abandoned like this. Afraid. His future completely out of his control. "It's only for a few months. We'll enroll you in school, you'll get your diploma here, and then you'll go to college."

"What if I don't want to go to college?" Ty's eyes narrowed.

"Then you'll get a job."

Tyler swallowed. "And if I don't want to do that?"

"You don't get a choice. You'll be an adult. Either you get educated or you get to work."

"You're one to talk. You're an adult, so where's your job?" Ty asked. "Look at what your fancy college education got you. No job, no house, just this hellhole of a cabin that neither of us want to be in."

"It gave me choices," Mason said, his jaw tight. "I chose to leave my job."

Ty shook his head. "What kind of idiot chooses to be poor?"

"Did you bring the cleaning stuff in?" Mason asked, ignoring the jab.

Ty shook his head. "Was I supposed to?"

Yes, but Mason didn't need any more arguments right now. "Actually, I'm going to head into town to pick up some heating oil. Plus some food and a cooler." He also wanted to get a door lock from the hardware store. "You can start cleaning this place while I'm gone."

"Why can't I come with you?" Ty asked him.

Because if we spend any more time together we'll end up strangling each other. "Because it'll be quicker this way. I'll tell you what, you clean up this room and I won't make you touch the bathroom."

Ty knew a good thing when he heard it. "Okay..." He looked around, his brow furrowed. "Hey, there aren't wolves around here, are there? Or bears?"

"There are black bears, but they'll be more afraid of you than you are of them."

"You think that's what came in here?" Ty asked. "A bear?"

"Maybe. Probably looking for food. They're solitary, they don't like people. More like Yogi Bear than grizzlies."

Ty's expression was blank. "More what?"

"Yogi Bear? You know," Mason said. "Smarter than the average bear..."

Ty blinked. "I've no idea what you're talking about."

Of course he didn't. They might be brothers, but Mason

was almost old enough to be his father. He'd been seventeen when Ty was born–the same age Ty was now. A boy in a man's body, angry at the world.

He was still pretty furious. He just liked to hide it more.

"Don't worry about it," Mason said, waving that thought away. "They're pretty lethargic at this time of year, so the likelihood of seeing one is pretty small. Just tidy up and I'll be back with food and supplies, okay?"

"Okay." Ty nodded. "Can I play some music while I do it?"

"Go for it."

Ty looked slightly mollified. "What's the Wi-Fi password?"

Mason rolled his eyes. "Gonna have to use your 4G, buddy. We're not connected yet."

Ty grimaced. "I don't have much data left. I'll play something I've downloaded."

"Good call." Mason pulled the keys to the truck from his pocket and headed for the door, looking over his shoulder at his brother. "I'll be back in a bit. Get as much cleaned as you can, okay?"

"Got it."

Pulling the door closed behind him, Mason exhaled heavily, his warm breath turning to vapor in the icy cold West Virginia air. In the distance, the snowy tops of the mountains sparkled in the winter sunshine. Between the cabin and the mountains was a thick line of trees. Between the evergreens there were red maples, their branches bereft of leaves.

From here he could just about see the balls of mistletoe clustered in the top branches. Or 'Kiss and Go' his dad had called it. Mason blinked the memory away. He didn't need sentimentality right now.

Or ever, really.

He'd done the right thing in bringing Ty here, even if his brother didn't know it yet. Sure, the cabin needed work. But it would keep Ty out of trouble and that was the point. To keep him away from temptation and make sure he got his high school diploma. If Mason could do that, then he'd done his job as an older brother.

And done more for Ty than anybody had ever done for him.

He pulled the truck door open and glanced toward the mountain peak. There was another house there. It was sturdier than the cabin. Brick by the looks of it. And almost sparkling new.

Ah well, whoever lived there probably preferred keeping to themselves, too. Why else would they build a house outside of town?

Climbing into the cab, he closed the door and rubbed his hands together to warm them up.

It was going to be okay. It had to be. For both their sakes.

Alaska Winter smiled as her favorite festive song blasted out of her car's speakers. Sure, it was only the first week of November, but as far as she was concerned you couldn't listen to Christmas music early enough. Especially when Mariah was hitting the high notes like the queen she was.

She sang along, taking a right onto the country lane that led to her new house. Well, it wasn't that new anymore. She'd moved in six months ago, much to the annoyance of her family. They hated the way it was so remote, but that was the exact reason she loved it. She felt peaceful here, away from the hustle and bustle of her job at the Winterville Inn.

Sure, the road could get cut off in a raging snowstorm, but she had skis. If she needed to, she could still get to town. But she was the baby of the family and even at thirty they still liked to coddle her.

As her house came into view, a large black truck passed her. She glanced in the rear-view mirror, watching it get smaller in the distance. She wasn't used to seeing other cars on this road. Since she'd bought the little house nestled into the hills, she was the only one who used it, apart from the mailman and her family when they came to visit.

As she approached the old cabin near her house, she could see that the door was wide open. She slowed down to look. In the summer, some kids had tried, and failed, to light a fire behind it. The last thing the volunteer firefighters needed was a pointless call out to deal with bored teenagers. She knew most of the firefighters since birth–that was Winterville for you. Everybody knew everybody, and they were always up in each other's business.

A flash of movement caught her eye. A man walked out of the cottage and onto the stoop. She slowed down enough to watch as he carried what looked like a box full of papers into the white-covered yard. That's when she realized he wasn't a man. Maybe a teenaged boy. Sure, he had the height and breadth of somebody in their twenties, but the softness of his face gave him away.

Bringing the car to a stop, she rolled down her window and leaned out. "Hey!" She put a friendly smile on her face because this kid didn't look like he was here to set fire to anything. "You moving in?"

The kid looked up, his eyes wide as they caught hers. "Uh, yeah. That's right."

So she was going to have neighbors. A little thrill rushed through her. She liked the tranquility of this area, but it was always nice to meet new people. She opened the car door and climbed out, her boots crunching against the snow on the side of the road. "Welcome!" she said, still smiling. "I'm your neighbor. I live up there." She pointed at her cottage, about two hundred yards up the road. "Are your mom and dad here?"

"No."

She blinked. "But you're not moving in alone, right?"

He shook his head and relief rushed through her. "My brother's gone to town to get some supplies."

He shivered, and she realized how cold it was. The boy didn't even have a winter coat on. Just a jacket that would do nothing to shield him from the bracing mountain winds. "You should go inside," she urged. "Warm up. Do you have something hot to drink?"

"The stove isn't working. My brother's gone to get some oil."

Well, she couldn't leave him here. Truth be told, she was annoyed at his brother—whoever he was–for leaving the kid here alone. "What's your name?"

"Should I tell you? You're a stranger." There was humor to his voice. It felt like she'd melted through a polar ice block.

"I'll tell you mine then you can tell me yours. My name's Alaska," she said.

He lifted a brow. "I'm Texas."

She laughed. "Stop that." She grinned, and he smiled back. It felt like another victory.

"I'm Ty," he admitted. "Tyler, but nobody calls me that."

"Well, Ty, how about you come to my place and I'll make us both some hot chocolate? I'll put the fire on and you can warm up there."

He glanced at the cottage in the distance longingly. "I shouldn't go. My brother will be mad."

"Did he drive into Winterville to pick up supplies?"

"Yeah."

"When did he leave?"

"About five minutes ago," Ty said.

That must have been the truck she passed.

"He'll be gone for at least half an hour. Just come and warm up for a little while." She lifted her brows. "I have hot chocolate and marshmallows. And homemade cookies."

"That's what all the serial killers say," he pointed out.

She laughed again and this time he joined in.

"Okay, look," she told him. "I'm a hundred and ten pounds. You're, what... a hundred and eighty?"

"Something like that."

"I think you'll be safe with me. But why don't you leave your brother a note? That way he can come join us when he gets back."

He looked at her for a moment, as though assessing her. "Okay, I'll come."

She climbed back into the car, turning the ignition on and cranking the heat. A minute later Ty was wrenching at the passenger door, breathless, as though he'd been running around the house.

"You left a note?" she asked.

"Yeah." He tipped his head. "How about you?"

"What about me?"

"You tell anybody you're taking me to your house?" he asked.

Alaska blinked. "No, why would I?"

He gave her a pointed look. "Because I could be the serial killer instead of you. Did you think of that?"

2

The last time he'd been in Winterville it had been the height of summer. Mason had been on school vacation and his dad had packed them both up and brought them to his little cabin in the mountains. He could barely remember the place. His memories were all hazy, like old photographs that had turned orange and faded.

It was still festive as hell, though. And full of people. Somehow, that put him in a bad mood. It was November. Halloween had just happened. Did he really have to listen to festive music as he attempted to fill his cart with food for him and Ty?

"That'll be fifty-seven dollars and eighty-one cents," the cashier said, putting the last of his groceries into a brown paper bag.

He handed his credit card over. The cashier smiled at him as she read his name embossed across the front. "Thank you, Mason." She said his name loudly.

He winced and waited for her to give him back his card.

"You're new here," she said, still looking at his name.

He really didn't want to make small talk. He wanted to get

home and get to working on the cabin. "Yup." He picked the brown bag up. "Just staying for a few months with my brother."

"And Mrs. Parker?" the cashier asked, leaning closer like a journalist attempting to get a scoop. "Is she staying, too?"

"No."

"But there *is* a Mrs. Parker?" the cashier asked, not getting the message that he didn't want to talk.

"Do you need anything else from me?" he asked, holding his hand out for his credit card.

"Oh, no." Her smile faltered. "You have a nice day." She passed the card back to him and he shoved it into his pocket with his free hand.

"Hope to see you again soon!" she called out.

"Sure," he muttered. Carrying the bags to his truck, he laid them in the flatbed, then walked over to the coffee shop and ordered two hot chocolates. The woman behind the counter smiled as she worked to make the drinks.

"I haven't seen you before," she said, frothing up the milk. "You here for the weekend?"

It was just another friendly conversation. He knew that. But he still didn't like people knowing his business. "Here for a while," he muttered. "Fixing up the old cabin on the road to Marshall's Gap."

"The Parker place?" the woman asked.

He blinked. "Yeah."

"I remember the owner. He and his son came in here a few times." She smiled. "Must have been back in the nineties, or maybe the early aughts." She wrinkled her nose. "Time takes on a different meaning at my age."

Mason shifted his feet. "I guess it does."

"So you bought the place from them?"

"Something like that."

She didn't seem perturbed by his shifty answers. "Wait a

minute," she said, squeezing whipped cream onto the hot chocolates. "Are *you* a Parker?"

No point in lying. The cashier at the grocery store already knew it. He had a feeling the whole town would know by nightfall. "Yes, ma'am."

"You're the boy who used to come in," she said, a smile pulling at her lips. "Oh my goodness, yes. I can see the resemblance." She put her hand across the counter. "I'm Dolores. We've met before but I don't expect you remember. You used to love my ginger cookies. Let me give you some to take back with you." She grabbed a paper bag. "A welcome home present. On the house."

"You don't have to do that." He couldn't remember the cookies at all. And to tell the truth, he wanted to get out of here and back to Ty. His kid brother might be in the middle of nowhere, but that didn't mean he couldn't get into trouble.

"Of course I do." She passed him over the cookies. "Are you here with your family?" she asked as he took the bag from her. Through the paper, the cookies were warm to the touch and the ginger smelled amazing.

"Just my younger brother."

"You'll have to bring him next time you're in town. See if we can tempt him with some cookies."

"I'll do that," he said gruffly.

He held out his card and she waved him away. "Everything's on the house today. Call it a welcome back gift."

"I like to pay my way."

"Then make sure you come back," she told him. "I'll charge you next time."

For the first time since he'd arrived, he smiled. It was small and yeah, a little grudging, but he owed it to her anyway. "I will."

"Good." She turned her attention to the customer behind him as he gave her a nod and took his drinks and cookies.

Taking them back to the truck, he placed them on the roof as he let himself in, then slid them into the cup holders and started up the engine.

"Ty?" he called out from the front steps of the cabin. "Get your ass out here and bring in these bags."

Nothing. Typical. Ty had probably put his ear buds in and cranked up the volume. He had an annoying habit of doing that. Shaking his head, Mason carried the hot chocolate and cookies into the cabin. Nobody was touching them until the truck was unloaded.

"Ty?" he said again, frowning. "You in the bedroom?"

Still no reply. Just weird silence. He put the cups and bag onto an empty space on the kitchen counter, the movement ruffling all the papers piled up on the side. "Ty?" he bellowed. "Where the hell are you?"

His heart raced. He went into the bedroom, then the bathroom, even wrenching the closet open in case for some bizarre reason Ty was hiding in there. Then he circled the exterior of the cabin, hoping against hope he'd find his brother peeing against a tree, but there was nothing. No tracks except the ones they'd made earlier.

Okay. Breathe. He exhaled heavily and tried to think about what to do. There was no sign of a struggle. Well, that wasn't strictly true. If there was any struggle, it wouldn't have made the cabin look any worse than it did already.

But there was no sign of animals. That was a good thing. Not that he thought a pack of wolves had eaten his brother. They'd probably choke on his scrawny ass.

He grabbed his phone from his pocket, frowning when there was no message there. But at least he had service.

Tapping his finger on the screen, he pulled up Ty's number, half expecting to hear his phone ring in the cabin.

The dial tone buzzed twice before it connected. And damn if his heart didn't almost leap out of his chest.

"Mase?" Ty's voice echoed from the earpiece.

"Where are you?" It came out terser than he'd intended. But dammit, Ty was supposed to stay in the cabin.

"Having hot chocolate and warming up with our neighbor."

"What?"

"At the house up the road. She stopped and offered me a drink. She's not a serial killer, I checked first."

He heard somebody chuckle. A woman.

"Come home now," he instructed. "You have chores to do."

"You should come here. She says she'll make you a drink. She has cookies, too."

"I have hot chocolate and cookies," Mason pointed out. "I bought us some in Winterville."

"Please come here and say hi," Ty said, his voice tight like he was gritting his teeth. "She's nice, and she's our neighbor."

The last thing Mason expected was a lecture from his brother on being neighborly. "I'll be there in five. But then you're coming home. We have work to do."

"Sure. Whatever. Just get your ass over here."

"He's on his way," Ty told Alaska, shoving his phone back in his pocket. He was on his second hot chocolate and fifth cookie. It always amazed her how much teenagers could eat.

She smiled, remembering when her guy cousins were teenage boys and used to send their grandmother crazy every time they stayed at the Inn. They'd clear the cabinets of her penthouse faster than a plague of locusts. There were three of them–North, Gabe, and Kris. Plus her sister, Everley, and her cousin, Holly, making them a band of six.

Well, more now, since Holly had gotten married and had a baby. And Everley had reconnected with her long lost love. Then there was Gabe, currently living in bliss with his new wife, Nicole.

"Does your brother prefer coffee or chocolate?" Alaska asked Ty.

"Chocolate. He has a sweet tooth even though he'll deny it." Ty pressed his lips together. He'd already told her that his brother was seventeen years older than him. Almost the same age as her cousins. Maybe she could introduce them. They all loved meeting new people.

"So listen," Ty continued. "He's been grumpy as hell for weeks. If he's horrible, it's not his fault."

She blinked. "Okay..."

"Seriously. I've pissed him off. His job has pissed him off. My mom... yeah well. He's dealing with a lot."

She nodded slowly. "I'll take that into account. Maybe I can charm him with cookies."

"Good luck with that," Ty muttered.

Two minutes later, they heard footsteps on the front porch, followed by a hammering at the door. Alaska shot Ty a smile, and he immediately stood up. "I'll get it," he blurted out. "You... ah... wait here."

Ty all but ran into her hallway and wrenched the door open. For a moment there was silence, followed by a low, muttered conversation. She could make out a few words.

"Be nice." That was Ty.

"I am." Gruff. Low. The sort of voice that sent shivers down your spine.

"No, I mean real nice. Alaska's a good person. And she makes great cookies."

She tried to not smile at Ty's description of her.

"I don't give a shit if she's a Michelin chef. You don't go off without asking me first." And then her smile melted, because that was her fault. And Ty was getting in trouble for it.

"Hi!" she shouted out. "I'm Alaska. Come on in."

Silence. The voices lowered until she couldn't hear them at all.

"Just a minute," Ty finally called out. "We'll be right there."

This was awkward. She couldn't sit and listen to this any longer. Not when she'd caused a misunderstanding between the brothers. Putting her half-empty mug down on the coffee table, she stood and smoothed her skirt down.

The conversation was still going on when she walked into the hallway. She painted a smile on her lips, ready to admit this was all her fault.

And then her eyes clashed with his.

They were icy blue and looked pissed as hell beneath his dark, cropped hair. If she thought Ty was big, this guy was a giant. She should probably be afraid. The man was built like a damn mountain. Probably best not to annoy him too much.

"Um... hi." She lifted a hand to wave at him.

He nodded. "Thank you for looking after Ty. We'll be leaving now." He glanced at his brother. "Get your coat on."

"But my drink..." Ty protested.

"Now!"

Alaska blew out a mouthful of air. They were her only neighbors for miles and she'd already annoyed him. "Please come in. Ty hasn't finished his drink and food. I've made plenty of hot chocolate. You can have some, too."

"I have drinks at the cabin."

"Oh, come on," she said, tipping her head to the side. "One little drink won't hurt you."

"We have work to do. And if we don't get it done before tonight, then we won't have anywhere to sleep."

"You could stay here," she said helpfully. "I have a spare room."

Ty turned to look at her, his eyes lit up. "We could?"

"No thank you," his brother said. "We can look after ourselves. And you shouldn't offer a room to people you don't know."

Wait until he learned that she ran the Winterville Inn. She tried not to laugh at that thought.

"Well, at least let me cook you dinner," she said, still trying to offer an olive branch. "That way you won't have to stop working until it's ready. Shall we say seven?"

"What are you cooking?" Ty asked, his voice hopeful.

"I bought canned chili. We're all good." The man's eyes connected with hers again. And yep, her heart did a little leap. Since when did she find grumpy-ass men sexy? She had no idea why she was being so friendly. Yes, he was pleasant to look at. Okay more than pleasant. But he didn't need to bite her head off at every turn.

"I'm Alaska Winter," she said.

"One of the Winters who runs Winterville, right?"

"Yeah." She nodded. "I run the hotel."

"Okay then. You're a busy woman. I'd hate to keep you from doing your work."

"Mase, let's come for dinner." Ty sounded exasperated. "It'll give us more time to work."

Ty's brother closed his eyes and pinched the bridge of his nose as though he was in physical pain. When he opened them again, she knew he was going to capitulate. His gaze was softer. Less furious. "Okay," he managed. "Thank you. Now Ty, get back to the house and start clearing up. We have a couple of hours of daylight left."

Knowing he was onto a good thing, Ty shot her a grin

then ducked under his brother's arm, heading out into the cold air. Leaving the two of them alone–Mr. Grumpy at the door, her in the hallway, thankful for the space between them.

"Miss Winter..." Mr. Grumpy said, looking back at her.

"It's Alaska," she corrected him.

He closed his eyes again. It was like he was on the edge of something. A nervous breakdown maybe. "Okay, Alaska..."

"I don't know *your* name," she pointed out.

"Mason Parker."

It suited him. A man of stone. "Yes, Mason," she said. "How can I help you?"

"Please stop distracting my brother. I'm trying to put him to work."

"He's seventeen. His whole life is distraction," she said lightly. "I remember being that age. Don't you?"

Was he rolling his eyes? "Yes, I do." There was something in his voice she couldn't put her finger on. It sounded twisted. Almost painful. "We'll come to dinner," he said. "But that's it. No more distractions, no more hot chocolates. Ty is here to work and finish school. After that we'll be gone."

She blinked. "Most people just offer to bring dessert."

Mason frowned. "What?"

Alaska folded her arms in front of her. "When somebody asks somebody else to dinner, they say yes and ask what they can bring. They don't give the host a lecture about distraction."

He stared at her. "Can I bring something to dinner?"

"What ya got?" she asked him chirpily.

"Canned chili," he replied, deadpan.

Her lips twitched. Was there a sense of humor in there? "In that case, just bring yourselves."

He inhaled sharply, his nose flaring. How the hell could he make that look sexy? Yet somehow he did. "Okay. We'll see you at seven. Thank you." He turned on his heel, his shoulders almost hitting the door jamb. She watched as he took her front steps two at a time, her eyes settling on his long, thick thighs.

"Oh Mason?" she called out.

He turned, frowning. "Yeah?"

"You guys can do the dishes."

3

It was just Mason's luck that they'd moved next door to Little Miss Sunshine. It irked him, because he knew her type. Always smiling, always neighborly, always interfering. And making him feel like an ass because all he wanted to do was mind his own business.

"She's nice, huh?" Ty said, when Mason had caught up with him. "Friendly, too. Do you think she'll invite us around a lot? Because I can't survive on canned chili."

"We'll clean out the living room and kitchen first," Mason told his brother, ignoring his question about their new neighbor. "Tonight we'll bunk down in there next to the fire. Tomorrow, we'll get the bedrooms ready and go into town to buy anything we need." Starting with new furniture. And a stove.

"We don't want to buy too much," Ty said, struggling to keep up with Mason despite his long legs. "I mean, we won't be here forever, will we?"

"Whatever we buy for your room you can take with you to college."

Ty blinked. "And if I don't go to college?"

"Then you can take it wherever you want to go." He wasn't having this conversation again. "Grab that box from the cab, can you?"

They reached the cabin, and he pushed the door open, Ty following behind with the cleaning supplies An entire box filled with cloths and brushes, bleach and Lysol, and thick trash bags they'd take to the dump tomorrow once they were full. That's if it was open on the weekend. He wasn't sure how this town worked. Maybe that had been the draw of the place.

Somewhere to hide away. Lick his wounds. Work out what the hell he wanted to do with the rest of his life while he tried to help his brother start his.

He picked up a trash bag and handed it to Ty, then unfurled the other one in his thick hands. "Okay," he told his brother. "You start with the fireplace. I'll start with the kitchen. We might be eating out tonight, but tomorrow we'll be cooking our own food." He looked carefully at his brother. "Did you call your mom?"

Ty shook his head.

Mason pressed his lips together. "You need to call her."

"She doesn't care about me."

There was an aching note to Ty's voice that made him sound like the kid he still was. Mason's throat felt tight. He wasn't used to dealing with emotions. He'd long since learned to ignore them.

"Call her," he said. "Or at least send her a message."

Ty shot him a sullen look, but still took his phone from his pocket. "All right already." He unlocked the screen, rolling his eyes. "Dear Mommy, made it safely to Disneyland. Wish you were here. And that you weren't a bitch."

"Ty!"

"What? She *is* a bitch."

"She's had enough." And so had Mason. "You really want

to annoy her? Because she could call CPS tomorrow and they'd come take you."

Ty swallowed. "No."

"Then send the message and get to cleaning." Mason turned his back on his brother, mostly because if he kept looking at him he'd probably explode. How the hell were they going to live in this enclosed space together for the next six months without killing each other?

Alaska prepared homemade beef pot pies. Two of them because she was used to the appetites of big, healthy men and she knew how pissy they could get when they were hungry.

Not that Mason needed hunger to be pissy. He seemed to be a natural at it.

And yet you thought he was sexy. Why is that?

She wrinkled her nose at that thought. She wasn't attracted to him, she was bored. And he was somebody new, somebody different. That was all. One of the problems about living in the small town you grew up in was that most guys were your friends, your exes, or the ones you'd been rejecting since you were a teenager.

She pulled the pies out of the oven to cool a little, before checking the roasted vegetables that were caramelizing nicely still in the oven. A huge pan of potatoes was boiling ferociously on the stove top, ready to be mashed when they reached the right tenderness. If nothing else, she was going to feed those boys well. Maybe then she might even get a smile from Mason.

She was draining the potatoes when they knocked at the door.

"Come in," she yelled. "It's open."

She heard the door open then slam closed. Followed by the telltale click of her lock.

"Shouldn't keep it unlocked," Mason said as he walked into the kitchen. She looked up from the stove. He'd put on a fresh shirt and it looked like he'd combed his hair. Her stomach did a little twist.

"Until the bears get opposable thumbs, I think I'm safe." She smiled at him, pouring the potatoes back into the pot. "Ty, how are you at mashing potatoes?"

Ty blinked. "Okay, I think."

"Great." She handed him a masher. "Cream and butter are in the fridge. Get them as smooth as you can. No lumps."

He didn't look surprised to be asked to help. More relieved than anything. Maybe it was the aroma of food.

"By the way, you look nice," she told him.

"Mase made me put on a clean shirt," he grumbled.

"It suits you."

She turned to Mason who was still hovering in the doorway, so bulky he blocked out most of the light from the hall. "Can I get you a drink?" she asked him. "I have wine and beer, or sodas if you prefer."

"A beer would be good." He lifted his hand up, and it was only then that she noticed the flowers. "These are for you."

She blinked as he handed her the roses. "They're beautiful. Thank you."

"It was my idea," Ty said, using both hands to push the masher into the potatoes. "Told him he needed to apologize for being an ass."

"That's a lovely gesture," she told Ty, then smiled at Mason. "I'll get you that beer."

She'd changed from her work clothes into a soft woolen dress and knit tights. Nothing fancy, just cozy and comfortable. Her hair was twisted into a messy bun to keep it out of the way of the cooking. She had so much of it that she dreaded a stray lock dropping into the food.

"Ty, what can I get you?" she asked as she pulled a bottle of beer from the refrigerator.

"I'll have a beer, too."

"No, you won't," Mason said gruffly. "He'll have some soda."

"Mom lets me drink beer at home," Ty protested, stopping his smashing of the potatoes.

"It's illegal," Mason said. "And you really don't need more trouble with the police."

She ignored the pulse of curiosity that went through her at the mention of 'more trouble' and sent Mason a sympathetic smile.

"So do you have any other siblings?" she asked, handing Mason his beer and Tyler a can of soda. She poured a glass of wine for herself and gestured at the kitchen table for Mason to sit down.

"Just the two of us," Mason said.

"How about you?" Ty asked. "Where's your family?" He took a sip of soda. "Or don't you have any?"

"Oh, I have lots of family." She smiled wryly. "Most of them live in Winterville or on the outskirts. I have a sister, Everley, and a cousin that's like a sister named Holly. Then I have three guy cousins. Two of them live in town and the other is in London."

She and her cousins owned a lot of the businesses in Winterville. They'd bought them after the matriarch of the family, Candy, had died. Candy had built Winterville up from a small town into the tourist attraction it was today, complete with a sprawling inn run by Alaska, the Jingle Bell Theater that Everley directed, a Christmas Tree farm run by their cousin, North, and now a ski resort that their cousin, Gabe, and cousin-in-law, Josh, had built and were running.

And Holly, their cousin with a head for numbers, oversaw the whole thing. Together, they made a formidable team.

"And your parents?" Ty asked. "Are they here, too?"

She blinked. "They live in Florida." And she barely saw them. They weren't so much snowbirds as permanent residents now. Had been for a while. "How about you?"

"My mom's in Baltimore," Ty said. There was a dullness to his voice that made her feel sad. "And our dad's dead."

"Oh, I'm sorry." She shot a look at Mason, worried about what to say. He shrugged.

"Do you have a boyfriend?" Ty asked her. Mason muttered something under his breath that sounded suspiciously like 'for fuck's sake'.

"No," she told Ty.

"Why not? You're pretty enough."

She wasn't sure whether to laugh or cry. "Thank you. I think. But I'm not really on the market. I enjoy living alone." She winked at him. "Nobody to tell me what to do."

"I long for those days," Ty said, letting out a deep sigh.

"Graduate from college and you can have them," Mason said. He was sitting on one of her wooden kitchen chairs, his body dominating it. His long legs were stretched out in front of him, the denim of his jeans tight against his substantial thighs. She lifted her eyes up quickly, and he was looking at her carefully.

Yeah, that was the word. Careful. Like his gaze could hurt if he didn't control it.

"So you're planning on going to college then?" she asked Ty. He'd added cream and butter to the potatoes and was stirring it through.

"I don't know. Mason wants me to, clearly."

"I just want you to get yourself settled. Get a job that pays your way. You don't want to be reliant on anybody else."

Ty let out a grunt. She sensed they were on dangerous

ground. "You're still in school at the moment though?" she asked, sensing a change of subject would be good right now.

"I start on Monday."

"At Marshall High?"

"Yeah." Ty nodded.

"That's where I went." She smiled at him. "You'll love it. You getting the bus?"

"I guess so."

"I know a few of the teachers there," Alaska told Ty. "And some students, too. Some of them work for me on weekends at the Inn."

"You run an Inn?" Ty asked, interested.

"Yeah. The Winterville Inn. Have you seen it? It's hard to miss when you drive into town."

"I haven't been there yet," Ty said. "Is it nice?"

Her face lit up. "It is. So lovely, especially at this time of year. It's our peak tourist season, so it gets busy, but there's always lots to do."

"And you employ teenagers?" Ty asked.

"Yes. We need the extra help on the weekends."

"Do you have any vacancies?" He suddenly looked excited.

"Um." She glanced over at Mason. His eyes caught hers and he shrugged. "We'd definitely welcome an extra pair of hands. Why don't I give you an application once you've settled in at school?"

"Yeah," Ty said, nodding. "That'd be great. I want to save up for a car. Nobody should ride the bus at my age."

"You'll probably make friends who can give you a ride," Alaska said. "And if I'm heading that way, I'm happy to drop you off."

Mason had been silent the whole time, but she could feel the burn of his stare. Was he always this quiet?

"Potatoes are done," Ty said, holding the pan up to show her.

"Thank you." She smiled at him. "Why don't you sit down and I'll serve it up."

Ty washed his hands–impressive that a teenager did that without being asked–and pulled out one of the empty chairs. Alaska pulled three plates from the rack and placed them on the counter, putting a generous helping of pie and potatoes on two of them and a smaller portion for her on the other. The roasted vegetables — carrots, turnips, and onions — smelled delicious as she placed them on the plates.

"This smells amazing," Ty said as she slid a plate in front of him. "I can't believe we almost had canned chili."

"Don't get too happy, we'll be eating that tomorrow." Mason nodded at her as she gave him his plate. "Thank you. It looks delicious."

She felt like she'd won some kind of prize. He didn't seem like the type that gave praise out easily.

"Dive in," she told them. "There's more where that came from, and I don't want to be eating leftovers for a week."

Ty lifted his silverware and gave her a grin. "There's no chance of that."

4

Mason pulled his truck into the Marshall High School parking lot the following Monday. They'd spent the entire weekend getting the cabin habitable and his body was aching. There was more to do, but it was a start.

"You're not walking in with me," Ty warned, releasing his seatbelt. "Wait five minutes and then you can come in."

"We have a meeting with the principal," Mason reminded him. "We need to be in there together."

Ty let out an annoyed grunt and climbed out of the car. It had taken from dawn 'til dusk on Saturday to clean out the cabin. On Sunday, he'd made a simple bedframe for Ty's room and installed the new stove—or at least new to them—that he'd bought off Craigslist from someone in Marshall's Gap.

Today he'd make his own bed. Simple, again, with wood he'd bought from Walker Woods, a local forestry company. Eventually, he'd replace all the furniture—though chairs would be trickier.

Ty couldn't understand why they didn't drive to Ikea like everybody else. But that wasn't the point. He wasn't like everybody else. He never had been. And he was okay with that. In fact, he liked it.

He'd always walked to the beat of his own drum. He'd had to.

The hallway was empty when they pushed open the front doors. The first class must have already begun. But it was the smell of it that hit Mason in the gut. How the hell could all high schools smell so familiar no matter where they were?

Reception was on the right of the hallway, a big gap in the wall covered with a sliding window. Ty gave Mason another warning look then walked over and pressed the bell on the counter.

Within five minutes they were being shown to Principal Tasker's office, a large room with a window overlooking the sports field. The walls were lined with shelves stuffed full of books and file boxes, and in the center of the dark green carpeted floor was an oversized desk.

"Tyler Parker," Principal Tasker said, standing from her enormous leather chair. She looked to be in her fifties, with pale blonde hair and a pair of red glasses balanced on the bridge of her nose. "And you must be..." she glanced down at a file on her desk, "Mason. Tyler's brother?"

"That's right." Mason nodded. Tyler was unusually silent.

"Please take a seat. We won't be long." She gestured at the chairs on the other side of her desk. They were formed from metal tubing with seat pads made of fuzzy velvet material that had clearly seen better days.

They both sat and from the corner of his eye Mason could see his brother swallow hard.

"It's very unusual for us to have somebody transfer so late in their high school career," Principal Tasker told Ty. "I've looked at the transcripts from your old school and have put you in what I think will be the right classes for you. But as our curriculums aren't exactly the same as your old school, each teacher will work with you to catch you up as quickly as possible."

Tyler nodded, still staying silent.

"I also noticed there have been a few disciplinary warnings as well," Principal Tasker continued. She looked up from the file, her eyes catching Ty's. "We don't tolerate fights here. No matter who started them."

Tyler shifted in his seat. "I won't be fighting."

"And you won't be getting in trouble with the police either?" she asked him, lifting a brow. So she'd seen that, too.

"No," he said in a small voice.

She smiled. "Good. I've scheduled you in for a meeting with the school counselor this week during your study hall. It's listed on your schedule."

"I don't need to see a counselor, I'm fine," Ty said, frowning. Mason nudged his foot against his brother's and Ty stubbornly moved his leg away.

"It's customary for all transferees. Usually you transfer for a reason. And settling into school so late in the year can be difficult. This is your chance to offload and find support if you need it. Go to the meeting and if you don't want to see the counselor again, then fine. But at least try it," she urged.

Ty crossed his arms over his chest. "All right."

She smiled. "Good." She held out a piece of paper. "Here's a printed copy of your class schedule. It'll also be online and you'll have access to that when you're given your login at lunchtime. If you flip it over, there's a map of the school." She smiled at him as Ty took the paper. "Why don't you go to your first class? Mr. Rayment is expecting you." She looked over at Mason. "Could you stay for a moment so I can finish up some paperwork with you?"

"Sure." Mason nodded. Ty scrambled for his bag, stuffing the schedule into the front flap. As he stood he caught

Mason's eye, sending him a stare that looked suspiciously like begging.

Please don't embarrass me.

"I'll pick you up at three," Mason told his brother.

"It's okay, I'll catch the bus." Ty reached the door. Mason wanted to tell him to thank Principal Tasker, but hell, he wasn't Ty's parent and he sure as hell had no place to teach him about politeness.

So he sat still until the door closed behind him and Principal Tasker turned her attention to him.

"Mr. Parker."

"Mason is fine," he told her.

A hint of a smile crossed her lips. "I see you've taken on temporary guardianship for Tyler."

"That's correct."

"Can I ask where his mom is in all of this?"

Mason exhaled heavily. "She had enough. Told me either I took Ty or he was going into foster care."

"That must be hard on Tyler."

He nodded slowly. "Yes it is. Nobody wants to be abandoned by their parents."

"And hard on you, too."

"I'm fine." His brow furrowed. "I'm an adult. I get to choose what I do." Or at least he kind of did. Whatever. He didn't need any sympathy, save that for Ty.

"We have a parents' group that meets every two weeks," Principal Tasker continued, ignoring his frown. "To talk through the problems that are encountered when raising teenagers. It's run by our counselor. I can give you the details if you want them?"

No, he didn't want them. He knew the problems teenagers had. He'd had a bucketful of them himself. "That's very kind of you, Ma'am, but I'll be busy."

"What is it you do again?" she asked, glancing down at the file on her desk as though it held all the answers.

"I'm a lawyer."

There was a momentary look of surprise in her eyes. She hid it well enough, but he was trained to read expressions. "That's wonderful."

No point in telling her he didn't have a job at the moment. It was none of her business. "You mentioned paperwork for me to sign," he reminded her.

"Oh yes." She took some forms out of the file. "Just enrollment forms and the medical form." She rolled a pen over to him. "The usual stuff."

He still read each one anyway. No lawyer worth his salt would sign a document without reading the fine print first. Then he scrawled his name in each of the boxes and dated them, pushing them back across the desk with his fingertip.

"Is there anything else you need from me?" he asked.

"That's it for now," she said brightly. "I appreciate you coming in."

"Thank you," he said, impatient to get out of there. Because it didn't matter how old you were or how many qualifications you had, going in front of the principal always made you feel about twelve years old.

Passing the reception window as he walked out, the woman standing there called out his name. He turned, blinking. Surely Ty couldn't have gotten into trouble this quickly.

It would be a record, even for him.

"Mr. Parker, this is Lisa Gaughran. She's the head of the PTA," the receptionist told him. "I was explaining to Lisa that your brother is new at the school."

"Hello." Lisa smiled at him, flipping her blonde hair over her shoulder. "I haven't seen you in town before. Are you new?"

"Yeah, that's right." He went to walk away, but she grabbed his arm.

"We'd love you to join the PTA. We never have enough men in there." She put an emphasis on *men*. "We meet every Thursday in the gym. Can I count on seeing you there?"

He pulled his arm from her hold. "I don't think so. I'll be home with Ty."

"How about Mrs. Parker?" Lisa asked, glancing down at his left hand. "Can't she look after Ty?"

"No." He wasn't about to tell her there wasn't a Mrs. Parker. It was none of her business.

"Oh it's just the two of them," the receptionist said. "Only Tyler and Mr. Parker. It's on the forms." Mason tried not to scowl.

"Is that right? Well you could always bring him along," Lisa suggested, tipping her head to the side. "Or he could come over to my place. I have a daughter around his age."

Mason didn't point out that he hadn't told her Ty's age.

Lisa reached out to touch him on the arm, her smile widening. "I'd be happy to cook dinner for you all afterward."

"Lisa's single," the receptionist said helpfully. "*Newly* single."

"Ah..." He'd only been here a day and they were already trying to couple him off. Not that he was interested. She might not know it, but this woman was better off without him. Relationships and him didn't mix. He'd learned that by now.

"Give me your number and I'll call you to make some arrangements," Lisa suggested.

"Why don't you give me yours instead?" he said. "I'll call you."

"Ooh, I like a man who takes charge," the receptionist said.

Lisa reeled out her number, and he pretended to put it

into his phone, knowing full well he'd never call. Then he gave a nod to them both and hightailed it out of there before they tried to sign him up for anything else.

He let out a long, low breath before turning on the engine of his truck. What was it with women wanting to cook for him?

Though he hadn't minded Alaska doing it in the end. She hadn't looked at him like he was a piece of fresh meat. Truth was, she'd been more interested in Ty than in him. He liked that.

He reversed out of the parking lot, putting the thought of the PTA out of his mind. Ty was at school. He was grateful for that. Now he just needed to keep going until graduation.

"North's been trying to get ahold of you," Holly told her, leaning on the counter of the hotel reception desk. They'd decorated the hotel for the holidays a few days ago. Tall nutcrackers stood at the entrance, and the high-ceilinged lobby was festooned with garland and ornaments. Holiday music was piping through the air, bells jingling merrily.

"I know. I'm ignoring him." Alaska shot her cousin a smile. "He's got a bee in his bonnet about me having a neighbor. Wants his name so he can run a background check on him."

Holly tried to hide a smile. "Sounds like North."

As the eldest of the six Winter cousins, North had taken it upon himself to worry about all of them. But Alaska always bore the brunt, being the youngest.

And because she'd once caused them all panic and nobody had ever forgotten it.

"He also wants me to order in some extra propane for the generator because he thinks I don't have enough," Alaska said. The memory of his messages over the weekend still burned into her brain. Thank goodness that his Christmas Tree Farm would come into its busy season soon, otherwise she wouldn't have put it past him to drive to the hotel and stalk her down. "Oh, and he's worried about a party of doctors we have coming in January. Because apparently doctors at a convention have a thing for the female staff in their hotel."

Holly was openly laughing now. "How would he know that?"

Alaska shrugged. "You tell me. I don't see him flying off for tree conventions."

"Can you imagine? Don't you have to be friendly at those kinds of things? You know, smile at people and stuff?"

"So I hear." Alaska grinned. North had been grumpy recently. "I'm going to head home early. I don't want him dropping in here on his way back from making deliveries."

"He'll come to your place instead," Holly warned. "You know what he's like when he's on a mission."

"He won't," Alaska told her. "Because a little bird told me that Amber has a date tonight. He'll be too busy waiting for her to come home to worry about me."

Amber was North's partner at the Christmas Tree Farm. Though she wasn't part of the Winter family, he was as protective of her as he was of his cousins.

"Amber has a date?" Holly's mouth dropped open. "Who? What kind of guy would be brave enough to face North?"

"Some guy from Marshall's Gap, apparently." Alaska shrugged. "I don't care. I'm just pleased she's taking the heat off me."

"Temporarily," Holly said.

"Yeah, well I'll take it."

"Take what?"

Alaska looked up to see her friend, Nicole, standing at the

desk. She was practically family, too, being engaged to their cousin, Gabe. Nicole also taught yoga classes in the hotel fitness suite, and from the redness of her face and her Lycra clothing, she'd just finished a class.

"North not harassing me about my new neighbor," Alaska said.

"Oh! I know all about him." Nicole lifted a brow. "Tall and built. Beard. Sexy as hell."

"You've met him?" Alaska frowned. "When?"

"Nope, never seen him in my life. But all the women in my classes have been talking about him. At least five of them have baked a cake or a casserole to take over to his place to welcome him."

Alaska blinked. "They have?"

"Mmhmm." Nicole nodded. "I don't know whether to be sorry for the poor guy or jealous that he's gonna have enough food to last him weeks."

"Jealous," Holly said. "Definitely jealous."

"He won't like all the attention," Alaska said. "I get the feeling he likes to keep to himself."

"Have *you* met him?" Nicole turned to look at her.

Alaska shifted her feet. "Yeah, the other day. I cooked dinner for him and his brother."

Holly and Nicole leaned across the counter, their eyes wide. "What is he like?" Nicole asked. "As handsome as they're all saying?"

"I don't know." Alaska frowned. "I guess he's good looking. But as I said, he doesn't like attention."

"It sounds as if he likes *your* attention," Nicole pointed out. "If he came over for dinner."

"Oh God, don't tell North he's been to your place," Holly said, grimacing. "If he finds that out, he'll definitely be running a background check."

"Well I'm not telling him, and neither are you," Alaska said pointedly.

Holly mimicked zipping her lips. "Your secret is safe with us."

Alaska rolled her eyes because it wasn't a secret *like that.*

"As long as you keep us updated on the cake situation," Nicole added. "I have this pathological need to know how many he actually gets delivered."

"How would I know that?" Alaska frowned. "He's not going to volunteer that kind of information." And she wasn't going to ask. He was an adult, he could deal with whatever the townswomen gave to him. It wasn't her business.

She looked up to see Martin, their evening receptionist walk into the hotel. He was wearing a padded coat, and as he made his way to the desk he unwound his scarf, his hands drawing circles in the air above his head.

"Getting cold," he muttered as she lifted the counter for him to walk through. He opened the door to the office behind the desk and hung his coat and scarf on the rack in there. Then he slid on his name tag and logged into the second computer behind the desk. "Anything I need to know about the new guests?" he asked her, scrolling down the list. "Oh, the Bannermans are back."

"Yep. And the Carltons. The ones from New York," Alaska told him.

"Did they bring their dog?"

"Bentley? Yeah."

Martin wrinkled his nose. "Does he still fart like a trooper?"

"Oh yes. If anything, he's worse." Alaska shrugged. "Is there anything else you need?"

"Nope, got it all under control. I'll see you in the morning," Martin told her.

"Bright and early," Alaska agreed. She grabbed her coat

and hat, along with the envelope that she'd filled earlier with papers, and slid it into her purse. "Oh, the Richardsons in the penthouse are checking out a day early." She looped her purse over her neck. "Have a good night."

"You too." Martin looked over the counter and smiled at a guest. She joined Nicole and Holly who were walking out to their own cars, hugging them as they all went their separate ways. It had been a long shift—she'd barely had time for lunch—and she couldn't wait to get home and cook herself something easy before getting an early night.

But first she needed to drop the envelope off for Ty. She'd promised him an application form once he'd started school, but she had no idea of his email address. So she'd shove it into their mailbox on her way home. That was easy enough. And if she bumped into Mason and his cake mountain, then she could report back to Nicole.

It was a win-win, right?

5

"You need to heat it for thirty minutes," the woman told him, holding a casserole dish out as though she was one of the wise men offering gold or frankincense–or whatever the heck the third one was. "In fact, I could just come in and do it for you." She smiled at him, tipping her head to the side, her highlighted hair falling over her shoulder.

He'd forgotten her name since she'd told him at the school. To be honest, he hadn't been expecting to see her again. Yet here she was, the latest in a long line of locals–all women–who seemed to think he and Ty needed help getting fed.

"It's fine. Thank you, I'll warm it up myself."

She tipped her head to the side. "Are you sure? I have a bottle of wine in my car. We could make an evening of it." Her lips curled. "Of course, that would mean I couldn't drive home, but that won't be a problem. As long as I'm not late for work tomorrow."

Mason swallowed hard. "My brother should be back soon. We'll both be having an early night." And that was thirteen more words than he wanted to say to her. "Thank you for the casserole." He tried to take it from her but she wouldn't release her grasp on the dish. For a moment he considered leaving her standing there on the stoop with that damn dish still in her hand, but he wouldn't put it past her to stay there until Ty got back. And knowing his brother, he'd let the damn woman in and they'd both have to deal with her for the night.

No, this situation needed delicate handling. He'd tried being an asshole, and she'd blinked it away. He'd tried taciturn, and she'd just done the talking.

Mason looked her in the eye. "Goodbye then." There. Politeness. The last resort.

"Actually, I have a minor problem." She pulled her lip between her teeth. She was pretty enough. But he wasn't interested. The same way he hadn't been interested in the other women who'd arrived at his door with baked goods and casseroles today.

All of them careful to show him their left hands so he could see they were free of wedding rings.

"That's too bad." His voice was dismissive. And she still wasn't releasing her vice like grip on the dish.

"My car was making some strange noises on the way here," she told him. "Could you check the engine for me?" He looked over her shoulder at the sleek gray SUV parked at the end of his drive. It was sparkling new. "I'd hate to get stranded on my way home. It'll be dark soon and I'm a single woman. Nobody will know where I am."

He wanted to walk back into his cabin and bang his head against a wall. Instead, he let out a long sigh.

"Miss..."

"Call me Lisa."

Yes. That was it. "Lisa," he drawled. "I'd suggest calling a mechanic. I think I passed a garage when I got to town."

A slow smile pulled at her lips. "Oh what a wonderful idea. You're so smart. Let me try calling."

She lifted her phone to her ear, though he couldn't hear any ring tone. He willed whoever it was at the other end of the phone to pick up. He was sure she was a nice person, but he really wasn't looking for any type of relationship.

Mason had come here to get away from people, not to throw himself at them.

The rumble of a car cut through the silence. He looked up, watching it turn the corner and his chest let out a little when he saw it was Alaska making her way up their road. At least he wouldn't have to find room for yet another casserole.

"Charlie's not answering," Lisa said, pressing the screen of her phone. "Maybe I could leave my car here and you could drive me home."

He opened his mouth and closed it again. There was a minute chance she wasn't lying. So tiny the human eye couldn't see it. But he didn't want to be the asshole who left a woman stranded.

Alaska's car slowed down. His gaze fixed upon it, his brows pulled tight. He hadn't seen her since the night they'd gone over for dinner. He'd seen her a couple of times coming and going while they were cleaning the cabin, and Ty had gone over with a thank you card for giving them dinner.

But she was busy, that much was clear. And that was fine by him. Nobody to bother him.

He waited for Alaska to drive past, but to his surprise, she pulled in behind Lisa's SUV. Well this was interesting. She climbed out of the car, her black leather boots hitting the ground, and shivered as she pulled something out of her bag.

And then her gaze landed on Lisa. She froze for a moment, the envelope still in her hand, then she looked at him.

"Help me." He mouthed at her.

Alaska's lips opened, but she said nothing. Her eyes were still wary as she glanced from him to Lisa. Before he could mouth the words again, Lisa looked up. "I guess I'll have to call Charlie in the morning. Maybe you could follow me home just to make sure—"

"Hi." Alaska made it to the foot of his steps, holding a brown envelope. Lisa blinked at being interrupted mid-sentence.

His smile was big. She blinked as though he'd dazzled her.

"Hi." His voice was warm and her shock deepened.

"Oh, it's you," Lisa said, her brows knitting as she looked at Alaska standing there. "What do you want?"

There was a tic in Alaska's jaw. "I've come to see my neighbor."

"Your neighbor?" Lisa pressed her lips together. "Oh, I forgot you're living up here." She lowered her voice, though he was sure Alaska could hear her. "She's a strange one. Always has been, you should probably watch out for her."

The circles of heat on Alaska's cheeks deepened until they were almost puce. Then she did the last thing Mason ever expected her to.

She walked up the steps, her eyes set on his, and reached out to put her hand on his neck. Her fingers were cool, but they felt like they burned his skin. Then she rolled onto her tiptoes and pressed her mouth against his.

Her soft, open mouth.

And damn if he didn't feel a shot of heat rush through him. For a moment he didn't know what to do, but she was looking at him through those honest blue eyes and the mixture of innocence and heat in her gaze made his chest do a little gallop. So he did the only thing he could think of.

Mason slid his hand down her padded coat, his fingers curling around her hip. He wasn't sure who he was trying to keep steady–her or him.

He parted his lips, his tongue touching the tip of hers, causing her to let out the tiniest of goddamn moans. She arched herself against him, her fingers tracing the nape of his neck where his hair met his skin.

He felt himself harden against her. She tasted like sugar and spice, and all things fucking nice. And her fingers, feathering against his neck. There should be a law against it. Because men would throw themselves under a truck just to feel that caress.

They'd fight wars for it.

Alaska arched herself into him, making a noise in her throat that made him want to scoop her in his arms and march her straight to his bed. She had to know he was hard, she was pushing herself right into him. And dear God, it felt good.

"So you know each other well then?" Lisa sounded like she was going to cry.

Alaska jumped out of his embrace like somebody had lit her on fire. His body immediately missed the warmth of her against him. Thank God he was wearing a thick shirt that covered the part of him that was... over emotional right now. From the corner of his eye he could see the brown envelope that Alaska had been holding now laying on the wooden slats of his stoop. He reached down for it at the same time Alaska did and the tips of their fingers brushed.

Her wide eyes locked with his, and he could see the heat in there. Could see regret, too. Then she pulled them away and yanked the envelope from his hand and it felt like a cold bucket of water being thrown over his face.

They both slowly stood, and she took two steps back.

"Alaska is my..." His brain still wasn't working right.

"His friend," she breathed. "I brought this for Ty." She held out the envelope she'd just snatched from his hand. "It's an application for the Winterville Inn."

He took the envelope from her. "Thank you." She

wouldn't meet his eyes. He wanted to take her shoulders and make her look at him.

Yeah, way to go. That would help the situation.

"So, you two are a thing?" There was disappointment in Lisa's voice. "That's... unexpected."

"We're taking it slowly," Mason said. Alaska pressed her lips together.

"I should probably go," Lisa said, looking at her phone. "I'm supposed to be somewhere."

"What about your car?" he asked her.

"Oh, it'll be fine. It's booked in for service next week." She glanced at the casserole she was still holding. "I'll still need this dish back. Actually, I'll just take it with me now. You don't want this food, do you?"

Mason looked her in the eye. "I'll survive without it."

Lisa nodded, then sent one last confused glance at Alaska, before aiming her frown to Mason. She shrugged as though she couldn't understand what the hell was going on, before turning on her heel and stomping down the steps.

Yanking the door open, she climbed into her SUV. Mason turned to look at Alaska.

She still wasn't looking at him.

"I..."

A forced smile pushed up her cheeks. "I hope I helped. I should go now. I have things to do in the house."

"Alaska..."

She shifted her feet. "Don't forget to give the application to Ty. That's if it's okay with you that he works at the Inn. I won't over schedule him. He'll still be able to get all his school work done because I know that's important to you."

"ALASKA!"

"What?" She blinked rapidly.

"Thank you."

A slow breath escaped from her lips. "It's fine. We're neighbors, that's what we do, right?"

Not where he came from, no. And he was pretty sure it wasn't normal business in Winterville to kiss your neighbor until your dick was so hard you could drill through the polar ice cap.

But whatever. It did the job. Lisa got the message, and he got a cheap thrill.

He should take it as a good thing that Alaska wasn't affected by it. He definitely shouldn't be standing here thinking that he wanted to kiss her again until every part of her was as flushed as her cheeks.

Let her go. Keep to yourself. Get Ty through high school and then you can disappear again.

"I'll give him the application," Mason said, reaching for his door.

She nodded, then almost ran down his steps, heading for her own car.

He yanked his door open and stepped inside, trying not to groan at all the things he still had to do to make the house habitable.

Well that was one way to get rid of a hard-on.

6

Alaska made sure her front door was closed before she dropped her bags onto the wooden floor, letting her head fall back onto the wall.

And then she screamed. Not loudly, because she didn't want anybody to hear her. Especially not the neighbor she'd just thrown herself at.

What the hell was wrong with her?

When he'd mouthed for her to help, the only thing she could think of was to pretend they were a thing. And then the bright idea to kiss him had come into her head.

And yeah, she'd thought a peck would do it. But somehow the kiss had deepened. And now it felt like her whole body was on fire.

She kicked off her shoes and slid her feet into her fluffy slippers, then walked to the kitchen, pulling her emergency supply of chocolate out of the cupboard. In the summer she kept it in the refrigerator, but at this time of year she liked it gooey. Breaking off a row—because a square wouldn't cut it—she shoved it in her mouth and closed her eyes, letting out a moan.

But that reminded her too much of the moan she'd let out when she'd felt his thick hardness press against her stomach. He'd been big–of course he had, because everything about him was big–but he hadn't looked embarrassed at all. He'd just kissed her back and her body had responded, and so had his.

How the hell could she face him again?

It was getting dark outside, and the light differential from the kitchen turned the window into a half-mirror. She caught her ghostly reflection staring back at her. Chocolate around her lips, cheeks so red she could be a damn clown, eyes wide with the memory of kissing her stupid neighbor.

No, he wasn't stupid, *she was.*

Because he'd taken that kiss for what it was supposed to be. Saving him from Lisa Gaughran, nothing more. She'd known the woman for most of her life. Lisa had been one of a gang of girls a few years older than her who'd made her life misery from the age of eight.

Remembering those days made her snap another line of chocolate from the bar. Then she sighed and only ate one square because she needed to keep some space for dinner. She was a grownup. She shouldn't eat chocolate as a meal, and she definitely shouldn't go around kissing guys who didn't want to be kissed.

Ignoring her better sense, she ate another square, stuffing it into her mouth as she stomped her way to the bedroom. A shower would do her good. And maybe a year or two of self-isolation. On a sunny island with no grouchy neighbors with impressive assets that she wanted to feel again.

She'd just stepped out of the shower when she heard a knock on the front door. "Just a minute," she yelled out, pulling some old black sweatpants from her drawer and yanking them on, kicking her legs to free her feet from the ends as she threaded her arms through a cream sweater.

Please don't let it be him. She couldn't deal with any more of Mason Parker tonight.

She slid her feet back into her slippers because it was cold and no amount of heating could warm them like pink faux fur could, then walked to the door, breathing a sigh of relief when she saw her sister standing on the other side.

Everley was just over a year older than Alaska. Growing up, they'd been close–Everley the outgoing one, Alaska the quiet and happy one. And as adults, it felt like they'd become even closer.

Then Alaska saw what was in Everley's cradled arms. A tiny puppy that was wriggling in a desperate attempt to get out of them. Alaska's lips broke into a grin.

He looked like a teddy bear, his fur thick and fawn around his tiny eyes and flat face.

"Oh my God!" There was nothing she loved more than animals. She leaned forward to stroke the puppy's downy fur. "He's beautiful. Whose is he?"

"That's the thing." Everley grimaced. "He's kind of homeless. One of my dancer's parents had him, but they gave him to her and she can't cope with him with her schedule. So I said I'd take him."

"You did?" The puppy was staring right up at Alaska. She couldn't help but lean in and nuzzle his fur. "Do you have enough time to look after him with your job at the theater and with Dylan away?" Everley's husband had recently left for Africa as a volunteer doctor, returning just before Christmas. And Everley's show at the theater had already opened.

"Um..." Everley looked her right in the eye. "I was hoping you could help."

"You want me to look after him?" Alaska raised an eyebrow.

"Only if you can spare the time. I know you're busy. But you're so good with animals and he's way too tiny to go to doggy daycare. I could give him back, I guess, but look at him." Everley stroked his back. "How could we reject a face like this?"

"You made me promise not to take in any more strays," Alaska pointed out, amused. She was the animal lover of the family. At one point, her house was constantly full of foster dogs and house cats and birds with broken wings. It was only when she moved to this little house in the mountains that she'd promised her sister and cousins that she wouldn't take any more in. They had visions of her sharing baths with wild bears.

"But he isn't a stray," Everley pointed out. "He's a pedigree chow chow. I just need your help for a while until the show is over. Not all the time, just when I'm performing. I don't want to leave him alone at the house."

She was right; the puppy was way too young to be left alone. "What's his name?"

"Leo."

It was perfect. He looked like a little lion cub, with his golden mane and pointy ears. "Hello, Leo," Alaska whispered, rubbing her thumb over his fur. He turned his head to lick her and gave what sounded like a purr.

"See, he likes you," Everley said, letting out a long breath.

"You'd better come in." Alaska stepped aside and let her sister walk into the house. When she closed the door, Everley put Leo on the floor and he started scampering around, sniffing the walls and the doors, before taking particular interest in the shoes Alaska had kicked off when she'd come home.

It was only when he started chewing on the leather that she gently pulled them away from him.

"So are you planning to cage train him?" Alaska asked her sister, scooping Leo up and carrying him into the living room. He scrambled on her chest and started licking her neck.

Damn, he was adorable. Everley was so sly, knowing she'd fall in love with him as soon as she saw him.

Her sister knew she couldn't turn down a little furball like Leo.

"Yeah. I was hoping you could help with that, too." Everley sat down on the sofa and Alaska took the easy chair. Leo jumped off her lap and onto the floor, determined to continue his exploration. "I feel terrible for asking, but you're the only one I'd trust with him."

"It's okay. I'd love to help." Alaska watched him sniff at her curtains. She already felt calmer. "Is Dylan okay with having a puppy?"

"He is. He can't wait to come back to meet him." Everley sounded wistful. She and Dylan had been childhood sweethearts. They'd married when she was twenty-one, but their relationship had quickly imploded thanks to their hotheadedness and stubborn ways. It was only a couple of years ago when Dylan discovered their divorce had never been finalized that they had reconnected and fallen in love all over again.

And now he was away for six weeks while Everley was appearing in a show at the Winterville Theater. Everley had told her how important his volunteer work was to both of them, and they'd decided this six week period would be the best time for him to go, since Everley would be busy performing every night anyway.

"So, when do you want me to look after him?" Alaska asked. Leo had found the glass doors that led out onto her back deck, and was licking them like a lollipop.

Everley's expression softened. "Are you sure you'll have time? I know you're busy, too."

"I can take him into work with me." She'd done it before with dogs she'd fostered. The guests would love Leo, she knew that much.

"Obviously, I could have him in the mornings," Everley

said. "Since I'll be home then. And maybe I could drop him off to you on my way to the theater at lunchtimes?"

Alaska nodded. "Of course."

"And then I'll drive over after the last show and pick him up from you to take him home."

"You can't do that," Alaska protested. "You'll be exhausted. Why don't I drop him off to you in the mornings on my way to work?"

"I can't ask you to do that," Everley protested. "That's too much."

"I'd be happy to." Leo was back at her feet, scrabbling at her shins in desperation to be picked up. It wouldn't be long before he was big enough to jump up himself, and then in a few months' time he'd be way too big to sit on her lap. Chow chows got huge, she knew that much. "He'll be good company for me." And maybe she'd be too busy taking care of him to think of how she'd embarrassed herself in front of her neighbor that evening. "When do you want me to start?"

"I was hoping tomorrow. But if you need a few days..."

"No!" Alaska ruffled Leo's ears. "I can start as soon as you need me to."

"You're a lifesaver," Everley said. "Thank you so much."

"Any time." But maybe Leo was the lifesaver around here. She'd forgotten just how much she loved being surrounded by animals. For the next few weeks at least, she was happy to remember all over again.

"I'm gonna take a shower," Ty said, passing Mason where he was working on his laptop at the kitchen table. Ty had come home just after six–he'd stayed late at school to take some catch up classes and had gotten a ride home with a friend he'd made this week.

He hadn't said much about how school was going, but at least he seemed in a good mood. Part of that was thanks to the food the women of Winterville had brought over. Ty was in heaven after his third slice of cake.

And yeah, Mason should probably be worried about his brother's sugar intake, but once the cakes were gone, they were gone. He wouldn't be whipping any more up, and he was pretty certain that after Lisa's visit there wouldn't be any more free food being brought to his door.

He could hear Ty stomping around in the bathroom. It was the one room he hadn't gotten around to doing anything about yet. Sure, it was clean–they'd done that much–but the fittings were old and the water supply was unpredictable. They'd both taken cold showers this morning. Or cold dribbles.

It was on his list of things to do next week. In the meantime, Ty would just have to stomp.

"Holy shit!" Ty shouted from the bathroom. "Mason, get in here."

Sighing, Mason closed his laptop, and pushed himself up, walking over to the bathroom door. "You'd better be decent. I don't want to have to wash my eyes out with bleach."

"Seriously," Ty protested. "I just fell through the floor."

"What the hell?" Mason pushed the door open. Ty was pulling his leg out of a hole caused by splintering in the wooden floor.

"Christ," Mason said, looking down at it. "The wood is rotten." He looked up at his brother. "Have you been using the bath mat when you get out of the shower?"

"Yes." Ty rolled his eyes. "And I don't think a few days of showers caused this."

Mason peeled back a corner of linoleum. Ty was right. The whole floor was probably rotten or getting there. Mason sighed. It looked like he was going to be renovating this room sooner than he'd planned. No point in replacing only the floor when the whole thing needed replacing.

"Okay, look," he said. "Just try to shower the best you can. And don't stomp on anything, just in case the rest of the floor gives way."

"I can't believe I'm having to live like this," Ty protested. "Isn't there a law against it?"

Mason shrugged.

"You're the lawyer," Ty pointed out. "Don't you know?"

"If you don't want to live here, you know what you can do."

Ty rolled his eyes again. "Call CPS."

"You know their number." Mason's stomach tightened. It was a pointless threat. He wouldn't let his brother go into the system, no matter how annoying he could be. He wouldn't let him be beaten up by the other kids. Wouldn't let him go hungry. Wouldn't let him go through anything like Mason had been through.

Ty scrunched his nose. "I can probably help you with the bathroom," he muttered.

"Okay. I'll see what I can buy locally and we can start this weekend. Oh, and did you fill out that application form?" He'd remembered to pass it to Ty at dinner time.

"Yep. I'm going to drop it off at the Inn tomorrow after school. I figured it's best to do it in person, show some enthusiasm."

Mason nodded. "Good plan. Call me when you're finished and I'll meet you. I'll be there and in Marshall's Gap tomorrow to get supplies."

"Sounds good." Ty shifted his feet. "Can I shower now?"

"Sure." It was a good time to part, before they started bitching at each other again. "Mind the hole when you get out."

"Yes, Dad."

Shaking his head, Mason left the bathroom, being sure to close the door behind him. He'd only just sat back down at his laptop when his phone rang.

And when he saw who it was, he wasn't sure whether to laugh or cry.

"Preach," he said, putting the phone to his ear.

"You were supposed to call me when you got there. I was on the verge of rounding up a rescue party to come save your ass."

Mason grunted a laugh because Preach had always been prone to exaggeration. They'd met at Mason's second foster home. He was two years older than Mason, but he'd been in and out of the system almost from birth. And when Mason had arrived, he'd taken him under his wing.

Not a lot of friendships survived foster care. When you escaped you wanted to forget you'd ever been in there. And yet somehow he'd kept in touch with Preach. Even when Mason had been in law school and Preach had been doing whatever it took to survive on the streets.

And here they were in their thirties, still friends, or something like it.

"Sorry I didn't call. There's been a lot to do," Mason told him, grabbing a notepad so he could start a list of everything he'd need for the bathroom.

"Like what?" Preach asked. "You're in the middle of nowhere."

"The cabin was worse than I thought it would be. We'll be doing repairs for a while."

"And how's my boy doing?" Preach asked. He had a soft spot for Ty.

"He's started school, so that's a win."

"And he's keeping out of trouble, right?" Another thing about Preach. He might be involved in things he shouldn't but he didn't want the same for Ty. Mason appreciated that.

"Right. He's working hard, or at least it seems like he is. And he's applying for an after-school job."

"Fuckin A," Preach said, sounding pleased. "That's my boy."

"He also just ruined my bathroom."

"That's teenage boys for you. All those hormones, not enough receptacles."

Mason grimaced. "Not like that. He just stepped through a rotten floorboard."

"Oh. That kind of ruin. Sure." Preach cleared his throat. "Anyway, you met any women yet?"

Another thing about Preach. He was always direct.

"Nope. Not interested."

"Ty messaged that they've been cooking for you," Preach told him, sounding almost smug.

"So you knew we were safe then," Mason pointed out. "If you talked to Ty already."

"Yeah, but I wanted to hear it from you," Preach told him. "Anyway, if you get sick of the meals, you can send me some. I'm starving here."

"What happened to Marina?" The last Mason knew, Preach was dating a chef.

"Ah, it was never meant to be." Preach didn't sound sad about that. "By the way. You're doing a good thing, man. For Ty, I mean. Not for you. You're doing exactly the wrong thing for you."

"Thanks for the vote of confidence," Mason said dryly.

"I mean it. You should never have left your job. You're an idiot."

"I thought you hated lawyers," Mason pointed out.

"I do. But not you. I could never hate you. I love you, man."

Mason rolled his eyes. "Uh-huh."

"Tell me you love me, too," Preach said, teasing now.

"Get out of here. I got things to do."

"Come on. Just once. Tell me."

"Goodbye, Preach. And try not to starve." Not that Mason could talk. He couldn't cook for shit either.

"Okay. Talk soon. And by the way I know you love me."

"Then stop asking me to say it."

"Sure." Preach ended the call and Mason stared at his phone for a moment, before Ty let out another yell.

Okay, so he'd forgotten to avoid the hole when he got out of the shower. Mason sighed and threw his phone on the table in front of him, then got up to save his brother.

But this time, there was a smile on his face.

❧ 7 ❧

It was almost three in the afternoon the next day when Mason pulled into a parking space outside the Cold Fingers Café in the center of Winterville. It was the only space left in this part of town–somebody must have just vacated it. He hadn't expected everywhere to be quite this busy.

Climbing out of his truck, he slammed the door behind him and checked the truck bed. He'd got some timber to refit the floor and had placed an order for a new complete bathroom suite that would be delivered in a few days. In the meantime, he and Ty would have to keep on hopping over that hole.

Or tiptoeing, just to make sure they made no more holes.

A yawn forced his jaw open. Coffee. He needed a vat of it, and he was in the right place. It was another hour before Ty was due to meet him here. His bus wouldn't get here for another half an hour, and then he'd have to walk to the Winterville Inn, and no doubt talk to Alaska.

As soon as he pushed the door open, the smell of coffee assailed him, making his stomach twist with a reminder that he'd eaten nothing since breakfast. He made his way to the counter–there was a line, and it looked like every seat in the café was full. That was just fine by him. He'd drink his coffee in the truck.

"Hello stranger," Dolores said when he reached the front of the line. "How are you settling in?"

"Pretty good," He nodded. "Got Ty into school and the cabin is cleaning up nicely."

"That's wonderful. I was hoping you'd come into town again. Maybe next time you can bring Ty."

"I might bring him in later for a hot chocolate," Mason said. "I'm meeting him here in an hour."

"Perfect." Dolores gave him a big grin. "What can I get you?"

"A flat white would be great. And a cookie." Because his stomach was going to beat him up if he didn't fill it soon. "Actually, make it two."

"You want to sit down and I'll bring them over?" she asked, then frowned when she saw all the tables were full.

"It's fine." He shrugged. "I'll take it to go."

Dolores was frothing up the machine when the door opened again, and a tall man around Mason's age joined the line. A moment later, another person walked in and Mason's stomach dropped.

Lisa Gaughran. Miss P.T.A. herself. Of all the people he didn't want to see, dammit.

Her eyes caught his and she blinked. Please God, let her say nothing. She turned her head and smiled when she saw her friends at a table waving at her. She pointed at the counter and they shook their heads.

Then she turned back to him and smiled. "How's Alaska?" she asked, her brows lifting.

His stomach dropped. "Fine, I think." He deliberately trained his gaze on Dolores as she scooped a metal milk jug under the frothing nozzle, hoping Lisa would get the message.

The man standing behind him shifted his feet.

"How do you know Alaska?" he asked Mason. "I haven't seen you around here before."

"Surely Alaska's told you about Mason Parker," Lisa said to the man. "She's your cousin, after all."

Fuck. A relative. Exactly the complication he didn't need. Taking a long, annoyed breath, Mason turned to look at the man. He was tall–almost as tall as Mason. With thick dark hair and a beard growth that somehow didn't look a mess. Like Mason, he was wearing jeans and a thick shirt.

But he wasn't smiling.

"I'm her new neighbor," Mason said, ignoring the way Lisa was watching them both, her breath fast with excitement. He felt like a lion in a Roman amphitheater. There purely for her entertainment.

"Oh, North, he's more than a neighbor. I caught them eating each other's faces yesterday," Lisa said gleefully. "Seriously, I had to leave before it turned into a porno."

For Christ's sake.

Alaska's cousin–North–looked visibly shocked. A moment later, the shock was replaced by an altogether more sinister one. His jaw was so tight it could cut a piece of granite in two.

"You did *what* with my cousin?" North asked, his voice low.

"Nothing," Mason replied. This was exactly what he didn't want. People all up in his business. Men built like brick shithouses annoyed with him because he kissed one of their damn relatives. "Is my order nearly ready?" he asked Dolores, because he was itching to get out of here.

"One minute," Dolores said, oblivious to the sense of

menace on the other side of the bar. "Just adding the milk now."

"Wait up," North said. "You're not going anywhere. I need to know what's been happening with my cousin."

"Why?" Mason asked him, because he was finally out of fucks to give. "She's a grown adult. I'm pretty sure she can kiss who she wants."

North's eyes narrowed. "So you *did* kiss her?"

"I told you so," Lisa said, excitement making her eyes shine. "I'm not kidding, it was like watching people have sex with their clothes on."

"Will you shut the hell up?" North snipped at her. "I don't need that kind of vision in my head." His hands curled into fists as he looked back at Mason. "Are you in a relationship with my cousin?"

"Define relationship." Mason was hedging for time. He could easily clear this up by telling North exactly what had happened. But it was none of his goddamn business. And he was sick of people sticking their noses in where they shouldn't.

And yeah, he didn't want Lisa to hear it was all a ruse either. He'd only just gotten rid of her.

"Are you sleeping with Alaska?" North said, his eyes boring into Mason's.

"Maybe you should ask her that," Mason said.

"I. Am. Asking. You." North's jaw ticked.

This man didn't know how to take no for an answer. He didn't need this right now. Alaska was pretty, and she kissed like she was a piece of heaven, but fuck this.

"What's going on?" Dolores asked.

"North found out that Alaska and Mason have been sleeping together," Lisa said, her voice so loud that everybody turned to look at them.

"Oh." Dolores' eyes went wide. "I don't want any trouble

in here." She passed Mason his drink and cookies. "Maybe you should drink this now. Outside."

"Was just about to," he said, lifting the cup and taking a long sip, because if he didn't get some caffeine in his body he was about to turn feral. "Thank you for the drink."

But North was blocking his way. "We haven't finished here," he said, his voice thick.

Mason had already had enough. "You really want to talk about your cousin in here where everybody's listening?" he asked him. "Don't you care more about her than that?"

"I care about her a lot," North hissed. "That's why I want to know your intentions."

"Then let's take this outside," Mason said calmly. "For her sake." Also where Lisa wouldn't be listening in. Then he could explain this once and for all and get the hell out of this place.

Well, as soon as Ty was ready.

He'd dealt with his fair share of angry fathers growing up. A kid from the foster system wasn't exactly the kind of boyfriend parents welcomed into their homes. But he'd never had an angry cousin before.

It'd be amusing if it wasn't so damn annoying.

Without saying another word, Mason walked past North, and the line of desperately curious faces, yanked open the door, and stepped outside into the ice cold air. Steam rose from the hole in his coffee lid. A moment later, he heard North's footsteps behind him.

"You gonna tell me now?" North asked.

Mason turned to look at him, but his attention was caught on what was happening in the coffee shop. It looked like half of the customers had run to the windows and were pressing their faces against the glass, desperate to catch the action.

"You know what?" Mason said, sick of it all. "I'm not. All I'm going to tell you is that your cousin's a grown woman. She can do what she wants, when she wants, with who she wants, and it's got fuck all to do with you unless she wants you to know. And she clearly doesn't, because otherwise she would have told you. So there you have it. If she wants to push me over and fuck me seven ways to Sunday, it's still none of your goddamn business."

Okay, that might have been too much. Because the next thing he knew, North let out a roar.

It was late afternoon and the line for check in was crazy. Alaska had put Leo in the back office, where she'd installed a cage because he had a thing for chewing every inedible thing he could get his jaws on.

There were three of them working the desk, taking details and payments and giving out key cards as fast as they could. So when a breathless Charlie Shaw ran into the hotel lobby, she barely noticed him.

At least not until he pushed his way to the counter.

She'd known Charlie since she was a tiny girl. He ran the Cold Start Garage in town, but more importantly he was Everley's father-in-law. So when he leaned on the counter and took in gulps of oxygen, she frowned, worried he was on the edge of collapse.

"Charlie? Are you okay?" She reached for his hand. "Should I call somebody?"

He breathed heavy again. "You need to come quick."

Her heart sank. "Why? What's happened? Is it Everley?"

"No." He shook his head. "It's North. He's fighting that new guy outside Dolores' cafe. Your neighbor. Mason, is it?"

Oh no. She winced at the line in front of her. What the heck was her cousin thinking, fighting somebody in the middle of town? They'd spent years building up their reputation as a family-friendly resort. She couldn't let him threaten that.

And she didn't even want to think about why the two of them were fighting. Because she had a horrible feeling it had something to do with her.

"Here you go," she said, her voice artificially light as she handed a key to the guest who was listening in, clearly entertained. "You're in room three-oh-four. The elevators are just past the Christmas tree. Go to the third floor and take a left when you get out."

She looked around, her eyes alighting on Carl, the Inn's cook, who was just coming in for the dinner shift. "Carl," she called out. "I need you."

"What can I help with?" He turned and walked toward reception.

"Can you take over at check in?" Thankfully, he'd done it before. "I need to do something."

He checked his watch. "Sure. As long as it's not for too long."

"It won't be," she said grimly. "Oh, and can you check on Leo if you get a spare minute?"

"Leo?" Carl frowned.

"He's a dog. A chow chow," Alaska quickly told him, wrenching the door to the office open to grab her coat. She slid it on as Carl walked behind the reception desk and smoothly took over the next customer.

Without waiting for Charlie–because he'd slow her down, she ran out of the Inn and down the impressive stone steps, her shoes clattering against the blacktop as she reached the top of the drive. What the hell was North thinking? He knew better than to beat up random strangers.

She didn't have to look far to see where the fight was taking place, because a crowd had already gathered around the two of them. She pushed her way through, fury making her strong, and then saw the two of them squaring up.

"You don't touch her, you don't talk to her, you don't even breathe near her, got it?" North was shouting. "In fact, why don't you just leave town? That'll make it so much easier on you."

Her chest felt way too tight. Yep, this was *definitely* about her. How the heck was she going to stop this?

"I'm not going anywhere," Mason said, his voice ominously low. He was as big as North and looked as strong, too. There was no way this fight would end in anything other than tears. "Why don't you take your goddamn nose out of business that has nothing to do with you before I break it?"

Okay, that wasn't helping. Not one bit.

"What's going on?" Alaska called out, stomping into the circle that was formed around them. She could almost smell the toxic testosterone. What was it with her family and fighting?

Or more specifically North and fighting. And now Mason, too.

"You tell me," North said. "I've been hearing about you and this idiot swapping saliva all over town."

She let out a sigh, because this was just embarrassing. "North..."

"What she does has nothing to do with you. I told you that." Mason's jaw was tight, just like his voice.

"Will you both shut up?" she said, folding her arms across her chest. "What the hell's wrong with you? Arguing in the middle of the street? People are here to have a good time, not watch a rerun of *Fight Club*."

"I'm just doing what any cousin would do," North told her. "Defending your honor."

"The way you defended Holly's?" she asked, her brow raised. North winced when she said that because the whole town remembered how he'd hit Josh, Holly's husband, square in the jaw when he found Holly's panties in his pocket.

But that was years ago, when North was a young hothead. He should be better than that now.

"Just stop it," she implored. "I'm a grown woman. I don't need you defending me."

"You're a woman who lives alone in the middle of goddamn nowhere. And now this asshole has moved in next door." North shook his head. "This is why we didn't want you living there. He could do anything to you and we wouldn't be there to save you."

Damn, he was frustrating. She loved North to death, but he could be such an idiot sometimes. "Mason is nothing but a gentleman," she said, ignoring the way Mason's brows lifted. "You don't need to worry about him."

"He took advantage of you," North said. "He needs to know that's not acceptable."

"Oh, for goodness' sake." Alaska sighed. "He didn't take advantage of me. I was the one who kissed him. And you know what? I'll do it again. Because I'm a thirty-year-old woman who enjoys kissing men. Who enjoys doing more than kissing them when she gets the chance."

Mason blinked right as North winced. At least she'd shut them both up. "Now, will you stop making a spectacle of each other and of me and walk away please?" She looked at Mason, her brow lifted. "That means both of you."

He put his hands up in surrender. "I wasn't the one who started this."

"You kissed her. You started it," North said, and she glared at him.

"If you don't move right now," Alaska warned her cousin, "I'll drag you across the square. I'm not kidding."

There was another scuffle in the crowd surrounding them. Everley appeared, flanked by their cousin, Holly.

"What's going on?" Everley asked. "Somebody ran into the theater and said there was a fight in the street."

"North's being an idiot," Alaska told them. "Can you make him leave?"

Everley's eyes darted from North to Mason, interest lighting up her face. "If I do, will you tell me what's going on?"

"I'll be delighted," Alaska told her.

"Okay then. Come on, North. Let's go get you a drink," Everley suggested, walking over to him and tugging at his arm. "The Tavern is open, and you look like you could use one."

North let her pull him away, because he was fierce but gentle. And he cared about his cousins more than he cared about himself. "Okay, I'm going," he muttered. "But Alaska, we need to talk."

"I'll join you in the Tavern just as soon as I get everybody to leave here," she said, resigned to having to explain herself. She turned around to the crowd of locals. "Okay, everyone, show's over," she shouted. "Go back inside and finish your coffees."

A disappointed groan washed over the crowd, but they did as they were told, slowly breaking off and walking back into the shop, where Dolores was grimly holding the door open.

"And as for you," she said to Mason, poking him in the chest with her finger. "What the heck were you thinking?"

He looked surprised at her annoyance. "I was thinking you're a grown woman who could kiss who she liked without it being anybody's business."

He was right. And she kind of liked his stubborn take on it. It mirrored her own.

"I don't need you fighting for me," she told him, her jaw tight. "I don't need anybody to do that."

"You're wrong. I wasn't fighting for you, I was fighting for me," he told her gruffly.

His eyes caught hers and she felt herself melting a little. She knew what North was like. Hell, Josh knew what North was like. Her cousin's husband said his jaw still hurt when the wind blew in a certain way, even ten years after North had hit him.

"Yeah, well, just stay away from him," she asked softly.

"I was trying," he pointed out. "But he made it rather difficult."

Yeah, that was North. She looked over her shoulder. Everybody had left, including North, Holly, and Everley. It was just her and Mason now. "That shouldn't have happened," she told him, her stomach twisting. "You shouldn't have to deal with my idiot family."

His lip quirked, and relief washed over her. "For what it's worth, it's nice that you have people who care. Not everybody does."

She nodded. "Well I should go over to the Tavern. I need to have words with my cousin."

"Sure." He glanced down at her lips. "Are you okay?"

"I'm..." Pissed. That was the right word. "I will be. I'm just sorry this all happened over a stupid kiss."

He gave her a tight smile. "You should probably go to the Tavern before they worry about you."

"Okay then."

"And Ty's bringing in his application to the Inn today. I know he wanted to see you."

She glanced at her watch. "I'll let the desk know to keep him there until I'm back."

"Thank you." Mason nodded. "He's a good kid underneath it all."

Alaska gave him a half smile. "He seems like a good kid on

top of it all, too. Well, I'd better go. I hope your evening is better than your afternoon." She started to walk away.

"Alaska?"

She looked at him over her shoulder. "Yeah?"

"That kiss wasn't stupid. It was good."

"It was?" For the first time she smiled.

"Yeah, it was."

A little thrill shot through her as she walked away.

8

By the time Alaska arrived at the Tavern, her family was already sitting in their favorite booth. North and Everley were whispering, and Holly must have called Josh because he was sitting next to her, holding her hand. And their other cousin, Gabe was at the bar, buying them all a drink. He gave her a sympathetic smile when he heard the door bang behind her.

"I see they called in reinforcements," Alaska said, joining him as he carried the tray of drinks over to the booth.

"Holly called Josh and Josh told me. I wasn't going to miss out on North getting an ear bashing from you, was I?" Gabe grinned at her. The two of them had always been close. He was so easy to get along with, and happy-go-lucky, especially since he'd gotten together with the love of his life.

At the thought, she asked, "Where's Nicole? Shouldn't she be here?"

"She'll be devastated that she isn't," Gabe said, deadpan. "But she's got a private client."

Gabe handed out the glasses as she slid into the booth next to Everley. Her sister nudged her with her shoulder.

"Why didn't you tell me about kissing Mr. Hottie Neighbor last night?" she whispered.

"Because it was no big deal. Or at least it wasn't until North went berserk." She shot him a dirty glance. He looked suitably embarrassed.

"I'm sorry," he said, his eyes imploring. "I overreacted."

"I'll say you did."

He put his hands up. "But hear me out. I worry about you being all alone out there. You know I didn't want you to live in the middle of nowhere."

"And that's exactly why I bought that house," she told him. "Because I'm so sick of everybody being in my business. I don't need protecting, North. You might not have noticed, but I'm a grown woman."

"I know you are. But I worry about you. Especially after..."

She put her hand in front of her. "Don't say it," she warned him. "Nothing happened, I was fine and it was over twenty years ago." She hated the way those forty hours still casted a shadow over all their lives. "Gabe nearly lost Nicole because he felt responsible for me. I don't want you losing your business because you can't keep your fists where they belong."

"I know." North raked his fingers through his thick hair. "I'm an idiot. I'm sorry."

"You need to back off, okay?" Alaska told him.

"I get it," he muttered, taking a sip of whiskey.

"Good." Her chest loosened. She hated disagreements.

"So, are you going to tell us what's going on between you and that guy?" Everley asked. "Are you a thing now?"

"No." Alaska shook her head. "That's the stupid part of it. There's nothing going on." She quickly explained her actions of the previous day. North looked appalled, Everley looked amused, and Gabe, Holly, and Josh just looked shocked.

"You really kissed a guy to get Lisa Gaughran off his back?" Everley asked. "Oh God, that's delicious. No wonder he looked so pissed with North."

North squeezed his eyes shut. "I'm an idiot."

"Yes, you are," Alaska told him. "He did nothing wrong. It was all me. And if you're so worried about me living alone, you should be glad he's moved in. At least if something happens, I have a neighbor to call on."

"You owe him an apology," Holly told North. "The same way you owed Josh an apology."

"Hey, don't bring me into this," Josh said. "North and I buried the hatchet years ago." They'd had to, because they were family now. And actually the two of them got along great nowadays. Alaska loved it when they all got together and had fun. Holly and Josh often hosted them all at their place.

"I'll apologize to him," North promised. "And I'm sorry to you, too. I just see red when it comes to you. I know I need to be less overprotective."

"Speaking of overprotective," Everley said. "How was Amber's date?"

"No idea," North grunted. Everley exchanged a smile with Alaska because they knew how much his business partner and best friend's new relationship would rankle him. And it was the perfect way to get the attention away from Alaska.

"Okay then," Alaska said, standing. "If everything is all cleared up, I need to get back to work."

Everley slid out of the booth after her. "I need to go, too. I have a show tonight."

Josh glanced at Gabe. "You want to stay for another?"

"Yeah." Gabe nodded. "I think North needs it. This way we can stop him from starting his own fight club."

But North was standing and reaching for Alaska's arm, his

gentle fingers encircling her wrist. "I really am sorry," he said softly.

"I know." She smiled at him. "Just don't do it again."

"Good luck with that," Gabe snorted.

Ignoring him, North nodded. "I won't." Then he pulled Alaska into a bear hug. She squeezed him tightly back.

"I love you. Just be safe, okay?" he whispered into her hair.

"I'll do my best."

"I can't believe you," Ty said, shaking his head. "How many lectures have you given me about not fighting people, then *you* do it? And in front of the whole town."

They were eating dinner at the small kitchen table. Mason had repaired it rather than making a new one. Sanded it down, stained it, and fixed a leg that was threatening to wobble off.

"I didn't fight anybody," Mason said calmly. "We had a discussion about a difference of opinion."

Ty rolled his eyes.

"So it's okay to hit somebody if I don't agree with their opinion?"

Please save him from teenage logic.

"No, it isn't." Mason spooned some chili into his mouth. He was going to have to mix up their repertoire. He liked chili, but he didn't want to be eating it for the next thirty weeks. "And you know that, because that's what got you in trouble at your last school."

That and the gang he'd been hanging around with. At least he didn't have to worry about gangs in Winterville.

"Yeah well I know you used to get in trouble when you

were a kid," Ty said, giving him an annoyed look. "Preach told me all the stories."

Of course he had. Preach loved talking about what a punk Mason used to be. But he'd learned the hard way that using your fists got you nowhere. He didn't want Ty to have to learn, too.

"I just don't get why you had to have a brawl in the middle of the street," Ty continued. "Everybody's talking about it."

Mason frowned. By the time Ty had gotten off the bus everything was over. North and his family had gone into the Tavern and Mason had slunk back to his truck and turned on a talk radio show to try to calm himself down. He hadn't planned on telling Ty about this at all. He should have known the gossip would spread like wildfire.

"Like who? Is there some kind of Winterville Forum? Did somebody take a video?" Mason asked.

"What century are you living in? Nobody goes on forums anymore. We use Snapchat and TikTok. Or Reddit. Or if we're feeling old school, we might go on Twitter." Ty shot Mason a look that you could only get from a teenager.

"Okay then." Mason wasn't going to get riled. He didn't like to lose control. It was bad enough that North had pushed him to the edge in the streets. "Have you been talking on Snapchat?"

"No. But everybody in the Inn was talking about it when I dropped off my résumé. I have friends who work there, you know?"

Mason blinked. "You have friends?"

"Yeah." Ty put his spoon down and frowned at his older brother. "Of course I have friends."

"It's just that you keep telling me you hate everything and everybody here. I guess that excludes your friends?"

Ty let out a sigh. "Okay then, they're people I go to school with. I don't hate them, but I don't know them. But now everybody knows me because I'm the kid whose brother beat up one of the town's VIPs."

"Okay," Mason said. "Let's get one thing straight. I didn't beat him up. He got the wrong information about something. I suggested we take it outside because I didn't want everybody up in my business and then somehow it escalated." And that didn't sound much better. He was supposed to be setting a good example for his brother.

He needed to do better. Keep a low profile. Avoid going into town wherever possible would help.

Avoiding Alaska Winter would help even more.

"Because you kissed our neighbor." Ty rolled his eyes.

"You know about that?" Mason's brows knitted.

"Of course I know about that. Everybody knows about that. I'm not an idiot, Mase. I'm not a little kid either. You do stuff and I hear about it." He picked up his spoon again, the metal clattering against the china of his bowl. "And believe me when I tell you, I really didn't want to hear that."

"It wasn't a real kiss."

"It was according to Laura Gaughran. She's Lisa's daughter. She said her mom saw it first-hand."

Mason winced. "It's not what you think. Lisa was being persistent and Alaska was trying to save me by pretending there was something going on between us." He looked Ty straight in the eye. "But there isn't."

Ty shrugged. "Makes sense why her cousin tried to smash you up."

"Why does that make sense?" Mason frowned.

"Cos you used her. If she was my cousin, I'd probably smash you up, too."

A weird tightness wound around Mason's chest. "I didn't use her. She's the one who kissed me."

"Did you push her away?"

No, he didn't. He'd kissed her hard and deep, and he could

still remember the hard-on he got. "It doesn't matter. It's over with. All of it. I'll avoid the Winter family and you should, too."

"It'll be tough. I got a text that I got the job. I start next Saturday."

He'd forgotten all about that. "Oh. Well done." He tried to sound pleased for his brother.

"Thanks," Ty said sarcastically. "I really appreciate your support. Especially the way you're building such great relationships with all my bosses."

He felt like an asshole, because Ty was really trying this time, and Mason was doing everything to make it more difficult. It was like he was the kid and Ty was the adult for once. He didn't like the way this whole situation made him feel out of control. Like he was on a boat, tilting to the right, unable to keep himself standing.

"I'm serious," Mason told him. "I'm proud of you. I know this hasn't been easy, but you're doing good." Ty had even gone to his counseling session. He'd made an appointment for a second session, too.

Mollified, Ty nodded and took another mouthful of chili. "You know the other good thing?"

"What?"

"I get to eat at the Inn whenever I work. And I'm not ordering chili." Ty looked pleased with himself. "And can I ask you a favor?"

"Sure," Mason said, expecting his brother to ask for a ride to the Inn on Saturday.

"Please don't kiss my new boss again."

9

Almost a week passed before Mason saw Alaska again. You could say he'd been avoiding her, but really he was busy putting the finishing touches on the house. All except the bathroom which he would start on this weekend.

After Ty left for school, Mason poured himself a mug of steaming coffee and walked onto the deck. It was his favorite place to drink in the morning, especially since the ground was covered with freshly fallen snow. The view of the white-capped mountains was breathtaking, reminding him exactly why he'd brought Ty here to finish his school year out.

The mountains had been here for centuries. Millennia maybe. They didn't care about the hopes or worries of the humans that stared at them. They just stayed strong. Immovable. Battered by wind and snow but never giving in.

And they'd be here long after he and Ty were just dust in the wind.

Maybe that shouldn't feel comforting. All he knew was that he'd avoided this place for so long, fearing the memories would eat him alive. But now that he was here he realized why his dad had chosen this cabin all those years ago.

Why he'd brought Mason here when he was eight years old for them to spend a few months together before everything would fall apart. He swallowed a mouthful of coffee, his eyes squinting at the steam that rose from the surface, then leaned on the rail of the deck and let out a sigh.

A bang of a door disturbed the quiet of the still, winter air. It wasn't his door, though. It came from too far away. Which meant it had to be Alaska's. He tipped his head to watch as a ball of what looked like blonde fluff came bolting off her deck and into the snow, followed by Alaska, wearing a pair of shorts and a tank and nothing else.

She hollered loudly, but the blonde animal kept moving. Then she did what looked like a frustrated jump on the deck–the kind that toddlers did when they didn't get their way–before pulling on her boots and running into the snow.

She was going to get hypothermia. He looked down at his own clothes–his usual outfit of jeans, working boots and a thick flannel shirt over a thermal long sleeved shirt. They had to wear layers to keep warm in the cabin, despite the workable heating system.

"Get back here!" Alaska yelled. The animal was hurtling through the snow, heading for the tree line that began a few hundred yards from their houses. A herd of deer lived in there–Mason occasionally saw one or two of them emerge from the wooded glade to look for food–but he hadn't seen any animals more threatening than that, despite his teasing of Ty when they first arrived.

Still, that animal–whatever the hell it was–would get lost within a moment. From here, he couldn't tell if it was a dog or a cat. It could even be a ferret, but who the hell would have one of those in the house?

"STOP!!"

Alaska's plaintive cry hit something in him. He put his half-drunk coffee on the rail and walked down the steps that led from his deck into what was supposedly a backyard, but really just led to the trees.

"What are you doing?" he yelled at Alaska. "Get inside, you're gonna freeze."

She did a double take when she heard his voice. Her head snapped to look at his. "I need to get Leo."

The animal had almost made it to the trees. Mason really didn't want to do this. He wanted to go inside and not be involved. He didn't want to be looking at a beautiful woman wearing only a pair of shorts and a tank, her blonde hair flowing down her back as she ran in thick, brown boots through the snow.

Because she did things to him that he didn't need right now.

"I'll get him," he said, starting to run. "You go inside. Now."

He ran like hell for the tree line. Which kind of hurt because he was thirty-four years old. And even though he hated to admit it, he couldn't run like he was a kid anymore. But he still did it, his feet thumping against the snow-covered ground, his breath puffing through his lips into clouds of vapor, as he closed the gap between him and... *Leo*?

A lion? It had better fucking not be, even if it was only three pounds of lion. He'd almost made it to the trees when Leo, what-ever-the-hell-he-was, ran into the shadows. It took another second for him to catch up with the damn animal and make a lunge for him.

The slippery little sucker slid out of his first grasp, but his second try was successful. His hands closed in around fur and more fur. Dammit, what the hell was this animal anyway? Huffing out another breath, Mason lifted Leo up to his chest.

Nope, still no idea what it was. It looked like some kind of teddy bear on acid. And whatever he was, he didn't want to be held. He squirmed and scratched against Mason's chest.

"Got him!" he shouted, walking out of the trees. Alaska was standing there, still basically half naked, her long smooth legs enhanced by the thick leather of her boots.

She looked like a sleepy dominatrix. Her hair was wild, her face flushed, her breasts perky. Not that he was looking. No, sir.

"What the hell is this thing?" he asked her, trying to avoid looking at her chest.

"He's a puppy. A chow chow," she told him, grinning.

Mason held him out at arm's length. Leo looked like a cross between a lion and a bear. Flat face, beady eyes, a thick mane of fur. He looked pissed, if that was possible. Like Mason had spoiled his fun.

Yeah, well I just saved you from being bear meat, my friend.

Leo twisted his body in Mason's grasp, letting out a high-pitched wail.

"You're hurting him," Alaska said.

"I'm just holding him," Mason grunted. "Unless you want me to put him down again."

"Oh God no." She shook her head. "I can take him now... oh."

"Oh what?" He frowned.

"You're bleeding." She pointed at his stomach.

Mason looked down at where his shirt was open, revealing his white thermal top. Sure enough, there was a rip in the white fabric, beads of blood spilling through. "I'll tell you what," he said, his voice low. "I'll clean myself up if you go inside before you die of exposure. Deal?"

"It is a little cold," she admitted.

"Then get the hell inside!" He marched over to her, still holding the demon dog against his chest with one hand as he put the other on Alaska's shoulder. He steered her toward her house, and she complied. Maybe she had some sense of self-preservation after all. "You need to get into the shower and warm up," he told her, feeling her ice cold skin beneath his warm palm. "I'm serious, Alaska. You could get sick."

"Okay, okay," she said, her teeth chattering. She was almost running to keep pace with his long strides. "But you need to clean up those cuts. When did you have your last tetanus shot?"

"I don't know." He shook his head. "And they're not cuts, they're scratches."

"Puppy claws are sharp. I can't walk him yet, and he's not had all his shots to go to a dog park, so there's nothing to wear them down into blunt ends."

"He walks pretty well by himself."

"Yeah, well he was supposed to relieve himself and come right back. But then he saw a bird and got distracted. He ran before I could stop him."

Yeah, distracted. That was easily done. Like he could get completely distracted by the way certain parts of her body were straining against the thin fabric of her pajamas. If he looked down, he could see the line of her cleavage disappearing below her top.

Do. Not. Look. Down.

His eyes weren't getting the memo, damn it.

When they made it to her back door, Mason wrenched it open and practically pushed her inside. Then he held Leo out to her like an offering.

"Could you bring him in?" she asked, shivering. "Just keep an eye on him while I shower?"

He tried to think of an excuse but came up blank. And anyway, he needed to make sure she didn't really have hypothermia. "Okay," he said. "But I'm not holding him the whole time."

She nodded. Her teeth were setting a fast rhythm. "I won't be long."

At least her clothes were dry. He was pretty sure she was

suffering from a case of the stupids rather than needing hospitalization, but he'd wait here. He put Leo gently on the floor and leaned against the wall as she ran out of her hallway and up the stairs.

"Stay in that shower for ten minutes," he shouted at her.

"You're so bossy," she said, leaning over the banister.

Yeah, she was okay. His lips twitched. Then he heard the shower turn on. Leo was darting around the living room, jumping like a cat at imaginary mice. Then he ran over to Mason and started trying to climb his jeans.

"No, thank you," Mason said, pulling his claws out of the denim. His stomach was stinging where the dog had scratched him. Sighing, he rolled his thermal undershirt up and grimaced when he saw the line of three scratches. It wasn't a mauling, but it had broken the skin.

And he really didn't want to get a tetanus booster. Shrugging his shirt off, and pulling his undershirt over his head, he walked to Alaska's kitchen and yanked open her cupboards until he found a first aid kit. Then he grabbed some paper towels and ran them under the faucet before cleaning off the scrapes.

What was it with him and the Winter family–pets included? They all seemed to want to injure him.

"Okay, I don't think I'm dying..." Her words trailed off as she walked into the kitchen. Mason was standing at the counter, shirtless, rubbing ointment into his stomach.

And she nearly combusted.

Hello abs! The man should come with some kind of warning. That kind of view shouldn't be allowed this early in the morning. His chest was sculpted, his stomach ripped, scant dark hair covering him from his pecs down to a thin line that led from his stomach to his...

She wanted to fan herself. Maybe she over did the hot shower.

He looked up at her, and her wide eyes were captured by his. A half-smirk pulled at his lips.

"Um..." She desperately tried to think of something to say.

"I thought I'd better put some antiseptic ointment on the scratches," he told her, his voice low. "In case your dog has cooties."

"You mean tetanus."

"I mean whatever it is you're worried about. I have it covered." Which was more than he could say for his chest. "Now I'm going to go home and finish my coffee."

Disappointment washed over her. This was the best view she'd had for years and she wasn't sure she was ready for it to end. "It'll be cold. I'll make us both one." She flashed him a smile. "I have pastries I can warm up, too. A peace offering."

"You don't owe me anything," he said. "It wasn't your fault your..." He frowned, as though he couldn't believe it was actually a dog. "Leo scratched me."

"Yeah, well I feel like we're all ganging up on you. With North nearly knocking you out, and me all over you before that. And now Leo." She pulled her lip between her teeth and his eyes dipped down to look at them. "Anyway, please stay."

"North didn't nearly knock me out," he said, his brows knitting.

She bit down a smile, because that's what he took from her words? He had a macho streak in him. Not that it mattered, she was used to those. Her cousins had practically trademarked the word.

Mason put the ointment back into her first aid kit and lifted it into the cupboard. As he turned, she caught the sight of a tattoo on his left arm, right beneath where it met his shoulder.

She swallowed as the muscle beneath it flexed. Damn, he was built.

"What's that date?" she asked, immediately regretting it, because seriously, curiosity was going to kill her in the end.

"What date?"

"On your arm." She scanned her eyes over it. There were two dates tattooed on his bicep in black script.

He glanced down at his arm, then back at her. "Those are the dates I went into foster care and the date I left."

They covered almost eight years. "How old were you when you went in?"

"Eleven." He ran the tip of his tongue along his bottom lip. "I got the tattoo the day I escaped from the system. Wanted a reminder that I'd never let anybody control my life again."

Alaska let out a long breath. She couldn't imagine this big, taciturn man being controlled by anybody. "I'm sorry," she mumbled.

He shrugged. "It wasn't your fault."

"I meant for asking. I was being nosey and I shouldn't have."

He pulled his white thermal over his head. She was glad, because now she didn't have to stop herself from ogling him.

"If I didn't want people asking I wouldn't have it permanently etched on my skin," he told her. "I'm not embarrassed about being in foster care. It wasn't my fault either. It's part of my story, not all of it." He slid his arms into his thick shirt, then ruffled his hair to get into some kind of order. "And if you're wondering why I went into care at eleven, which most people do, it's because my mom died when I was eight and my dad was sent to prison three years later."

He lifted his head, as though he was waiting for something. She wasn't sure what he needed though.

A little voice in her head told her she could tell her own story. The one that started her own kind of imprisonment.

But she didn't want him to see her differently. She liked the way he treated her like she wasn't some kind of fragile doll.

"What did you do after you aged out? Apart from heading straight to the tattoo parlor?" She turned on her coffee pot–she'd filled it last night the way she always did–and grabbed some milk from the refrigerator.

"I went to college on a full scholarship. Worked my ass off and went to law school."

She blinked. "You're a lawyer?"

"I was."

She glanced at him over her shoulder. He was watching her. She liked it. "So what's this, a sabbatical or something?"

"Something like that," he said gruffly.

Okay, so he had limits when it came to her curiosity. She could live with that. "It's nice that you get to spend time with Ty." She grabbed two pastries and slid them into the toaster oven, flicking the timer on for ten minutes.

"Nice isn't quite the right word. Aggravating, maybe. Gray-hair inducing for sure."

Her lips twitched. "Did you never want kids of your own?" Okay, so apparently her curiosity didn't have an off switch.

"Nope."

The coffee machine was sputtering. She grabbed two mugs and put them on the counter. Mason was leaning against the breakfast bar on the other side, his arms folded across his chest. He didn't look annoyed at her questioning. More bemused than anything.

"How about you? I can see you surrounded by a dozen of 'em."

"You can?" She smiled, liking that picture.

"Yeah. And you'll probably lose at least one or two a day. They'll run for the forest like Leo."

She laughed because she could picture that, too. "I'll remember to lock the doors."

His eyebrow lifted. "You should remember to do that, anyway. You're a single woman living in the middle of nowhere."

She rolled her eyes. "I already have my family telling me that. I don't need anybody else. And I'm more likely to get eaten by wildlife than have anything else happen. I don't think animals check if you're single or married before they devour you for dinner."

"Smart ass."

"Yeah, well, you can't live your life dictated by fear, can you?" she asked him. "Sure, I'm careful. I don't know any woman who isn't. But I will not cower in a little cottage on my cousin's estate just because there's a one in a million chance that somebody might come along with ill intent."

"Your cousin asked you to live on his estate?" Mason asked.

"He wanted to build me a house."

"Figures." He lifted a brow.

"Right?" She sighed, grabbing the now filled coffee pot. "How do you take it?"

"Black no sugar."

She shot him a smile. "Figures."

"What? Why?" He looked suddenly interested. "What does my coffee choice tell you?"

"That you've had to train yourself to like coffee black because you never have cream in the house. And now you tell yourself that's exactly how you like it, because anything else would be admitting a weakness."

"Did you do a psychology course?" He seemed amused.

"Nope. I just deal with a lot of people in my job. I get insights that other people don't. From how they like their pillows to the newspapers they read to the screaming arguments I have to break up in the middle of the night." She passed him his coffee, and he took it with a nod. "And don't get me started on the number of people who turn up at the hotel with somebody who clearly isn't the person they're married to."

"Sounds like my job. You get to see the worst of humanity."

She sipped her coffee. "And the best, too. Especially at this time of year. The families are my favorites. Seeing the kids' faces light up when they see Santa around the tree. Or hearing everybody come back from the Jingle Bell Theater after a show." She smiled at the thought of it. "It's magical."

He swallowed down a mouthful of coffee, his throat undulating. "It sounds it." His voice was hoarse.

And for a moment he stared at her and she stared back. Then he dragged his eyes away and pointedly looked at his watch. "I should go. I need to start work on the bathroom." He hadn't even drunk half his coffee.

Ugh, she'd said too much. She always did. "Of course. And I need to get this little guy to my sister."

"He's not your dog?"

"I'm dog sitting. Well dog sharing really. And doing it badly if this morning is anything to go by." She wrinkled her nose. "He's never run off before."

"Yeah, well he'll have a taste for it now."

"That's what I'm worried about. He'll make a bolt for it every time until he's trained." She sighed. "I guess I'll have to put him on a leash every time nature calls."

"Or at least put some clothes on first."

She rolled her eyes again. He didn't quite smile, but his lips threatened it.

As though he knew they were talking about him, Leo abandoned the rubber bone he'd been chewing on and padded over to her, scrabbling at her legs. She reached down to ruffle his mane, and he licked her palm, making it tickle.

"I'll make you a run," he told her. "That way you'll avoid hypothermia."

"What?"

"A run. A little enclosure that you can put against the door so he can only go so far when he needs to potty. You won't need it for too long, just until he's trained."

She rolled her bottom lip between her teeth. "You don't need to do that. I know you're busy."

"I do need to do it. If I see you running in the snow in your pajamas again, I'll probably have a heart attack. Call it self-preservation."

There was something in his voice. A deep roughness that made her body clench. One thing about Mason Parker–he seemed to hate offering help as much as she hated accepting it.

"It'll take me a couple of days to get everything I need," he told her. "In the meantime, please put a damn coat on or something."

"Okay. But at least let me pay for the materials and your time."

"Not happening."

Of course it wasn't. But it was only polite to offer. But she figured politeness didn't matter a lot to Mason.

She was starting to wonder what did.

10

Mason was drinking coffee on the deck early the following Saturday when Ty opened the kitchen door, wincing as the ice-cold air hit his face.

"How do you knot this freaking thing?" Ty asked, a red necktie wrapped around his hand. From its wrinkled state, he'd been trying–and failing–for a while.

"Give it to me." Mason held his hand out. Ty's face was stony, but he said nothing as he handed the tie to Mason, then let his brother wrap the tie around the back of his neck where the collar was upturned.

"It's just a matter of practice," Mason told him, threading the fabric first under, then round, before sliding it through the loop. "Under, around, and through. That's the easiest way. There are more complicated ones, but you don't need to learn them now."

Ty nodded. He looked nervous. Mason's chest clenched because he knew how much this job mattered to his brother. It wasn't just the money, it was the chance to meet new people. To get out of this goddamned cabin and into the world.

"Did Dad teach you how to do this?" Ty asked.

"Nope. One of my foster parents, I think. Or a girlfriend. I can't remember." Mason shrugged. It was all so long ago. All he knew was that his dad didn't teach him very much about being an adult.

As he straightened the tie, his brother glanced over his shoulder and let out a slow whistle. Mason glanced to where his brother was looking. There was Alaska again, in her short pajamas, her hair tumbling over her shoulders. She opened the gate to the enclosure Mason had made for her and shuffled Leo in.

"She's hot for an older woman."

"She's your boss," Mason said sharply. "That kind of talk will get you fired before you've begun."

Ty rolled his eyes. The teenager was back. "I'm not planning on saying it at work, doofus."

"Call me a doofus again and you won't be getting a ride to work."

"Oh yeah?" Ty mock-squared up to him. He was almost as tall as Mason. His features were still rounded, waiting for that testosterone boost to sharpen his jaw and nose, and to hollow out his cheeks, but he was nearly a man.

Where had the time gone? Mason could still remember the day Ty was born. Though his dad was out of prison by that point, Mason had still been in foster care. They wouldn't release him to his dad no matter how much they'd both pleaded.

There'd been no room for him in his dad and Ty's mom's studio apartment, anyway. But he would have slept in a closet if he'd been given the chance.

He blinked that thought away, because that was so many years ago. They were here, and they were both okay.

Mason's lip quirked as he looked at his brother. "Think you're a big man?" he teased, the memories gone now.

Ty smirked. "I know it. I could take you, old man. Any time I want."

"Try it."

Before the words had finished coming out of his mouth, Ty swung his arm around Mason's shoulders and hooked it around his neck, pulling him into a headlock. Mason went to buck out of it–Ty's hold wasn't that strong–but then he saw the absolute delight on his brother's face.

He thought he was winning. And damn he deserved that. God knew he hadn't won at life.

Not yet.

"I got you!" Ty sung out, pure joy in his words.

Mason's stomach tightened. "Yeah, you did." And then it came out. Unbidden and unexpected. A wave of emotion he didn't know what to do with. "You're a good kid, Ty." He wanted to say more but he couldn't. Even the thought of talking about feelings made Mason's throat feel constricted. But he cared for this kid. More than he would ever know.

Ty swallowed. "Yeah, you're all right yourself." He released Mason's neck, and he stood, pretending it was painful to roll his neck.

"Your tie's askew," Mason said gruffly, reaching out to straighten it. Ty swallowed as he did, his eyes not quite meeting Mason's.

"You know the other thing about Alaska?" Ty said, like he was as desperate as Mason to get away from the subject of feelings.

"What?" Mason steeled himself for a description of her body. Because that's what teenagers did. Not that he needed a description. Those curves were burned into his memory. Every time he saw her it made his body tighten.

"She's so kind. And she doesn't have to be. Not when she's the boss. And especially after what happened to her."

Mason blinked. "What happened to her? What are you talking about?"

"The abduction."

Mason froze. "What abduction?"

"When she was a kid. Somebody took her for two days. Nobody knows who or why." Ty looked at him carefully. "Are you okay?"

"I'm fine," he grunted. "Did Alaska tell you this?"

"No. I heard somebody talking about it at the hotel."

There was rushing in Mason's ears like he was on an out-of-control train. "You sure? It was definitely Alaska?"

"Yeah." Ty's voice wavered. "You're not gonna say anything, are you? I wasn't supposed to overhear that conversation I don't think."

"I won't say anything," Mason said, a hundred thoughts racing through his head. He wouldn't ask her about it, but he sure as hell had questions that needed answering.

And there was only one person he knew who could help him with that.

He waited until Ty had disappeared back into his bedroom, then grabbed his phone and sat out on the back deck, staring at the snow-tipped mountains and gray sky. Preach answered after the first ring.

"Sup?"

"I need your help with something."

"You need me?" Preach asked. "That's a first." He sounded stupidly pleased. "Okay then, hit me with it."

"I need you to find out some information for me." Mason was still trying to get everything straight in his mind. "A girl disappeared for a couple of days here in Winterville a while back. I want you to find out what happened."

"Legally or illegally?" Preach asked.

"Whatever it takes." He needed to know the truth.

Preach chuckled. "Got it. Text me the details and I'll get to work. Wanna tell me what this is all about?"

"No. Not yet." Mason needed to know more first. His next stop was the library in Marshall's Gap. He'd already checked and they had a newspaper archive there.

"The little girl. Did she get hurt?" Preach asked him. "Killed?"

"She's still alive." And he didn't know how hurt she'd been. "Grown up. Still lives here."

"Send the details over to me. She a friend of yours?" Preach sounded interested now.

"Just an acquaintance. I gotta go, Preach. Thanks for doing this for me."

"Any time, buddy. But you're gonna give me the full details soon, right?"

Maybe he would. Mason wasn't sure. All he knew was that he had to find out the truth. Even if it changed everything.

Alaska put the crate of beers down on the stoop and knocked on Mason's door. She knew he wouldn't accept money, but she couldn't let him make something for her without giving him something in return.

Beer seemed innocuous enough. He couldn't turn those down, could he? And then she'd feel better because the run he'd made for Leo was like some kind of fine carpentry. The man had skills.

He swung the door open, three lines pinching the top of his nose when he saw her standing there. Her smile wavered.

"Hi, I just wanted to say thank you for making the run," she told him, nudging the crate with her toe. "So I bought you some beer."

He looked down at the crate like it was a meteor that had landed from space. “Uh, yeah, thanks.”

“I should have brought them sooner, but we’ve been busy as heck at the hotel,” she told him. “This is my first day off. I get tomorrow off, too, so that’s some kind of compensation. I’ll probably sleep all day.”

Mason shifted his feet. “Right.”

Ugh, he didn’t want to hear about her days off. She wanted to hit herself for being so chatty.

He lifted his head from the crate, but didn’t meet her gaze.

“Did I do something wrong?” she asked him. “Should I have called first?”

“What?” His head snapped up, and finally those warm eyes met hers. “No. I’m just... I’ve got things to do. I need to head out to Marshall’s Gap.”

“Oh. Sorry for interrupting you.” She tried to keep the hurt from her voice. “I’ll let you go.”

He winced as though he could hear the hurt, anyway. “You don’t need to be sorry. Thanks for the beer. You didn’t need to do that.”

“And you didn’t need to make me a run for Leo, but you did.”

“I did need to make that run,” he told her stiffly.

“Okay then.” She let out a mouthful of air. “So that’s it. Thanks and... yeah. See you later.” This time she didn’t hide the hurt. She didn’t know why his grumpiness affected her so much.

Actually, yes she did. He was treating her like he treated Lisa. Keeping her on the step, looking at her gift like it came with obligations. She’d thought they were friends–or at least that they could become friends.

She didn’t need his bad mood. And she didn’t need him.

Without saying another word, she turned on her heel and walked down the steps, the icy wind whipping at her hair.

"Alaska," he called out, his voice hoarse.

"What?" She wasn't in the mood for any more of this.

"I'm sorry. It's a bad morning..." He looked straight at her, running his thumb over his jaw. "Thank you for the beers. I appreciate them."

She nodded. "Okay."

"Okay." His eyes were still on hers. "I have to head out for a few hours. Do you have Leo with you?"

What a strange question. "No, he's with my sister. She's bringing him over later."

"Ty should be home in a few hours. If there's any trouble before then, make sure you call me. Or your cousins."

She blinked at his mention of them. "What's going on? Should I be worried?"

Mason shifted his feet. "No. I just like knowing... that you're safe."

"You're being weird. You know that?" She tipped her head to the side, trying to read his expression.

"I know," he said, shrugging. "But humor me."

She rolled her eyes, and he rolled his back, making her smile. Then she turned again, her back to him as she walked down the pathway to her car.

He liked knowing she was safe. That was interesting. It was also tantalizing.

Yes, he was grumpy. And he had no people skills. But damn if that man didn't make her feel hot inside. And outside. Not to mention all the spaces in between.

11

It was just after five that evening when Alaska heard a knock on the door. She'd spent the afternoon getting some laundry done. It had piled up during her busy time at work, and took a good three hours to run it all through the washer and then the dryer, shaking it all out to avoid having to iron it.

Everley had dropped Leo off between her shows. She hadn't had time to talk, and maybe Alaska liked it that way. Her mind was too full of thoughts to talk.

Mostly about Mason Parker. Why was she so intrigued by him? From the start, she'd felt an attraction–though to be fair, most warm-blooded women would. In fact, they did–the single women of Winterville proved that by lining up to give him baked goods.

He was a handsome man. Grumpy, sure, but she didn't mind that. In fact, it suited him, like a well-fitting jacket. She couldn't imagine a sunshiney Mason.

It would be weird. And maybe less attractive. An over-the-top happy Mason wouldn't have kissed her like she was the air he needed to survive. He wouldn't have frog marched her back to the house because he was certain she was going to get hypothermia.

The only problem was, a happy Mason wouldn't set her body on fire the way a growly, taciturn Mason did. He treated her like she was his equal. They sparred. She liked it way too much.

Except today he'd felt different. She wasn't sure what that meant.

Walking to the door, she opened it fully expecting to see the man she couldn't get out of her mind. Instead, Ty was standing there still in his hotel uniform, holding out some papers.

"The chef asked me to deliver these," he said, as she took them. Glancing down, she could see they were next week's menus. The man had a severe allergy to email and always insisted on hand writing them for her approval.

"Oh, thank you." She smiled at him. "How was your shift?"

"Good." He nodded. "I got to try out the booking system. I even took some payments."

She smiled broadly because he looked happy about that. "That's wonderful. We'll make a receptionist out of you yet." She looked over his shoulder at his house in the distance. Mason's truck wasn't there. "Who dropped you at home?"

"Grace did. Said it was on her way."

Grace was one of their long-standing Saturday workers. She was a single mom and worked whenever her kids were with her ex-husband. "That's right. She lives in Marshall's Gap."

"I tried to give her gas money, but she refused." Ty didn't look too pleased about that. Maybe there was more than a touch of Mason in him.

"She wouldn't have wanted anything. We take care of each other at the hotel." She smiled. "If it becomes a regular thing, you could always get her something for Christmas. She loves candles."

Ty nodded. "Okay then. I guess I'll see you around."

She glanced over his shoulder again. The daylight was fading, and the clouds looked thick above. They were in for another covering of snow tonight. "Will Mason be back soon, do you think?"

He shrugged. "No idea. He told me to message him when I got home."

She didn't like the idea of Ty going back to the cabin alone. Yes, he was seventeen, old enough to take care of himself. But she still felt strange letting him leave.

"I was just about to have a coffee. You want to come in and have a drink?"

"No, it's okay," Ty said quickly. "Mason says I shouldn't bother you too much."

Her chest clenched. "You're no bother. It's nice to have company. You can message Mason to let him know you're here and head home when he gets there."

Pressing his lips together, Ty nodded. "If it's really okay with you?"

"It is." She opened the door wide, and he stepped through, following her down the hallway to her living room. As soon as she opened that door, Leo came barreling toward them, launching himself at Ty's legs.

Ty laughed and reached down, stroking Leo's fur. "Mason told me you had a dog. Said he's like Houdini in animal form." Leo started licking his hand and Ty's eyes crinkled.

Her chest clenched. "He just needs a little training. I'm working on it. But my sister, his owner, keeps spoiling him stupid."

Ty looked at her over his shoulder, still playing with Leo. Something in his expression reminded her of Mason. "How many sisters do you have again?" he asked.

"Just one sister, but lots of cousins."

"Yeah, I remember you had a big family." Leo rolled onto his back and Ty tickled his stomach, causing Leo to let out what sounded like a purr.

"I do. You'll probably meet a lot of them working at the Inn. Holly runs the business side, and Nicole runs the yoga classes in our fitness suite. The others are always dropping in, because they have nothing better to do than annoy me." She did a mock grimace and Ty laughed.

"It must be nice to have so many people who care for you." He sounded wistful.

"Yeah," she breathed. "It is. But you have your brother. That must be nice."

Ty lifted a brow. "Sometimes."

"That's families for you. Can't live with them, can't live with them."

"You said that twice."

She grinned. "I know. I meant to." She pulled her lip between her teeth, glancing out of the window at the tree line beyond. "Is Mason okay?" she asked Ty. "He was weird when I went to see him earlier. I wasn't sure if I'd upset him."

"Weird in what way?" Ty asked her. He was laying on the floor now, Leo clambering over him.

"It doesn't matter," Alaska said quickly, because she shouldn't be discussing Mason with his brother. "I'm sure I was imagining it."

Ty tilted his head, Leo licking his jaw. "Did he say something to upset you? Because I can hit him if he did."

She laughed. "No violence, please. And he said nothing. It just looked like he didn't want me there. Like he couldn't wait to get rid of me."

"Oh." Ty blinked and lifted Leo from his stomach, rolling onto his knees. "I told him not to say anything." He sighed. "I told him about you disappearing when you were a kid and he got real angry about it. Maybe it's something to do with that?"

Alaska swallowed even though her mouth felt dry. "He knows about that?"

"I'm sorry." Ty blinked. "I overheard someone talking about it at the Inn and mentioned it to him."

She shook her head. "You don't need to be sorry. It's not exactly a secret. Most people around here know about it. I just..." She just didn't want Mason to know. To treat her the same as the others. Like she was glass about to shatter in his hands.

Ty still looked guilty.

"Seriously, don't sweat it," she told him. "You haven't done anything wrong." There was no way he should feel bad about telling his brother the truth. "It's just that people treat me differently when they hear about my disappearance."

"Differently how?" Ty asked, interested.

Alaska tried to think of the right words. "Like I'm fragile and full of secrets and maybe they're scared that it might be catching."

Ty nodded slowly. "I get that. People were like that after my dad died."

"They were?"

"Yeah. I guess that's why I decided to say 'to hell with it all' and do what I wanted. The only people who didn't treat me like I should be crying all the time were the bad kids. They were too busy drinking to care about that."

She eyed him carefully. "Is that why you had to come here?"

He shrugged. "Mase said I got in with the wrong crowd. I stopped going to school, failed my classes. And then I got arrested."

"I'm sorry."

"Don't be sorry. I was an asshole." His brows knitted.

"You're not going to treat me differently, are you? Just because my dad is dead?"

"No, I'm not," she promised. "If you promise not to treat me differently because I disappeared for a couple of days."

"I won't," he said, his expression sincere. "I'll treat you exactly the same."

She smiled at him. "Good. Now how about that drink? I've got soda or coffee." She lifted a brow. "But no beer."

He laughed. "Coffee would be good. With lots of cream and sugar."

Ah, he took it like her and not his brother. She winked. "That's exactly how I like it, too."

Mason stared at the documents Preach had emailed to him. And there it was in black and white. Alaska Winter had disappeared for almost forty hours when she was eight years old, before walking into the police station, a cut and bruise on her head, and her body grimy from being wherever the hell she'd been for almost two days.

And she'd lost all memory of what had happened to her.

Jesus. He shook his head because no kid should go through that. But knowing it was her... it was killing him.

Thank God for Preach. Mason's trip to the library had turned up nothing at all. There'd been nothing in the papers about a little girl disappearing, even though it had to be the biggest thing that had happened around here for decades.

"The stuff I'm sending through was suppressed," Preach told him. "I got it, but I shouldn't have it. Once you read it delete it, okay? Don't get me into trouble over this."

"What do you mean suppressed?" Mason asked.

"I mean it's restricted access. I assume because this little girl's grandma was famous."

"You think she paid people to suppress it?" That would explain the lack of newspaper articles. And he didn't even want to think about how Preach had gotten the information. He knew people, but those people weren't exactly law-abiding citizens.

Still, Mason was glad he had.

"I dunno how it got suppressed," Preach said. "Either she had friends in high places or they were worried that it was some kind of kidnapping or extortion attempt. Whatever it was, they had this locked down tight."

But Preach had gotten it. And Mason knew he should feel bad for making his friend take the risks he had to get these documents. But Mason needed to see them for himself.

"You gonna tell me what this is about now?" Preach asked. "Because I also ran a check on this Alaska person. And I found out that she happens to live in the next house to yours."

Of course Preach had run a check. He was a nosy bastard. Mason sighed. He owed Preach an explanation, even if he didn't really want to give it. Standing, he glanced at Ty's door. He'd been in his bedroom pretty much since he'd gotten back from Alaska's house, just after Mason arrived back from town. It was shut, but he still didn't want his brother hearing this conversation. "Give me a minute, I just need to find somewhere quiet," he told Preach.

"I can wait."

Pulling the back door of the cabin open, Mason walked onto the deck. He immediately looked over at her house. The lights were blazing, but the curtains were closed. He resisted the urge to walk over there and check that she'd locked the doors.

"Okay then," Mason said clearing his throat. "So you might want to sit down for this."

Ty was in the kitchen when Mason walked back inside. The cold air rushed in with him, lifting the papers on the table.

"Hey," Ty said, pulling a mug out of the cupboard. "I'm just making some hot chocolate. You want some?"

"No thanks." Mason picked up the papers. They were where he'd left them, thank god. He didn't want Ty seeing them at all.

"You been over at Alaska's?" Ty asked him.

Mason blinked. "No. Why?"

"Dunno. Just thought you'd go over and apologize or something. She said you'd been an ass to her."

"She said that? When?"

"When I was at her place earlier." Ty rolled his eyes. "So what were you doing if you weren't at Alaska's?"

"Just getting some air." Mason looked at his brother. "Tell me exactly what she said about me."

Ty shot him a look. "She was right. You're being weird."

Mason raked his fingers through his hair. Ty was right, he was being crazy. But after finding out what he'd found out today...

"Anyway, she was upset. She thinks you think she's weak." Ty shrugged.

"What?" Mason frowned. "Why would she think that?"

"Because you found out that she'd disappeared and are now treating her different," Ty told him, spooning chocolate powder into his mug. "She says that happens a lot. That people think she's some kind of fragile woman because of something that happened when she was a kid."

Mason's throat tightened. "That's not true," he said gruffly. "I don't think she's fragile at all."

"You should tell her that, not me," Ty said. He'd made his

drink and had lost interest in the conversation. "I'm going to head to bed."

"Sure." Mason nodded. "I'm glad today went well for you." He'd at least remembered to ask about that when he'd gotten home from Marshall's Gap. Ty's first day at work was important.

"Thanks." Ty shot him a small smile. "Hey, did you hear about the storm?"

"What storm?"

"They were talking about it at the Inn. There might be a storm tomorrow or Monday. We might not have to go to school." Ty looked excited about that.

"Yeah, well do your homework anyway. Just in case." And Mason would check the generator oil to make sure they kept warm.

"Will do. Good night, bro."

"Night, Ty." Mason watched his brother disappear into his bedroom then sat down again at the small kitchen table, staring blankly at his laptop.

Ty was right. He owed Alaska an explanation. But the fact was, he didn't know what to say.

He'd wait until next week. Maybe inspiration would hit him by then. And in the meantime, he'd read these documents all over again.

12

Alaska cancelled her Sunday off and went into the Inn to help them prepare for the storm they'd forecast to start overnight. She'd spent the morning making sure their food supplies for Monday were delivered early, then organized for the driveway and paths to be cleared once the storm had passed. And just when she'd thought she'd be able to go home, North had walked into her office.

"Hey."

She smiled at him, because she knew exactly why he was here. "Hey. Before you ask, yes I'm going home to sit out the storm and yes, I have enough oil and the backup generator is ready in case the power goes out."

North had the good grace to look embarrassed. "I just wanted to make sure."

"I know, and I appreciate it. But I'm a big girl and I've lived through storms before. This isn't even going to be a big one." She stood and gave him a hug. "Now, go to work. You have trees to worry about."

"I know. And I will. Amber is there already."

"Her boyfriend let her out then." Alaska grinned, because she knew it would rile North up.

"He's not her boyfriend. They're just dating." North rolled his eyes.

"Yeah, but he will be. She's a great catch. And she deserves to be happy, right?"

North swallowed hard. "Yeah, right."

"Okay then. If that's all, I'm going to get Leo home and batten down the hatches before the storm starts."

Leo looked up from the bed where he'd been dozing, at the sound of his name being called.

"You stay safe, okay?" North said gruffly.

"I will. And you too."

She watched as he ambled out of the office, no doubt on his way to see Everley at the theater to make sure she was safe, too.

For a moment, she thought about sending Mason a message to make sure he was ready for the storm. She could pick them something up on her way back from Winterville if they needed anything. But then she remembered his weirdness yesterday. He hadn't said a word to her since.

And yeah, that hurt a little. But he didn't owe her anything. She was a big girl, and she certainly wasn't going to beg for his attention.

Let him be grumpy, she was used to that.

Pulling on her coat and grabbing her purse, she took Leo's leash in her hand and walked out of the office with the pup in her arms.

"I'm heading home," she told Martin. "If there are any problems, call me okay?"

"Of course. But we've got this." He winked. "It's not even a big storm."

"That's what I said." She grinned. "Have a good night, Martin."

"You too." He nodded. "And stay safe."

Oh she would. If only to prove to everybody that she could.

The wind started whipping around the cabin right after one in the morning. She lay beneath the covers, listening to the rattle of the roof tiles and the soft snoring coming from Leo's cage. Something was loose on the porch, banging against the wall, but she couldn't find the energy to fix it.

The wind howled. And a moment later, Leo let out a howl, too. Groaning, she rolled out of bed and pulled her robe around her pajamas, tiptoeing into the kitchen and flicking on the lights.

"What's up, honey?" she whispered, opening up Leo's cage. He scrambled out onto her lap. "It's just a storm," she told him. "Nothing to be scared of."

Another howl. Leo looked around the room, then curled back into her lap. The lights flickered.

And then they died.

Damn. She'd need to start the generator before they froze to death. Sliding Leo back into his cage with promises of cuddles once she was back, she felt her way to the cupboard where she kept a flashlight, flicking it on to illuminate her way.

Leo let out a growl. "It's okay. We'll be okay," she told him. "I just need to put on some clothes." Thankfully, she'd left yesterday's joggers and sweatshirt in a pile on her floor. She pulled them on over her pajamas, along with some thick socks and her boots.

Then her phone lit up with a message.

She glanced at it, unsurprised to see who it was from.

. . .

Did you just lose power? – North

She typed back quickly.

Yes, but turning the generator on now. – Alaska

I'll drive over and get you. You can sleep here. – North

Don't you dare. I'm fine and I just want to get some sleep. I'll message you in the morning. – Alaska

There was a pause. She imagined him deciding just how pissed she'd be with him if he showed up, anyway. Better to nip this in the bud early.

I'm serious, North. If you come here, I won't forgive you. I'm a grown woman. I have a generator and a dog here. Now go back to sleep and I'll message you in the morning. – Alaska

You sure? – North

I'm certain. I love you. x – Alaska

Love you, too. Call me if you need anything. – North

. . .

I will. Now go to sleep and stop worrying! – Alaska

She was pretty sure North would do exactly that. If she'd have asked him, he would have picked her up without complaint, but she knew how to start the generator. She'd already used it once this year, when they'd had a power outage after a tree had fallen on the lines between here and Marshall's Gap and she'd needed the air conditioning to keep herself cool.

Pulling her coat on, she slid the flashlight back into her hand, checking on Leo who was already back snoring in his cage. Grabbing the keys to the generator shed, she pushed open the back door, having to use extra effort against the wind that was determined to keep it closed.

She maneuvered herself through the gap, gasping as the frozen air hit her face. It was so dark out here, the flashlight only illuminating one or two feet in front of her through the falling snow. Almost tripping over the run Mason had made for Leo, she managed to get down the steps and onto the path that led to the shed.

The gusts of wind were thick with snow, sticking to her coat and face, a few landing in her mouth when she took a deep breath. Pushing her way against the wind, she heard a plaintiff howl come from the trees. She couldn't blame whatever animal it was.

It was only ten yards between the house and the generator shed, yet it seemed to take forever. She was almost there when her foot slipped on a patch of fresh snow, the sudden skid whipping her legs out from under her. She landed with a hard thump on the ground, her pants already wet from the blowing snow.

Alaska scrambled to her knees, looking around for her

flashlight, breathing a sigh of relief when it was still lit up. Annoyed with herself for being so careless, she snatched it up and pushed to her feet, fighting against a painful gust to stay upright.

"Alaska!" The wind almost swallowed the deep voice.

For a moment, she thought that North had ignored her. She whipped her head around, snow still battering her skin, frowning when she saw the yellow circle of a flashlight bobbing toward her.

"I told you I'm fine!" The flashlight got closer. Enough for her to see the outline of its owner. As tall as North but broader. And she knew it wasn't her cousin.

It was Mason Parker.

"Why the fuck are you outside in this?" he shouted over the wind.

"I need to start the generator," she shouted back. "Go home. I don't need your help."

He caught up with her, tipping his flashlight so he could see her face. Her eyes blinked at the sudden onslaught.

"I'll do it," he told her. "Is it in there?" He angled his light at the shed.

"I don't need your help," she told him. "I can do it." She didn't need North, and she certainly didn't need Mason. She was stronger than that.

"Stop being stubborn. I can do it faster than you can." He was still shouting through the whistle of the wind.

Aggravation washed over her. She ignored him, grabbing the keys from her coat pocket, trying–and failing–to slide them into the lock. She jabbed them in again, and this time they slid into the locking mechanism.

But when she turned them to the left, they refused to budge. The goddamned lock had frozen.

She twisted again, still failing to turn it and then Mason's fingers curled around hers. Annoyed, she whipped around. "Are you still here? I thought I told you to go home."

He narrowed his eyes, not letting go of her hand. "I'm still here because you need help."

She gritted her teeth as he yanked the key to the left, and the lock released. She could feel him so close to her, his large body almost cradling hers from behind. Like he was trying to shield her from the storm as well as open the door.

Jerking the handle, she let out a sigh as the door released. It took strength to hold it against the push of the wind, but the last thing she needed was for the door to fly off and the generator to get covered with snow.

She stumbled inside, followed by Mason, who pulled the door shut. And yeah, she was grateful because she wasn't sure she could've done that. Even so, she would have tried.

His flashlight bobbed over the generator, as though he was assessing what needed to be done. She walked over to it, using her own light to find the fuel valve. Thank god that she'd ordered enough propane to power it up.

"Hold this." Mason held his flashlight out to her. "I'll start it up."

"I can do it." She wanted to roll her eyes. She knew how to do this. It was one of the first things she'd learned when she'd moved out here.

"I know you can," Mason said, his voice softer now that they were sheltered from the wind. "But you're shaking and freezing and I need to get you back inside."

Ignoring him, she turned the choke to the left. Mason sighed, but stepped forward, aiming his light at her hands so she could see what she was doing.

And yeah, she appreciated it. She'd tell him later once she was warm.

After she flipped the ignition on, she grabbed the cord and pulled it fast. It didn't work on the first pull. Or on the second either. She waited for Mason to say something but he didn't. He just kept his light aimed at her hands and waited.

Mustering her strength, she curled her fingers around the handle and yanked the cord as hard as she could. There was a moment's pause, and then the generator kicked on. It sounded like standing next to a motorcycle being revved, except the noise was constant, filling her ears.

"You have a gen tent?" Mason shouted.

"Over there." She pointed at the corner. The gen tent would protect the generator while it was running, in case any snow got into the shed.

This time she let him help, the two of them unfolding the plastic cover and fitting it over the generator. When it was done, she let out a long, low breath. She'd done it. Now she could get back to Leo and check that he was okay.

Mason trained his light on her. "You okay?" he asked, still shouting over the sound of the generator.

"I'm fine." A little exhilarated, a little annoyed, a whole lot exhausted. "I'm going back to the house. Leo is in there."

"I'll come with you." Mason turned to the door.

"You don't need to come with me. I'm fine." Or she would be if all the men surrounding her would trust that she could take care of herself.

"I know you're fine, Alaska." He didn't look annoyed at her rebuff. "You've told me ten times. But maybe I'm not fine. Maybe I'll feel better if I make sure you get home safely. Now, are you ready for me to open the door?"

"I know what Ty told you," she said, just as he yanked the handle. The wind howled, and snowflakes danced in the halo of their lights, before falling to the concrete floor of the shed.

Mason stopped dead. "What?"

"I know Ty told you about me disappearing. I know that's why you suddenly think I need all this help." She had to shout for him to hear her.

He turned his head. She lifted her light to his face. He was frowning. "That's not what I think," he shouted back.

"That's why you hightailed it over here in the middle of the night, isn't it? Because you think I'm weak just like everybody else does." The cold air was whipping around her face, making her eyes sting.

His jaw tightened. He closed the door and turned, taking two steps toward her. Despite the ice cold air she felt herself flush at his nearness. Felt her body respond to his as that never-ending need washed over her.

"Alaska." He said her name like a prayer. It sent a shiver down her spine. "You are the complete opposite of weak. I've never met anybody stronger. I should know that more than anybody else."

"You should?" Her voice was low now. Her brow pinched as she tried to understand him. "Why would you know that?"

"Because I was there the night you disappeared."

13

Alaska stared at him for a moment, then walked past him out of the shed, striding through the snow as he locked it back up.

And for a moment he wondered whether he should go back to his cabin or to her house. Because this was not the way he'd planned to tell her.

"Are you coming or what?" she yelled at him. "We need to get inside before we freeze to death."

This wasn't how he'd expected her to respond, either. He'd thought she might scream at him. Hit him. Something other than look beautifully serene.

He followed her back to the house, the wind whipping their faces. She pulled the door open and walked inside then turned to look at him.

"Come on. Before the snow gets in."

And that's how he found himself standing in Alaska's kitchen, taking off his soaking coat and boots as Leo rubbed himself against his legs.

Alaska removed her coat, along with the sweatpants that were damp and sticking to her skin. Beneath them her legs were bare and red. He wanted to rub them until they warmed, but this wasn't the time.

"You going to ask me about what I said?" he asked her, steeling himself for the screaming.

"In a minute. When we're warm."

He couldn't work her out. She was so calm. He'd dropped a bombshell and here she was, pulling a pan out of the kitchen cupboard and filling it with milk.

"I'm going to make us both some hot chocolate." She put the pan on the stove, lighting it up. "Is Ty okay in the cabin?"

"He's fine. Sleeping like a log."

She nodded and grabbed two mugs, spooning chocolate powder into each one. "You should message him and let him know where you are in case he wakes up."

"Already did."

Once the milk bubbled on the stove, Alaska took it off and poured it over the chocolate powder in the mugs, stirring until the grains dissolved. Putting the pan back on the stove top, she handed a mug to Mason and took the other for herself. "I assume you don't want whipped cream and marshmallows like Ty."

"This is good. Thank you." He blew on the surface, vapor rising, then looked over at her. She was still wearing her hoodie, along with her shorts and bare feet. She looked like she should be on a beach in California, not in the center of a storm in Winterville.

"If you want to call the police you can," he told her.

"Why?" She looked genuinely confused.

"Because I told you I was there when you went missing." Was there something wrong with her? She wasn't reacting like a normal person would. It was exasperating.

He'd just told her he'd been there at the worst moment of her life and she was behaving like they were discussing the weather.

"And you were a kid, the same as I was. So I'm sure there's a good explanation. Drink your hot chocolate and then we'll talk." She inclined her head at the living room and he followed her in, sitting on an overstuffed easy chair as she took the sofa. She curled her legs under herself, still cradling her mug, then took a sip. Leo jumped on the sofa next to her, nestling against her legs.

He wasn't sure he'd seen anybody look more beautiful than she did right now. There was a calm to her that seemed to suffuse the room. How the hell could she think she was weak or that anybody else thought that? She had a quiet strength to her that awed him. It seemed to awe Leo, too, who had already fallen asleep. He was letting out gentle snores as his fur rose and fell.

"How old were you when it happened?" she asked.

"Eleven."

She nodded. "I was eight."

"I know."

Her lip quirked. "Was I...?"

"You were okay. Nobody harmed you. You were just lost, that's all." All day he'd been trying so hard to remember all the details, but it was like a haze in his mind. Sure, he could remember the big stuff, but the rest was almost impossible to grasp.

"How do you want to do this?" he asked her. "You want to ask questions or do you want me to just tell you?"

She pulled her lip between her teeth. "I don't know. I'm still... shocked, I guess."

Of course she was. He leaned forward, his elbows resting on his legs. God, this was difficult. He'd never thought she was *that* girl. His dad had lied to him. And he'd never be able to get all the answers now.

But at least he could give her the answers he had.

"Shall I just tell you what I know?" His eyes caught hers and she nodded.

He took a deep breath. "Okay then. I'll start at the beginning." Or at least their arrival in Winterville. He could still remember it. The way his dad had thrown their luggage into the truck and made him climb into the cab. They'd played sixties music all the way from Baltimore to West Virginia. "They knew how to make music back then," his dad had said. "Not like the crap they play on the radio nowadays."

Despite the lawsuit hanging over him, his dad had seemed almost carefree. They'd stopped for slushies on the way, the hot summer sun beating down on them as they'd enjoy them at a picnic bench.

It was probably the happiest time of his life.

"My dad and I came here because he was about to go to trial for fraud," Mason told her, his voice low. "My mom had already died and there was nobody else to take me. We both knew I'd go into the system as soon as they found him guilty."

"You were sure he would be found guilty?"

"He *was* guilty. He knew it, I knew it, all the people he defrauded knew it. It was only a matter of time before the law caught up with him. So he brought me to the cabin, a kind of last-minute father-son bonding. And one night we found you."

"You found me?" she leaned forward, interested. "Where was I?"

"On our stoop. We didn't know how long you'd been there. You were curled up underneath one of the blankets Dad kept in the box outside our front door. He used to come outside and smoke at night, and used them to keep warm. The thing is, we'd been out hunting since the early morning, and this was late at night. You could have been there all day."

"What day was this?"

"It was a Saturday night. I know because we left town on

that Sunday and never came back. Dad panicked when he saw you. Tried to wake you up, but you were fucking exhausted, Alaska. So he carried you into the cabin and put you in my bed. I slept with him that night."

"I slept in your bed?" She blinked. "I don't remember that."

"I know." He nodded. "And if I'm being honest, I barely remember what happened next. All I remember is dad saying he couldn't call the police because they'd think we'd taken you since he was already charged with fraud. And he couldn't just drive off and leave you somewhere because you were asleep and somebody really could take you. So he decided to let you rest and drop you off somewhere in the morning. We spent the night packing up because he didn't want to bring any suspicion on us. He said I'd be arrested and end up in jail if they thought we were involved."

"But you were a kid..."

"And he couldn't protect me. Nobody could. I learned that as soon as I entered the system." He caught her eye. The strength of her compassion was making him feel all kinds of things. Emotions he hadn't felt since he'd locked them away at eleven years old.

Things he wasn't sure he'd ever be ready for.

"In the morning, we dropped you off about two hundred yards from town and watched from a distance until you made it into the police station. Then we drove away and never came back." He pressed his lips together. He'd had so many questions his dad hadn't wanted to answer. They hadn't listened to sixties music on the way home. Every time Mason had tried to ask his dad something he'd snapped and told him he was trying to concentrate.

That day had felt like the beginning of the end. He'd sat in the truck's cab, still as a statue, afraid of what was coming next.

And maybe it was good he hadn't known. Because he'd have wanted to disappear, too. Nothing had prepared him for being a foster kid.

He looked at Alaska again. There was so much softness in her eyes. He wanted to lose himself in them. "Two weeks after we left Winterville, Dad's trial started, and they took me into foster care," he told her. "And after that, I learned never to talk about anything that might cause people to notice me." He ran the tip of his tongue over his dry lips. "And I regret it so damn much."

"Why didn't you say anything about it before? You must have known it was me."

He shook his head. "I didn't know your name back then. I just knew it was some kid in Winterville. I tried to Google it when I was older, but nothing came up."

"My grandma suppressed any reporting of it. She had friends in high places."

He nodded. "And then before my dad died earlier this year, I asked him about it. Said we needed to make it right. So he paid for a private detective. He told me the report said the little girl and her family moved out of the country when she was eleven. That nobody in Winterville knew where she'd gone."

Alaska blinked. "But that's not true."

"I know that now. He lied to me. I don't know why. Maybe he was trying to protect me, I don't know. All I know is that I can't ask him. He's gone, and he's taken that knowledge with him." Mason shook his head. "I'm sorry, Alaska. I'm so fucking sorry."

"It wasn't your fault." She put her mug down on the table and lifted Leo from her lap. "None of this was your fault."

"You've lived all these years not knowing what happened. I should have come back. Tried harder. This is all on me."

She uncurled her legs from beneath her and stood,

walking across to where he was sitting. He looked up, confused, then she dropped to her knees and slid her hands into his.

Her face was inclined, her pretty eyes catching his. He wasn't sure he'd ever seen such pure goodness before. He wanted to bathe in her light. To let her wash over him like the ocean washed over the beach.

Wanted to lose himself in her so he could only think good thoughts again. But he couldn't. Because he'd been there when her life got tipped upside down forever.

"You saved me," she whispered. "You found me and you saved me."

He shook his head. "That's not true." Even if he wanted to believe it was.

"Yes, you did. You and your dad. I was lost, that much is clear. I must have wandered for miles to get to your cabin. I'd been camping outside the Inn the night before. By the time you found me, I'd been missing for almost a day. And you took me in and made sure I was safe."

"I'll go to the police tomorrow," he whispered hoarsely. "Tell them everything I know."

"No." She shook her head vehemently. "Nobody's going to the police."

"But the case must still be open." He knew it was. Suppressed but open. Because of him.

"Nobody's bothered with it for years. Let it stay open," she whispered. "I must have known somewhere deep inside this is where I found safety. I couldn't have chosen this house by accident. Some part of me must have remembered that I was out here that day." Her gaze flickered to his. "The same part that must have remembered you."

His stomach tightened. Every part of him wanted to touch her. As if she understood, she slid her fingers from his hand and reached out to cup his cheek, her palm warm and soft.

She was soft everywhere. And he was hard. So hard. Not just physically–though that was bad enough. He was hard in body and hard in soul. He didn't want to hurt her any more than she'd already been hurt.

But he couldn't stay away either.

"It's the right thing to do," he said hoarsely, so aware of her fingers as they traced the roughness of his jaw.

"Is it?" Her brow puckered. "Because I don't want it all brought up again. And even if I don't matter, think about Ty. It's hard enough being the new kid in school, imagine if this came out. He's had enough to deal with, let him get through senior year at least."

"You care so much about everybody," he whispered.

"I'm thinking of myself." She pulled her other hand from his, sliding her palm up his chest, to his shoulder. Without thinking, his free hands cupped her hip. He could feel the heat of her skin through her shorts, the jut of her hip bone, the softness of her curves. He wanted to trace every one.

"How about you?" she whispered. "Who thinks of Mason?"

"*I* do. I think about nobody but myself." He ran his hands up her side, and her lips parted, a little sigh escaping from them. She was on her knees in front of him but she'd never looked more powerful. Growing up, he'd had to learn to temper his strength, like all big men did. Learned the power of his muscles, discovered how to control them. Understood that to be gentle wasn't a weakness.

It was power. And she had it seeping out of her.

"You're a liar," she whispered, though there was no malice in it. "Look at what you've done for Ty. Look at how you keep trying to save me. But when are you going to save yourself?"

His throat felt tight. She must have seen the emotion in

his eyes because she scrambled onto his lap, her legs straddling his. Both hands cupped his jaw, as though she was sending up a prayer.

Maybe they both were. Even if nobody was listening.

Then she slid her hands down to his shoulders, her palms tracing the hardness of his biceps, the thick cords of his wrists. She looked at his chest, her thick eyelashes sweeping down, then slid her hands inside the v of his shirt.

There was a thermal undershirt between her palms and his skin, but he felt exposed anyway. Raw and revealed. His breath caught in his throat as her thumb scraped against his nipples, making the thick ridge of him harden even more.

"Alaska..."

"Just let me touch you," she whispered. He gave a half nod in acknowledgement. Of course she could touch him. He felt like her property already. "I didn't understand," she whispered. "But now I do."

"Understand what?" He was confused.

"This connection. Do you feel it?" Her gaze swept up to his.

"There's no connection. You don't remember me. How could we be connected?"

"I'm not talking about that night. I'm talking about afterward," she whispered. She pulled her hands from his chest, unbuttoning his shirt. He watched her, letting her touch him.

He trusted her. And wasn't that something weird? He didn't trust anybody, least of all himself.

But this woman, she deserved his faith. She deserved everything. She was a little piece of sunshine he never wanted to subdue.

Alaska pushed the flannel from his shoulders, and he got the message. He shrugged it down, sliding his arms out, then looked back at her to decide what she'd do next.

"And the undershirt."

He quirked a brow. It made her smile. "I'm not gonna molest you, Mason. I just want to show you something."

Curious, he did as she told him, tugging at the hem of his undershirt and lifting it over his head. She leaned back on his thighs, her weight solid but not heavy, then let out what sounded like a squeak when he threw his undershirt on the floor. There was a darkness in her eyes, and her cheeks flushed as she stared at him. Then she traced her finger down his arm to his tattoo.

"This date," she whispered. "You've been in a prison of somebody else's making since this date." She leaned forward, her lips pressing against his arm. It took every bit of control he had not to curl his arm around her and crush her into him. His body ached for her.

"And so have I," she said, kissing her way to his chest. "We're the same, you and I."

"No we're not," he told her gruffly. But he still couldn't find the strength to push her away. "I'm damaged. And somehow you aren't."

She brought her eyes up to his. "We're all damaged, Mason. It's how we rebuild ourselves that count." And then she brought her lips to his nipple, and he knew this had to stop now.

"No." He pushed her away, letting out a low groan. "We can't do this."

It felt like he'd slapped her. Her body–so warm from his–felt suddenly cold as he lifted her from his lap. Tears stung at her eyes because she felt so humiliated.

She'd thrown herself at him when he was just trying to be kind.

Again.

What the hell was she thinking?

"I'm sorry," she said, stepping back, trying to blink the tears away.

"Don't cry. Please don't cry." His voice was plaintive. "I can't stand to see you upset."

She looked away, gritting her teeth together because he still thought she was weak. And it hurt so damn much.

"You should go," she told him, her voice rough. "Leo and I need to get some sleep."

"Alaska..."

"I'm sorry for touching you when you didn't want me to," she whispered. "That was wrong of me."

"You think I didn't want you to touch me?" he asked her, his voice lifting. "Are you crazy?"

Finally, she looked at him. He was pulling on his shirt. "You've made it clear," she told him. "Several times. I'm sorry, I won't bother you again."

"For fuck's sake." He shook his head, anger suffusing his skin. "You think I don't want you? I want you, Alaska. But you shouldn't want me. Not after this. Not at all, in fact. You deserve somebody better."

She wanted to laugh. "Like who?"

"Like... I don't know. A good guy who treats you the way you should be treated." He looked even angrier about that. But she didn't care because she was angry, too.

"What, like making a run for my dog because he keeps running into the woods? Or starting my generator because he's scared I'll end up freezing to death?" she asked, her eyes wide. She stepped toward him, shaking her head. "Maybe you only like me when I'm weak."

"You're the strongest woman I know," he told her. "So fuck that."

"Then prove it."

"How?"

"Stop treating me like I'm breakable," she told him. "Stop treating me like everybody else does. If you want me, show me."

His eyes were stormy, like there was a war being waged in his mind. For a moment he stared at her, as though trying to decide what to do. But then he stalked toward her, his jaw tight, his eyes narrow, and her breath caught in her throat.

"You want me to show you what I want?" he rasped.

"Yes, I do." Her heart was racing in her chest. She didn't care about the past. She didn't care that they'd both been paying the price of it ever since they were kids.

She wanted him. More than she wanted anything in her life.

His mouth closed upon hers and she let out a low groan. His hand cupped her jaw, and he kissed her hard and deep, her body arching against his until she wasn't sure where she ended and he began. She could feel the hard ridge of him against her stomach, could feel the pulse of need between her legs. She raked her fingers against his scalp, and it was his turn to groan as they kissed until they were breathless.

And when they parted his eyes were full of fire.

"I want you, Alaska," he rasped. "But I'm not going to have sex with you. And that doesn't mean I don't want to," he said gruffly. "Because, fuck, I want to."

"Then why don't you?" She looked at him, confused.

"Because I'd be taking advantage. I just told you something life changing. You need to think about it. Need to consider what we do next. And if you're still set on this direction." He gently pushed a stray lock of hair behind her ear. "If you're still set on me, then come tell me."

"You're giving me the brush off."

"I'm giving you the chance to back out." Because he knew that once she was in, he couldn't let her go. "I'm going to leave in a minute and tomorrow I'm going to work on my bathroom. I'll be busy all day and won't bother you at all."

"And if I have questions?"

"Then text me. You have my number, don't you?"

She nodded, her brows dipping. "And if I still want this? After I've thought about things?"

"Then you know how to find me." And if she didn't? The thought made his chest feel tight. But if she didn't then he'd done the right thing, hadn't he? Stopping her before she did something she regretted. Walked away before he messed her life up any more.

"You know what the answer will be," she whispered. "You have to know it."

His lip quirked. "We'll see." Gently, he released her, stepping back. Her body complained at the sudden loss of connection. He kissed her on the brow, stroking her hair softly. "Get some sleep, okay?"

He was right. She knew he was, even if part of her ached for him to carry her to bed. "Okay," she agreed. "I'll try."

14

By early morning, the storm had died down, but Mason still hadn't gotten back to sleep. Every half hour he'd look out of the window at Alaska's house, checking that the outside lights were still on and that she hadn't suddenly decided to replace some roof tiles in her skimpy pajamas, or something equally as stupid but Alaska-like.

Just before six, he heard the rumble of an engine. Glancing out of the window he saw a truck with a Cold Start Garage logo on the side and a plow on the front, clearing the road of the snow that had accumulated overnight.

"School's shut," Ty announced happily, walking into the bathroom. "The buses can't get here from Marshall's Gap."

"Your teachers give you any work?" Mason glanced up at him from his position on the floor. He had the wood he needed to close this gap, but there was no point until he'd checked the plumbing.

"Nope. A few kids are talking about meeting in Winterville. Maybe get a coffee or something."

"You don't drink coffee," Mason pointed out.

Ty rolled his eyes. "I don't mind it. I just don't like it the way you make it."

"How you gonna get there?" Mason waited for Ty to ask him for a ride. He'd willingly give it. Sure, he could use Ty's help with the bathroom, but he felt like being alone for a while. He had a lot to think about.

"Someone's mom is driving. Said they'd pick me up."

Mason's eyes met Ty's. "Definitely somebody's mom? Not a seventeen-year-old who's only just learned to drive? Because I don't want you out in this weather with an inexperienced driver."

"Definitely. You can meet her if you like."

Mason winced. "No thank you."

Ty smirked. "Thought so." He did that trick that kids have, of hanging around with something on their mind but not saying it. Instead, he shifted his feet and scratched the back of his neck.

"What is it?" Mason asked him.

Ty shrugged. "I dunno. Just wondering why you were with Alaska last night."

"I wasn't *with* Alaska last night. I was helping her set up her generator. Didn't you get my message?"

"Yes, I did. But then you didn't come home. Not for a good hour."

Of course Ty noticed. You couldn't hide anything from a teenager. They were like mini Columbos, with an attitude instead of a rain coat. "I wanted to make sure she and Leo were okay."

"That took an hour?"

For the first time, Mason realized why teenagers rolled their eyes so much. "It took what it took. We talked a little."

Ty tipped his head to the side. "What about?"

"None of your business." Alaska had been right about one thing. Ty didn't need to know what had happened all those years ago. Certainly not until he'd graduated. "Now, are you going to get ready to head out or are you hanging around here? Because if you are, you can help me take this floor up."

"I'm going to get ready," Ty said. "But I could use a shower."

Mason sighed and stood. He needed coffee anyway before he could really start working on this room. "Okay, but avoid the hole."

"You know what?" Ty said sarcastically. "That's a great idea. Don't know why I didn't think of that."

"Smart mouth." Mason ruffled his hair.

"I bet that's what she said."

Mason blinked. "What? What who said?"

Ty shot him an amused look. "It's a joke. From *The Office*. On Netflix."

"Okay." Mason nodded quickly, walking past Ty into the living room. "Good. That's good. I'll leave you to it."

"Did you think I was talking about Alaska?" Ty asked, turning to look at his brother.

"No. Why would you say that?" Mason shifted his feet. He needed another coffee. Possibly ten.

For a moment Ty said nothing. Just stared at Mason like he was trying to work him out. Then he ran his thumb over his jaw, a smile pulling at his lips. "Is there something going on with you and Alaska?"

"No." Mason frowned. "Definitely not. And don't go spreading that kind of gossip around Winterville."

The smile faltered. "I wouldn't do that."

Ty looked hurt, being accused of something he wasn't responsible for. Mason wanted to kick himself in his own ass. They'd been breaking through their barriers. Getting closer. He was all too aware that one wrong step, and they'd be at each other's throats again.

"Okay. I'm sorry." Mason nodded. "It's just that she's a private person. That kind of talk would hurt her."

Ty swallowed, his eyes still on Mason's. "Yeah," he said gruffly. "Well I'm not going to hurt her." His gaze narrowed. "And maybe you shouldn't either."

"Hey, you heading for the café?" Nicole called to Alaska from across the square. Alaska stopped and turned, seeing her cousin's wife hurrying past the thirty-foot Christmas tree erected in the center, a yoga mat slung over her coat.

"Yep. First break I've had all day," Alaska told her when Nicole caught up with her, breathless. "How was class?"

"Quiet. Most people are staying at home with all the snow. I should probably have cancelled but a few hotel guests had booked in."

"I bet Gabe wasn't happy with you driving here."

"Nope." Nicole grinned. "That's why he insisted on driving me. I'm going to grab a coffee and message him that I'm still alive. Join me?"

"Sure." Alaska nodded. "Sounds good." She adored Nicole. The Yoga teacher from Washington D.C. had temporarily moved in with Alaska's cousin, Gabe when her boyfriend had cheated on her and she needed to leave their shared apartment.

And then she'd fallen in love with Gabe – and with Winterville – and stayed. And now they were blissfully married. The way Gabe looked at his wife always made her feel wistful.

She and Nicole walked toward Cold Fingers Café. It had been busy all morning. There'd been a flurry of calls from guests booked for check in, worried about whether they'd be able to make it up the mountain. Then a line of guests due to check out, worried about taking the trip the other way round.

On top of that, yesterday's delivery of eggs had gone missing, sending the chef into a frenzy. By the time she'd calmed him down, and they'd put out a reduced lunch menu, it had been almost eleven o'clock.

And she hadn't had a chance to do the only thing she wanted. Think about last night. Sure, she'd lain awake until the early hours thinking about everything Mason had told her. Everything they did.

How he'd kissed her so softly yet so deeply she thought she might explode while fully clothed.

The café door opened and a gaggle of teenagers spilled out, carrying Styrofoam cups and laughing at each other. She saw Ty with them, and smiled at him. He smiled back but didn't say anything.

It warmed her heart to see him with some other kids.

"Hey Miss Winter." She looked up to see another of the students who worked at the Inn – Eloise – smiling at her.

"Hey Eloise. No school today?"

She shrugged. "Buses couldn't get here on time."

"Sounds like a win." Alaska smiled at her warmly. Then she noticed Ty was smiling, too. Looking directly at Eloise who was completely oblivious to his scrutiny.

Interesting.

"Well, I'll let you enjoy your day," she said. "You guys going sledding later?"

"Maybe." Eloise nodded. "We thought we might go behind the Inn." There was a big slope there, leading down to the trees. "If that's okay with you."

"Of course. Have fun."

She gave them a wave and followed Nicole into Cold Fingers Café, the warm air inside greeting her like an old friend. The café was full, as usual. In the corner she could see

Lisa and her friends, thankfully too busy talking to notice her. Or at least they were until Everley called out her name, beckoning her over. Her sister was sitting with their cousin, Holly, along with Holly's daughter, Candace, who was sitting in a high chair happily chewing on a cookie.

"Hey," Alaska said, leaning down to kiss their cheeks. "You guys survived the storm okay?"

"Yep," Everley said. "We even managed to finish last night's show without having to cut it short. How about you? Is your electricity okay now?"

"It's fine." It had come back on by early morning.

"I hear you had a little help getting the generator started." Everley lifted a brow.

"Where did you hear that?" Alaska frowned.

"A couple of kids were talking in the line in front of me. One of them must be your neighbor. The other was a girl who works at the Inn. Louise?"

"Eloise," Alaska corrected her.

"That's right. Anyway, she was asking him if everything went okay out there, and he said it was fine and that his brother helped you in the middle of the night."

Alaska swallowed. "That's right."

"Does North know about that?" Holly asked, not bothering to hide her grin.

"North, North, North," Candace sang.

"It's no big deal. Just a neighbor helping a neighbor," Alaska said, smiling at Candace who was dribbling chocolate down her chin. She grabbed a napkin and dabbed it off, then blew Candace a kiss.

Candace smacked her lips back.

"I ordered you a cappuccino," Nicole said, joining them at the table. "A large one. Hope that's okay."

"Large is perfect," Alaska told her.

"That's what I always say," Everley quipped, grinning.

Nicole and Alaska sat in the two free chairs, and within a minute Dolores came over to give them their coffees.

"You ladies need anything else?" she asked them.

"Nope, all good here." Alaska smiled. "Thanks, Dolores."

"So," Everley said. "Speaking of North. Has he beaten up any of your other neighbors recently?"

Alaska shook her head. "It's not funny."

"I know. He's like a bear with a sore head at the moment. I went down to the Christmas Tree Farm shop to pick up some new decorations and I could hear him and Amber shouting at each other in the staff room."

"They were shouting?" Alaska frowned. She hated when the people she loved didn't get along.

"Well, not shouting," Everley conceded. "Because I had to put my ear to the door to hear them. More like having a heated debate."

"About what?" Holly asked. She looked slightly shifted, like she knew they shouldn't be gossiping about their cousin. But they all loved North and wanted the best for him.

Even if he drove them crazy sometimes.

"About this guy she's dating. North doesn't like him," Everley said. "I walked away after that. I only wanted to tease him about hitting two of his cousins' guys."

"Mason isn't my guy," Alaska said quickly.

"Okay. Well he is your neighbor."

"And he *is* hot," Holly added, shrugging. "If you like the big beefy type."

"Help me out here," Alaska said to Nicole, who was watching the three of them, smiling.

Nicole shrugged. "Holly's right. The guy is gorgeous."

"You've seen him?" Alaska asked. Her stomach felt tight.

"Well, no. But he's still been the hot topic of conversation in most of my classes. I think Lisa's regrouping, deciding how to approach him next." She glanced over to where Lisa and her friends were sitting. Alaska realized they'd come straight from class to have a drink. "She was talking about how to get her tire to blow out when she's outside his cabin."

"Ooh," Everley said, her eyes wide. "You'll have to kiss him again."

"Already did." The words escaped her lips before she thought them through.

"What?" All three of them snapped their heads to look at her.

"Can you keep it down," Alaska whispered. "Everybody's looking."

Everley lifted her hand up, as though to quieten them all. Then she grabbed her phone and quickly tapped something on her screen.

The next moment, Alaska's phone buzzed. So did Nicole's and Holly's. When Alaska slid her finger across the screen, she saw Everley had created a new group chat.

And called it *Mason Parker's Talented Mouth.*

Great.

Shooting her sister an exasperated look, Alaska typed into the chat.

Rename the group or I'm leaving it. – Alaska

Everley smirked and tapped on her phone. The group name changed.

Hottie McHotpants.

I like that one. – Holly

. . .

Me, too. – Nicole

Then we keep it. It's democratic. And if you leave the group I'm going to use my outside voice in here. – Everley

That's blackmail. – Alaska

I'm your big sister. It's just the way I roll. – Everley

Spill, Alaska. When did you kiss him again? – Holly

...is typing... – Alaska

You just typed that. It's not how it works. – Everley

If I tell you, you have to promise not to tell North. – Alaska

Okay. – Everley

And Holly, you can't tell Josh. Nicole, you can't tell Gabe. – Alaska

Josh is the epitome of discretion. – Holly

. . .

Actually, he and Gabe have a bet on how long it'll take until North hits Mason again. Best not to tell either of them. – Nicole

Okay, but I'm not going to lie to my husband. If he asks, I'll tell him. – Holly

He won't ask. C'mon Alaska, just tell us already. I have a show to perform in two hours. – Everley

All right, all right. It was last night. After I got the generator started. – Alaska

Details. We need details. Where did you kiss? – Everley

She felt like she was walking a thin line. The fact was, their kiss didn't make sense without the revelations beforehand, but she didn't want to tell them about those. Not when she hadn't had a chance to think them through herself.

At my place. I made him a hot chocolate to warm him up. – Alaska

Of course you did! – Holly

. . .

It wasn't like that. Anyway, one thing led to another and... – Alaska

AND??? – Everley

And it was nice. – Alaska

So then what? – Holly

Nothing. – Alaska

They're gonna need more details. Give them a time, a location, and an approximate heat level then we can all stop messaging and drink our coffee. – Nicole

Alaska looked up. All three of them were looking at her expectantly. She gave a little huff and went back to her phone.

We kissed for a minute or so. In my living room. And it was good. That's all you're getting. – Alaska

This time when she looked up, Everley was grinning at her. "Good for you."

"You think so?" Alaska asked softly. Because right now she didn't know what was good for her. It would be easy to become obsessed with Mason Parker. It wasn't just that he knew exactly how to set her on fire. Or the fact that every time he walked into the room his masculine energy filled it.

And filled her, too.

It was something deeper. The connection neither of them realized they'd had. It felt weirdly like coming home, but to a home you didn't know existed until the moment you saw it.

Everley's phone buzzed again. She gave Alaska a quizzical look then checked her screen, her brows pulled together. For a moment she read silently, then looked up at her sister.

"Have you heard from Mom and Dad recently?" Everley asked her.

Their parents lived in Florida, permanent snowbirds who hated the cold. They barely visited Winterville, despite both of their daughters living there.

"I'm due to call them on Sunday," Alaska told her. "Why?"

"I just got a message from Mom." Everley glanced down at her phone again. "They're planning on visiting for Christmas.

"What? Why?" It was the season they hated the most. Her dad had never liked the tourists and her mom never liked it when it snowed.

"She didn't say. Just that they've booked their flights." Everley frowned. Her relationship with their parents was as fractious as Alaska's, especially since they tried to sell the town to a developer after their grandmother's death.

Winterville had been built and owned by Candy Winter, and when she'd passed she'd left it to her children, which included Everley and Alaska's dad. But they'd wanted nothing to do with it and had agreed to have it redeveloped as a ski resort.

The six Winter cousins – Everley, Alaska, and Holly, plus their boy cousins, North, Gabe, and even Kris, had to intervene to save the town.

Relations with their parents hadn't really been the same since.

Alaska's eyes met Everley's. "We won't have any rooms left to put them in," she said softly. "We're booked for the season."

"Can you bump somebody out?" Holly asked. "Maybe we'll get a cancellation."

"I don't think so," Alaska said, her stomach twisting because she hated surprises like this. "We'll have to find them something else."

"Can't they stay with one of you?" Nicole asked, looking from Alaska to Everley.

Everley grimaced. "Ugh, I can't think of anything worse. And anyway, I'll be working constantly." She lifted a brow at Alaska. "You will, too. Why the heck did they decide to visit now?"

"I've no idea." Alaska shook her head. She should be pleased they were coming.

But instead she was filled with anxious trepidation.

15

Mason spent the day pulling the old bathroom suite out. Half of the floor came with it, of course, and the stench of the sewage pipe had made him gag. And there'd been a pile of trash in the crawl space beneath the floor that he'd had to clear out, ready to burn when he had a chance. But still he hadn't stopped. He needed to dispel the energy, needed to take his mind off her.

Needed to get away from the thoughts that kept swirling around his brain.

It had been the longest day. Part of him had expected the cops to turn up at the cabin. Or for her cousin to arrive, this time swinging his fists liberally.

But instead there had been nothing. No visitors, no messages.

No word from her.

He was glad. He'd asked her to think about what he'd told her and he meant it. He hated that he'd had this knowledge about her life and she hadn't. Mostly because he knew how she felt. What was it she'd said?

You found me and you saved me.

His chest clenched, because it wasn't true. It just wasn't. They'd done what they needed and hightailed it out of town. Truth be told, he was too concerned about himself growing up to worry about what happened to that little girl.

Too busy trying to survive in a system that was constantly beating him down.

She'd told him they were the same. That they'd lived under the same life sentence. But she was wrong.

She'd thrived and he'd survived. That was the difference.

Alaska had reacted to trauma by following the light. Whereas he'd chosen the darkness. And yeah, maybe he'd had no choice.

"I Googled you."

He looked up from where he was kneeling on the bathroom floor. She was standing in the doorway, her golden hair twisted into a messy bun, her work clothes still on. She must have just gotten home from the Inn and tried his front door. He never bothered locking it – there was nothing of value in here, and Ty never remembered his key.

"You did?"

She nodded. "And I thought about what you told me. Like you asked me to."

"Did you come to any conclusions?"

"That you need me."

He laughed, because maybe there was some truth in her statement. "Yeah, but you don't need me."

"Can you tell my body that?" she asked softly. "Because it thinks it does."

"What else did you discover?" he asked, ignoring the way his muscles tightened at her words.

"I already knew you were a lawyer." She tipped her head to the side. "But you're not lawyering anymore."

"Nope."

"Why not?"

If it was anybody else in the world he'd tell them to fuck off, and attack the bathroom pipes like they were out to get him. But he didn't want to do that with her. It wasn't just that she deserved to be treated better than that. He wanted her to know the truth.

He wanted her to know *him*. The real Mason Parker, not the one he hid under layers of grouch and annoyance. She made everything feel good.

He didn't want to push her away.

"Because I got pissed at a client and sabotaged their case."

She blinked. "Who was the client?"

"A chemical company who'd fucked a whole community over. Pretty much left the town a stinking cesspit."

"Oh."

He looked up at her. He needed to be honest about this. About who he was. "It wasn't the first company I'd represented in a case like that. I'd done it before and won. I was the go-to guy for defending the undefendable. If a company messed up, they asked for me."

She didn't flinch. "It was your job."

"Yeah, but no job is worth selling your soul for."

"So how did you sabotage their case?" Her eyes didn't leave his.

"The defense was that they had no idea of the contamination until it was too late. I discovered a report they'd commissioned that said otherwise. Then released it to the other side."

"I bet they were pissed." Her lips curled. Damn if his didn't, too.

"Something like that." He put the wrench he'd been holding down. "It's funny," he said softly. "How easily you get sucked into something that pays well. I always thought I was different than my dad. That I'd be on the right side of the law where he'd been on the wrong side. And yeah, I was on the right side, I guess. But what I learned was the law doesn't care. It doesn't have morals. It doesn't lose any sleep when a town can't drink its own water and can't afford to make it right."

"So you got fired?" she asked him.

"Fired. Walked out. All the same thing."

"And here you are," she said, stepping forward gingerly, avoiding the holes in the floorboards. He stood up immediately, panicked.

"Careful of the hole in the floor."

She ignored him, stepping closer.

"If you fall in I'm not pulling you out," he warned.

"Yes you will." She was still smiling. "That's what you do. Pull people out of holes. Me, Ty, the companies you used to work for..." She reached out for him, her hand cupping his cheek. "But when do you get to climb out of your own hole?"

He blinked, not understanding. The touch of her hand on his skin was making him burn. Hot blood rushed through his veins, and all he wanted to do was scoop her up and throw her onto his bed.

And her eyes. Those pretty, trusting eyes. They never left his and it made him want her more.

"I don't want to hurt you," he whispered, voicing his biggest fear.

"Then stop pushing me away. I'm not breakable, Mason. I'm not fragile. I'm a woman. I'm strong. I want you to show me how strong I am."

She was so close that he could smell the scent of her shampoo. Something sweet and flowery. Then she rolled onto the balls of her toes, inclining her head until their eyes caught, and he knew.

He just knew.

One of them was going to get hurt.

But he couldn't ignore the aching need anymore. The call

of her body to his. She wobbled on her tiptoes and he reached down to steady her, his hands curling around her hips, pulling her close until their bodies crushed together.

Damn she was soft. It sent a shiver of need through him. To kiss every part of her skin, to hear her gasp out his name. To see her hair fanned out on his bed like she belonged there.

His lips were a breath from hers. Her eyelids fluttered then closed. He moved closer until he could feel the softness of her lips, the stutter of her breath, the parting of her mouth as he slowly submitted to the inevitable.

And then he messed it up.

"Ty..." he rasped, pulling back. "He'll be home soon."

She opened her eyes. There was a haziness in them he recognized. It was in his own eyes, too.

"He's sledding on the slopes behind the Inn," she told him, her gaze holding his. "Then they'll all have dinner in the kitchen. I've made sure he's got a ride home, should be back in two hours."

"Do you think of everything?" he asked, his thumbs caressing her sides.

"I like to be organized."

"I'm getting that feeling." It wasn't just the thick, hard part of him that ached for her. There was this weird flip in his chest, too. He couldn't explain it even if he tried. It was just there.

"So are you going to kiss me now?" She lifted a brow.

"Yeah." He nodded slowly. "I think I am."

He brushed his lips lightly against hers, marveling that this woman was standing here willingly, despite everything she'd been through. That she wanted him to hold her, that she wanted him to kiss her.

It was a miracle. One he'd never fully understand.

"Harder," she whispered. "Kiss me harder."

And damn if those words didn't unleash the beast in him.

From the moment she'd seen him from the doorway, she'd been on fire. It wasn't just the way his muscles flexed or the way he frowned when he concentrated. It wasn't even the fact he could repair things without blinking an eye.

It was that he'd bared himself to her. Shown her the chink in his armor that he hid from the rest of the world. Trusted her with his secrets, trusted her with his pain.

He saw her as his equal. And that hadn't happened in a long, long time.

And now he was devouring her, his lips sliding from her mouth to her neck, his hands feathering her sides, holding her up because her legs were trembling so hard she might tumble if he didn't.

He kissed the taut dip between her neck and her shoulders and it made her nipples tighten. As though he knew the effect he was having on her, his hand reached up to cup her breast, his thumb brushing her nipple, making them both groan.

She threw her arms around his neck, pushing herself against him, needing to feel his hardness against the soft swell of her abdomen. He groaned again, the vibration rumbling against her neck, as he unfastened the top buttons on her blouse, sliding his hand inside, the roughness of his palm making her shiver.

She wasn't inexperienced. She'd had boyfriends. But that's what they'd been. Boys. Sure, they were in their twenties, but they'd never known how to touch her like this. Never understood what she needed.

But Mason did. He understood exactly how she needed to be touched. With rough hands and demanding lips. Not like she was fragile. Not like she had a family they were afraid of. Not like she was a victim.

It was glorious.

She pulled her hands down, then pushed them beneath his t-shirt, tracing the ridge of his abdomen before sliding her palms to his chest. Her fingers feathered his nipples and he groaned, then recaptured her mouth once more, his tongue teasing and sliding against hers.

Everything about this man was hard. She loved it. Loved feeling him. Basked in the way he cupped her breast with his hard, demanding hand.

She stepped back to give him more access. But instead of a floorboard there was nothing, her body flailing into the void beneath the bathroom.

"Jesus, Alaska." Mason jerked her back up, pulling her against him once again. Using her hand to steady herself against his chest, she felt the race of his heartbeat through the thin fabric of his t-shirt. "You gotta look where you're going."

She smirked. "I don't have eyes in the back of my head."

"Yeah, I can see that." He was still holding her, his arm circling her waist. He used his free hand to brush the hair from her face. "You're going to give me a heart attack."

"That's the plan."

It was his turn to smile. The Department of Defense should bottle his smile and use it on their enemies.

They'd be begging for mercy.

"Bedroom?" he asked. She nodded so fast she was giving herself whiplash. Before she could second guess herself, he was sliding his hands down her back, then lifting her into his arms. "Only way I can make sure you don't fall down a hole," he muttered.

And yeah, she could protest, but she got the idea he liked carrying her. Truth was, she liked being carried. Liked being able to concentrate on his delicious face as he dodged around the holes and walked them into his living room.

He set a good pace, clearing the small room in three strides. Then he kicked open his door and pretty much threw her on his bed.

His made bed. Well that surprised her.

"You make your bed every day?" she asked, looking up at him.

His brows knit. "Is this a test?"

"Nope. I'm just surprised, that's all."

"Foster kid. It's like being in the army. You learn to keep a tidy room." He reached down to unlace her boots, his fingers surprisingly adept. Once they were off, he slid off her socks, placing them neatly in her boots.

And her heart did that little twisty thing again.

She scrambled to her knees, making little indentations in his coverlet, then reached for him. He kicked off his own shoes, letting her pull him toward her, her fingers bunching in his t-shirt. She tugged at it until he got the idea, letting her lift it over his arms and head, throwing it on the floor because she was in no way as well trained as he was.

She opened her mouth to make a smart remark, but the ridges of his abdomen took her breath away.

"Oh wow."

The quirk of his lip told her she'd said that out loud. Before he could say anything, she pulled her own top off and the smile melted from his face.

His eyes darkened, his gaze darting from her face to her body. His lips parted and he moistened them with the tip of his tongue. The expression on his face was so intense it made her body shiver.

"You're beautiful." He kissed her stomach where it emerged from her waistband. "So fucking soft. Jesus, Alaska." He gently pushed her until her back met the mattress once more, then kissed his way up to the wire of her bra.

She threaded her fingers through his hair, her own head

dropping back on the pillow as he slid his mouth over the swell of her breast, sucking at her nipples through the fabric of her bra. She let out a long sigh and his lips tugged harder, his teeth scraping until she was a heartbeat away from pain.

And damn if that didn't make her ache for him.

Still kissing her chest, he managed to burrow his hands between her back and the mattress, cursing as he tried to unclasp her bra. When it gave, she felt the sweet release, then the hot demand of his mouth as he sucked once more.

She tugged at his hair and he lifted his head, his eyes as glassy as hers. "Use your teeth," she begged him. "Mark me. Make me yours."

"Fuck." It was like she'd unleashed something inside him. Maybe inside of her, too. An animal-like need she hadn't known existed. He tugged at her pants at the same time she ripped open the buttons of his jeans, their mouths clashing, tongues whipping, bodies wriggling in an attempt to strip off.

It probably took longer than if they'd both stripped themselves, but she loved the way he looked at her body as he peeled the pants from her thighs. Like she was something amazing. Something breathtaking.

Like he was trying to imprint every inch of her into his mind.

His fingers tugged at her panties, sliding inside them, and he squeezed his eyes shut when he felt how wet she was.

"That for me?"

"Yes," she breathed. Then he slid his finger inside of her and all thoughts flew out of her mind. His mouth covered hers, kissing her hard and hot, as he circled his thumb against the most sensitive part of her, making her thighs quake with desire. She opened her eyes, and he was staring at her, eyes heavy-lidded, a little glazed. Her hips hitched, matching the rhythm of his fingers, as pleasure built in the pit of her belly, sparking and coiling as he coaxed her to her peak.

She reached down for him, letting out a squeak when she felt the thick hardness of his desire against her palm. He was still wearing his boxers, and somewhere in her consciousness she knew he hadn't quite kicked his jeans from around his ankles, too busy giving her pleasure to think of his own.

And then she felt it. A spark that licked into a flame. Burning her from the inside out, until she convulsed around his fingers, letting out a long, aching moan. Fireworks exploded behind her eyelids, her back arching as he continued to slide his fingers against her. She clung to him, her body shaking, her mouth whispering begging words against his.

"Mason..."

"That's it, sweetheart. Say my name."

As she came down from her high, her body sinking into his mattress, Mason pulled his fingers from inside her. Without blinking, he lifted them to his mouth, his eyes squeezing shut as though he was drinking a vintage wine.

It was dirty but delicious. She loved it. Still breathless, she watched as he shucked his jeans from his ankles, then slid his hands up her thighs, yanking the panties from her legs.

Then she was naked. And he was – well almost. The shorts he was wearing couldn't contain his obvious desire. His cock jutted against them, the velvet smooth head pushing through the waistband, and she climbed to her knees, reaching out for him, enjoying his groan as she slid her thumb over the tip.

He was wet, too. She spread it over him, loving the hard heat of this man who knew exactly how to make her feel good.

Her fingers curled around his waistband, yanking it down, the sudden movement making his hardness slap against his ridged stomach. She pressed her palm against him, taking him into her grasp, then lowered her mouth over him, until he let out an almost-roar.

"Jesus, Alaska. Warn me."

She would have smiled, but her mouth was full. Instead, she slid her lips down him, her tongue teasing, her warmth welcoming, and he tangled his hands into her hair, whispering her name like it was a prayer.

She'd only been teasing him for seconds when he pulled out. She frowned and he shook his head. "Not gonna come in your mouth."

"What if I want you to?"

"Soon," he told her. "But right now the only place I want to be is inside of you."

That's what she wanted, too. What her body was aching for. "I didn't bring..."

He nodded, understanding. "Condoms in my drawer."

She scooted across his bed, rifling through his sock drawer. The box was in the bottom, and she tried to not feel satisfied when she realized it was unopened.

Enough time to think about that later.

Pulling a foil disc out, she ripped it open, then rolled the latex onto him, trying to not smile again as he let out a strangled moan. She curled her hand around him, pumping him twice, before he batted her hand away and pulled her up until their faces were touching. He slid his hand around her neck, pulling her in for an aching kiss, his breath hot and heated against her skin.

"You done this in a while?" he asked her.

"Nope," she said honestly.

"Me either."

"I hear it's like riding a bike," she whispered.

"Get back on the bed, woman. I'll show you what I like to ride."

She did as she was told, her gaze heated as he climbed

over her, his hands spreading her thighs as he knelt between them. He took himself in his hand, sliding his cock against her once, twice, then three times. Then he was there and her breath caught, because she hadn't been lying.

It had been more than a while since she'd done this.

"You okay?" he asked. "I lost you for a minute."

She nodded. "Just wondering how part a fits into part b."

He grinned. "I hear it's like riding a bike."

"Which is fine if you're the rider. But if you're a bike..." What the hell was she talking about? She wanted to slap herself. She was about to make love to this delicious, complicated man and she was talking about bikes?

"We can stop at any time," he told her, his expression suddenly serious. "Right now. No problems, no worries."

"No!" She reached for him. "I want this. I want you."

He let out a low breath then leaned over her, his mouth kissing her jaw, her cheek, her lips. "We'll take it slow. I'll need to anyway."

"And then after that we'll take it rough," she murmured.

"We'll take it any way you'd like it, baby. Just say the word."

He was giving her the power. It was intoxicating. "Just fuck me, Mason."

She felt him against her again, her body parting to welcome him in. He slid about an inch inside, then looked at her. She nodded breathlessly as he pushed his hips until he was all the way to the hilt.

There was a pinching pain for a moment, but then she relaxed, her body accommodating the width of him, the length of him, the sheer power of his hardness in her. His eyes caught hers and she nodded again, until he pulled out and pushed in, the rhythm lighting something between her legs. The base of him dragged against her in the most delicious way, making her thighs tremble, her nipples harden.

"Alaska," he whispered. "So good." Without breaking rhythm, he slid his mouth to her neck, to her collarbone, to the needy swell of her breasts. As he closed his lips around her nipple she gasped.

She tipped her head back, overwhelmed by the sensation of him inside her. On top of her. Around her. He knew every angle she needed, every stroke she desired. Her breath quickened as the length of him moved inside of her.

She wasn't sure how much more she could take. He slid his hands beneath her, angling her until all she could see was stars. And then he scraped his teeth against her nipple and she was gone.

Her nails dug into his back as she screamed out his name, her body quivering and milking until he was groaning, too.

"I'm gonna..." His words strangled in his throat as his body froze above her, his mouth releasing her nipple as he spasmed inside of her.

"Too good, too fucking good," He squeezed his eyes shut and she could feel him still coming. "I hadn't meant to come that quick."

"I came quicker," she pointed out. "Twice."

A smirk pulled at his mouth. "Next time will be better."

Her eyes widened. "Stop making promises you can't keep."

He kissed the tip of her nose, still inside of her, his hands cradling her face. "Oh I intend to keep this one. Very goddamned much."

16

Mason nailed the last floorboard down right as he heard the front door of the cabin open. Alaska had gone home about an hour earlier – they'd agreed Ty didn't need to walk in and find them in bed together, even though the last thing Mason had wanted to do was get up. It had felt too good, laying in his bed and stroking her hair, listening to her talk about Leo and the Inn and her cousins.

She was so different to him. It was enticing.

"Mase?" Ty called out, his voice echoing through the living room.

"In here." Mason gathered up the nails that were strewn on the floor, throwing them into a jar. Neither of them needed to be stepping on one of those barefoot in the middle of the night.

Ty opened the door. He looked in as good of a mood as Mason – though he hoped to God it was for a different reason.

"How was sledding?" he asked his brother.

"Good." Ty's smile widened into a grin. "Well actually,

pretty crazy. Had to dodge a few trees and nearly landed in a lake."

"Glad you didn't," Mason said mildly. "Woulda hated to pay for those hospital bills."

Ty rolled his eyes, but it didn't ruin his good humor. "I'm on Mom's insurance."

Brushing the dust from his hands, Mason stood and looked around the bathroom. Another couple of days and he'd be finished. He needed to plumb in the new toilet, but the bath was in and so was the basin. Once everything was up and running he'd retile, paint, and be done.

It was strangely satisfying.

"Can I ask you something?" Ty said, his voice dropping low.

Mason steeled himself for questions about him and Alaska. "If you have to."

"What kind of thing do you wear for a formal dance?"

Mason lifted a brow. "I dunno. A suit or tux I guess. Why do you ask?"

Ty shrugged. "No reason."

"Is there a formal happening at the Inn?" Mason stood, rolling his neck to ease the ache in his muscles.

"No. At school. The senior winter formal is the weekend before break. The others were talking about it..." Ty trailed off, shrugging. "A few of my friends are going."

"Okay..." There was something Ty wasn't saying. "Do you want to go, too?"

"Maybe."

Mason bit down a smile. Ty wouldn't be talking about it if he didn't. He'd been a kid once himself, if you didn't want to do something you definitely didn't mention it. Just tried to fly under the radar.

"You'll need a suit. Or maybe a tux. There's probably a place nearby."

"It's next month. Will I have time?"

"It's fine. We can get it done." Mason looked at him carefully. "Is there somebody you want to take?"

Ty blinked. "What, like a girl?"

"I was just wondering." Mason was out of his depth here. Was it too late to grab Alaska and ask for her help?

Ty shifted his feet. "Eloise doesn't have a date. I thought it would be the right thing to do to ask her."

"Eloise?" Mason repeated. "Do I know her?"

"She works at the Inn. She's one of the friends I was out with today."

Okay then. That explained the good mood. "Is she your girlfriend?"

"No." Ty frowned. "It's not like that. We're just... friends. For now."

Mason was swimming in uncharted water. He didn't have girlfriends when he was Ty's age. Not for long anyway. One trip home to meet the parents and he'd be out on his butt. No father wanted a foster kid for his daughter's partner.

Romance wasn't an option. Dirty sex was. And yes, he'd grown out of it, but for a while there it was the only human contact he could get.

"Are you hoping she'll be your girlfriend?" Mason asked.

"I don't know. Maybe." Ty pressed his lips together, thinking. "I mean, she's really pretty."

"I bet she is."

"And she's nice, you know? Kind. I like that."

Yeah, Mason liked that, too. "Then you should ask her."

"Okay." Ty nodded. "I will."

"And I'll call around to find out about a formalwear shop."

"You'd do that for me?" Ty's eyes caught Mason's.

"Of course." Mason nodded. "I'm your brother. We'll get you what you need. You'll be the coolest guy in the school gym."

Ty rolled his eyes again. Okay, so maybe that was a bit too far. But still, the fact he wanted to go to a dance was a good thing. It showed he was getting settled. He had friends.

He was succeeding. And maybe Mason was, too.

"Thanks." Ty nodded at him. "Oh, I saw Alaska earlier."

"You did? Where?" Mason asked quickly.

"At the coffee shop. She was with a friend. She chatted with Eloise."

"Alaska knows Eloise?"

"Of course." Ty made a 'duh' sound. "I told you, Eloise works at the Inn."

That could make things easier. Alaska would know the low down on her family. Whether they'd be cool with Ty asking her to the dance.

But there was something else, too. The fact he had no idea what Alaska did with her days. Sure, she worked in the Inn, but he'd slept with the woman and she hadn't even mentioned having coffee with a friend.

He wasn't the kind of guy who had to know everything about a woman. Who wanted to be controlling like that? But dammit he should show more interest. Ask more questions about her life.

Isn't that what guys were meant to do?

"You okay?" Ty asked.

Mason blinked his thoughts away. "I'm fine. Why?"

"You looked weird for a minute."

"I was just thinking," Mason told him.

Ty smirked. "As I said. You looked weird."

"Do your homework," Mason told him. "Or read a book or something."

"Sure." Ty's grin didn't waver. "And you relax. Looks like all that thinking's giving you a headache."

"The Gunnersons in room five-eighty-two are complaining about the heat," Glenda from housekeeping told Alaska. "They say they've turned it down to the lowest setting but it's still too warm."

Alaska was in her usual spot at reception, working out staff schedules on her laptop while everything was quiet – or fairly quiet – in the Inn. Breakfast was over, checkout time had passed and it would be a few hours before new guests arrived.

She always loved this part of the day.

"Thanks, I'll get maintenance to check it," Alaska said, making a note on her pad.

"It isn't hot in there," Glenda said, lowering her voice to a whisper. "I think they just like to find something to complain about. Yesterday it was the towels. One of them had a pull. A pull! You'd think I was asking them to use sandpaper to dry themselves."

Alaska bit down a smile. "I'll still send Rich up. It'll make them feel loved." Alaska had worked here at the Inn for as long as she could remember. When she was a small child, her grandmother – who'd built the town and the Inn, had picked her up and let her sit on the reception counter, so she could charm the guests as they checked in each day. And when she was a teenager, she'd worked weekends and holidays here. All of the cousins had.

"Nobody gets a free ride," Candy Winter had always told them. It was up there with "The guest is always right." Damn, she missed her.

"Okay then. Do you have the rosters for the next two weeks?" Glenda asked.

"Just doing them now. I'll send them over in about an hour if that works?"

Glenda nodded. "Yep, works for me. Some of the girls

want to know what they're working over Christmas so they can make plans with their families."

That was understandable. One of the hardest parts of working in a hotel was that your busiest times were always the times you'd want to spend with those you loved. On Christmas Day, every Winter cousin worked in the Inn so they could give as many of the staff time off as possible, at least on that one precious day.

They'd man reception, serve in the restaurant, and sing songs around the huge tree in the center of the large lobby area. Then, when the sun went down and the final guests had been served, they had their own family celebration. She loved every moment of it, especially as their family grew with husbands and wives and now another generation into the mix.

Glenda gave her a wave as she headed to the staff restroom, and Alaska went back to her rosters. She'd only made one change before her phone vibrated with a message. She smiled when she saw who it was.

Mason Parker.

Yeah, that was the other reason she was in a great mood. Not just because this was her favorite time of year, but because she'd pretty much had the best afternoon of her life with him yesterday.

And spent all last night talking softly with him on the phone, while he pretended to have a headache and told Ty he needed to get to bed.

Sliding her finger on the screen, she opened up the message.

I've serviced your generator. Topped up oil, greased the starter motor, and covered it up until you need it again. Although hopefully you won't. – Mason

. . .

That was so typically Mason. Practical to the end.

Is this some kind of sex talk? Because I have to say you're turning me on. – Alaska

She grinned as she sent her reply. It was fun imagining his expression when he read it.

If it was sex talk you'd know it. – Mason

Brusque and to the point. Yep, that was her guy. Wait, *her guy*? No, not that. Just a friend. Or… oh this was confusing.

You can't just say something like that and not follow through. Now I'm intrigued about your sex talk. – Alaska

What do you want me to say? That I'm still dreaming of the way your skin was creamy and soft? The way your nipples hardened in my mouth every time I scraped my teeth against them? The way you came so hard on my fingers I get stiff every time I look at them? – Mason

Yeah, that would do it. Now she knew how the Gunnersons felt. She was getting overheated herself. She lifted her hand to fan her face.

. . .

Yes, I want you to say that. But probably not while I'm in public. I'm kind of blushing here. –Alaska

Okay then. Back to the generator. I've locked the shed and put the key back in your drawer. It's there the next time you need it. –Mason

How could he switch so easily from making her blush to making her feel taken care of? He'd even put the key back.

Actually, wait a minute...

How did you get the key in the first place? –Alaska

I kind of let myself into your house. I didn't touch anything else, I promise. –Mason

But the house is locked. BECAUSE YOU TOLD ME TO! –Alaska

Yeah, and I've spent a lot of time with law enforcement officers. There's a trick to every lock. –Mason

You broke into my house? I should call the cops. –Alaska

That's what I told you days ago. Call the cops, tell the truth, and get me out of there. –Mason

. . .

Yeah, but that was before I knew about your talented fingers. They're too good to be in shackles. – Alaska

How about I show you how sorry I am tonight? – Mason

What about Ty? – Alaska

He's out with some friends at the movies. Shouldn't be back until ten. – Mason

Okay. But you can come to my place. I have hot and cold running water. – Alaska

And a generator. Don't forget about that. – Mason

I won't. I'll show you my appreciation later. With my mouth. – Alaska

... Mason Parker is typing... – Mason

Don't try that trick on me. I'm the queen of that one. – Alaska

. . .

You're the queen of everything, baby. I'll see you tonight. –Mason

"What's got you smiling like you've just won the lottery?"

Alaska looked up to see her sister leaning over her phone.

"Nothing," Alaska said hastily, shutting it off,

Everley eyed her carefully. "Are you having sex with your neighbor?"

"What gives you that idea?" Damn her family was nosey. Alaska was, too. If the shoe was on the other foot she'd be giving her sister the third degree right now.

"He called you baby. And he's seeing you tonight."

"Maybe he has the wrong number."

"I'd go with that theory," Everley said, "if it wasn't for one thing. I just asked you a question and you avoided giving me an answer. Which means the answer is yes, you are having sex with Mason Parker."

Alaska widened her eyes. "Can you keep it down?"

"I mean, sure." Everley grinned. "But we both know you can't keep a secret in this town. Give it a few days and everybody will know."

"No thank you. It's nobody's business but mine." Alaska shook her head. "And for your information, we've had sex once. Well... twice. But in one sitting."

"You were sitting?" Everley was grinning.

"No. Yes." Exasperated, Alaska shook her head. This was payback for all the times she'd teased Everley about her relationship with Dylan. "It doesn't matter. All I'm saying is it's happened one time so nobody should be interested in that."

"But after tonight it'll be two sittings." Everley wriggled her brows. "Am I right?"

Alaska shook her head, and Everley gave her a knowing look.

"Anyway, as much as I'm intrigued by your sex life, that's not the reason I'm here," Everley told her.

"I'm glad to hear that," Alaska said. "So what's up?"

"Mom's just sent through confirmation of their flights. They're arriving on the nineteenth of December and staying until the twenty-sixth."

Well that was a way to dent her good mood. "Don't they realize we'll all be working? That's our busiest time of the year."

Everley sighed. "I called her last night and told her that. But she insists on spending Christmas with us. I don't know why this year is so different."

"And has she said where she's staying?"

Everley wrinkled her nose. "With me and Dylan."

"What? No!"

"I offered," Everley told her. "Because otherwise she was going to stay with you."

Alaska paled. The thought of her parents staying with her, so close to Mason and Ty, felt like a bucket of cold water being thrown over her. Not just because it would mean no more night visits from the sexy guy next door, but because of who Mason was.

What he knew. Having her parents next door to the man who knew all the secrets of her disappearance was way too close for comfort.

"I'm going to owe you for this, aren't I?" Alaska asked her sister.

"Yep. Big time." Everley grinned. "Not least because we already have one extra in our house to deal with."

"Leo?"

"I wasn't including him. But maybe you could keep him while the folks are here. Dad's allergic to fur, remember?"

Yeah, she did remember. It was one of the reasons they weren't allowed any pets when they were children. It had broken her heart, but she'd made up for lost time as soon as she'd moved out.

"I'll look after Leo," Alaska agreed. "But who's the extra person."

"You can't tell anybody yet..."

OH! Alaska's mouth dropped open. "You're..."

"Pregnant," Everley confirmed. "Only six weeks. We don't want to announce it until I'm in the second trimester. Just to be sure."

"Oh my God!" Alaska practically ran through the gap in the counter, throwing her arms around her sister. "Congratulations. How exciting! How are you feeling?"

"Pretty good. I think I've been sleeping through the morning sickness. And Dylan is calling to check up on me every day."

"As he should. You're carrying precious cargo." Alaska grinned at Everley. "How about the show? Are you still able to do that?"

"Yep. I'm not even tired. I think I'm one of the lucky ones."

"Maybe you're like Candy," Alaska said, referring to their late Grandmother. "She always said she sailed through her pregnancies. Never felt better."

"Well there's a while to go still, but if I can be a trooper like her, I'm up for that." Everley rubbed her still-flat stomach. "Anyway, I just wanted to give you a heads up. You know what Mom's like, she'll expect a tour of your place, and she'll probably hang out here with you when I'm working."

"It's okay. We can handle them. And it's only for a few days."

"Right." Everley nodded. "What could possibly go wrong?"

17

He'd never get tired of watching her reach to a peak of pleasure as she rode him. Alaska let out a cry and collapsed onto him, her naked body boneless as he caught her in his arms. He felt his own orgasm surge through his body and pulse inside of her. She let out another cry and he kissed her, swallowing her pleasure as it met his own.

And when they got their breath back, she still didn't move from him. He liked that. A lot.

"Oh my God," she murmured against his chest. "I think I just died."

"You're the prettiest corpse I've ever seen." He smiled at her and gently laid her down, pulling off the condom and tying it up. He hated this part but it was necessary. And he'd be back and holding her again before they knew it. "I'll be back," he promised as he climbed out of bed.

"You'd better be." She gave him a satisfied smile. "Because I don't think I can move again."

It took him a minute to clean up and dispose of the trash before he walked back into the bedroom with a warm, wet cloth and started to clean her up.

"What are you doing?" she murmured, her brows knitting.

"You're sticky. From me and you. Just making sure you're comfortable."

Alaska blinked. "Would you rather I took a shower? Do I smell bad?"

He stopped cleaning her for a moment. "No, sweetheart. You smell good. Like sex." He gave her a lopsided grin. "But I'm not just gonna come inside of you and leave you to clean up the mess."

"You came inside a condom."

"And the condom was in you. And if you're kind enough to invite me in, it's only right that I clean up when I leave."

She started to laugh.

"What?" He tipped his head to the side, sliding the cloth over her smooth thighs. Damn, he was getting hard again. What was it about this woman? He wasn't sure he could ever get enough.

"I don't know. Nobody's ever cleaned me up after sex before."

He lifted his gaze to hers. "You wanna talk about you having sex with other guys while I'm cleaning you up?" And yeah, a bolt of jealousy hit him. They were both adults, they had histories, but it didn't mean he wanted to hear about it.

"You make it sound like there were a line of them," she said, watching him as he started to move the washcloth again. "Three. There have been three."

He nodded slightly. Still didn't like it.

"How about you?" she asked. She didn't sound jealous. He didn't like it.

"More than three."

"More than ten?" she asked him.

"A few more than that."

She tipped her head to the side, smiling. "How many is a few?"

"I don't know. I'm not proud of my history. There was a time after I got out of foster care where I just longed for some human contact, you know? My dad was busy with his new wife and Ty. I felt lonely. So I played the field, hurt and got hurt. Then I concluded that the only way not to get hurt was to play a different game." He put the cloth on the side, scrambling up the bed so he could look her in the eye.

He didn't want to hide from her. Not even the stuff he regretted. She deserved his truth.

"What was the different game?" she asked him softly.

"Finding women who wanted the same thing I did."

"Which was?"

"To have sex and leave." He winced. "It sounds so goddamned awful, I know. And eventually I didn't even do that. I wasn't lying yesterday when I told you it's been a while."

"You don't have to explain yourself to me," she said. He could tell by her tone she really meant it. But he wanted to explain himself. Wanted her to know him. And that included his darkness.

"I'm not doing that with you. You know that, right?" He tipped her head up, her beautiful eyes meeting his. There was so much trust in them it was killing him.

"You're not?"

He shook his head. "No." And he wished he could say more. That he could even define the emotions rushing through him. But they felt alien. And he didn't like that.

"Well I like you cleaning me up," she said.

He nodded, feeling raw. "Yeah, I like that, too."

She smiled. "I wish you could stay longer."

"We need to get Ty to a sleepover."

She laughed. "Do seventeen-year-olds have sleepovers?"

"Not the kind of ones I'd approve of, no." He grimaced.

"Then I guess we'll just have to steal the time when we

can." She laid back, her hair fanning out on the sheets. "That's if you want to keep doing this."

He frowned. "Did I not just make that clear?"

"Not really, no."

He winced. This was why he avoided relationships. Why he'd sworn them off after hurting too many people. He didn't know how to say the right words. How to tell people what he was feeling.

He'd spent too long trying not to feel anything at all.

And the last person he wanted to hurt was Alaska. She was too good for that. She deserved more than he could give. But he was a selfish asshole, so he wouldn't walk away.

Not when this felt so good.

His chest felt like a band was pulling around it. But he ignored the ache and reached out, brushing a stray lock of hair from Alaska's forehead. "You're beautiful," he told her. "Inside and out. Any man would be lucky to have you. And when I say lucky, I mean the luckiest sonofabitch alive. So if you'll let me come visit you and talk to you and service your generator from time to time, then yes, I want to keep seeing you."

She slowly nodded. "Yes, I want that."

"Thank Christ." The band loosened just a little. "I'm not good at this. I'll try to be better. I will. I've just spent so long looking after myself I've forgotten how to do it for anybody else."

"Bullshit. We've already had this conversation and you're wrong." She lifted a brow. "You just don't want to admit you care."

"Maybe." He blinked. "But either way the result is the same. People get hurt."

She rolled onto her side, propping her chin on her hand as she looked at him. "People get hurt all the time. The only way to not get hurt is to stay wrapped in cotton and never leave the house. You think people aren't hurt because you avoid them? Maybe that hurts them more and you don't know about it."

He swallowed. "Maybe you're right."

"Do you know how many people have tried to not hurt me in my life?" she asked him. "I'm so sick of being treated like I'm fragile. Or even worse, broken. I'm not broken. I'm somebody who had something happen to her as a child. That's it. It doesn't mean you have to treat me like glass. I'd much rather you'd fuck and leave me than treat me like that."

"Alaska..." His voice was rough. "I'd never treat you like that."

"But don't you see, by treating me differently you're saying I'm broken."

He shook his head. "No. I'm saying you're special."

Her eyes looked glassy. "You think I'm special?" she asked softly.

He nodded because he couldn't find the words.

"I think you're special, too," she whispered.

"No, baby. I'm the damaged one."

Her eyes narrowed. "No! You don't get to call me special then twist it around when it comes to yourself. You know what we both are? Survivors." She ran her fingers down his arm, tracing the dates on his tattoo. "We were lost for a while, but we climbed out and we survived. Hell, Mason, you survived more than anybody. You were alone, with no love, no human contact, yet here you are. A beautiful, kind man who'd do anything for anybody but is too afraid to show it in case people think he's weak. But I don't think you are." A single tear ran down her cheek. "I think you're the strongest person I know."

The tightness had returned. Along with the pounding of his heart against his ribcage. He couldn't remember ever talking to somebody like this. He didn't let people in.

And yet here she was. Beautiful, soft Alaska. Inside him without him even knowing it.

"Don't cry," he said roughly. He ran his finger along the track of her tear, drying it away. "I'm not worth your tears."

"Yes you are. You always will be."

It was his turn to lay on his back. He stared up at the ceiling, his eyes seeking out the imperfections in the paint in an attempt to push out the emotion. He wasn't good at this. He couldn't deal with it.

But maybe he'd have to learn.

"Can I ask you something?" Alaska said, sliding her arm over his stomach. It wasn't sexual, just human to human.

"Yeah, you can."

"Why did you come back here?"

He blinked. "To Winterville?"

"Yeah. Of all the places you and Ty could have gone, but you chose here. The place where you had a secret you never wanted to come out. So why?"

"I didn't have a whole lot of choice. I needed to get Ty out of Baltimore. And this was the only place I owned."

"That's not true. You still could have gone anywhere. Sold this place. There are plenty of cheap places to live if you know where to find them."

"I didn't need cheap. I have money."

"There you go then. Even stranger that you chose to come here."

Yeah, maybe it was. And yet it had seemed so obvious when he realized he needed to get Ty out of town. "I guess..." His brow furrowed. "Maybe I brought him here because it was the last place I felt truly happy."

She rolled onto her front, draping her upper body over his until they were face to face, eye to eye.

"You were happy here?"

"It was a stolen couple of months with my dad. Before he

went into jail and I went into the system. We were like a couple of kids, you know? Buddies more than father and son. We'd swim in the lake and eat cereal for dinner and go hunting for turkey because they were the only thing in season." He gave a half smile. "Can you believe it? My dad was about to be jailed for years but he couldn't bring himself to hunt illegally."

"Maybe he just didn't want to bring attention to you guys. Imagine him getting arrested and you not being able to spend those last days together."

"Maybe." He nodded. "I guess I hadn't thought of that."

"It's the same reason you didn't take me into the police station, isn't it? Because he was trying to fly under the radar."

"Yeah, that's right. It makes sense."

"So now you've brought Ty here. To make him happy, too."

"I'm not sure that's possible," Mason said dryly. "He's a teenager."

She gave a gentle laugh. "So true. But at least you're trying. That's a good thing."

"I just want him to have what I didn't, you know?"

"I know," she agreed. "And you're doing great. He seems content."

"He seems horny. He's got the hots for a girl."

"Eloise?"

He shot her an amused glance. "How did you know that?"

"I saw them outside the coffee shop the other day. It was in the way he looked at her."

"Jesus this *is* a small town. Nobody gets away with anything here."

Alaska shrugged. "It is what it is. At least Eloise doesn't have three boy cousins to scare Ty away."

"I don't think that would affect him. I'm pretty sure he's falling for her. He wants to take her to the winter formal."

"He does?" Alaska grinned. "Oh that's so sweet."

"Hmm."

"Oh come on." She shook her head. "Even you can't be cynical when it comes to young love."

"I don't want him getting hurt."

She rolled her eyes. "He's going to get hurt, Mason. It's how we learn. How we grow. The trick is to be his soft landing when he falls."

"I hate how you're so wise." He pulled her close, cupping her face as he kissed her softly.

"No you don't."

"You're right. I don't." He kissed her again. "We have twenty minutes left before I have to get back to the cabin. Shall we spend it talking about my teenage brother, or can I push my face between your thighs until you scream my name?"

She grinned. "Well the first one does sound tempting..."

"Shut up, woman, and spread your legs."

"I will, but only because you asked so nicely."

"Hey!"

Mason was outside his cabin when he heard the low shout. Cutting up logs so they'd have enough for the next few days. He looked up to see North Winter walking toward him.

He hadn't seen him since that day in Winterville when they'd nearly thrown punches. According to Alaska, North wanted to apologize but she'd told him to leave it for a while.

Probably for the best.

"Hi." Mason nodded, his expression unchanging.

"I came over to check on Alaska's generator. Looks like somebody beat me to it. Was it you?"

Was the man going to get worked up about a generator

now? Mason didn't have the patience for this. "Yeah, it was me."

North nodded. "Thank you."

It took a moment for the words to sink in. "For what?"

"For taking care of the generator. It was a nice thing to do."

Mason put his axe down and looked North in the eye. He didn't have time for guys who played games, but it didn't look like Alaska's cousin was doing anything other than being genuine. "She's a neighbor." He shrugged. "It would be rude not to help."

North shoved his hands into his pockets. He was wearing work boots – the same as Mason – and a thick parka that covered his top half. But his head and his hands were bare. "Yeah, well, I appreciate it. It's a worry for us, having her out here alone. I'm glad she has somebody else looking out for her."

"She doesn't need anybody looking out for her. She can take care of herself. I just happened to have some oil and a bit of time to spare."

North looked at him carefully. There was a control to the man that Mason recognized from the court room. Somebody on their best behavior. He wondered who'd had a word with him and told him to be nice to Alaska's new neighbor.

"I... ah... also wanted to apologize," North said. "After my behavior the other week. I shouldn't have squared up to you. It was wrong."

"Apology accepted."

North caught his eye and nodded. "Thank you."

"But you know, if I *was* interested in your cousin, your caveman act wouldn't stop me one bit," Mason said, lifting a brow.

North looked surprised.

"She's a good woman. She's gonna make a guy very happy one day."

"Yeah." North swallowed. "I guess she is."

"So maybe you should give her a break. She doesn't need protecting by you or by me."

North looked over his shoulder. "Anyway, I have to go. Got some deliveries to do."

"Christmas trees?"

"Tis the season," North said. Somehow those words made Mason want to laugh. Because North looked the exact opposite of somebody infected by the Christmas spirit.

Damn, he was grumpier than Mason, and that took something.

"Okay then. I have more logs to cut so..."

"Yeah. I'll see you later."

"Sure."

"And you probably need to get your axe sharpened. It's leaving dents in the cuts. Come over to the farm sometime and you can use my sharpener."

Mason blinked. "Okay..."

North didn't wait to hear anything else. He turned and walked away, his big feet leaving imprints in the freshly fallen snow. Mason watched him for a moment and then picked up his axe again, swinging it against the log.

And dammit, North was right. The thing really did need sharpening.

"I called a formal wear place this afternoon," Mason told Ty as he slid a plate in front of him. Frozen pizza. Well, not frozen any more since he'd just taken it out of the oven, but it was still only one step up from eating cereal for dinner. But he was too tired to cook anything more complicated, and Ty seemed happy enough to eat a cheap pizza.

"Uh huh." Ty shoved a slice of pizza in his mouth.

"They're open on Saturdays. I checked with Alaska and you're scheduled at the Inn until one. I'll pick you up and we'll drive straight there. I gave them your size and they have some suits there."

"No need. I'm not going."

Mason blinked. "What?"

"I said I'm not going." Ty didn't look up. "There are no tickets left."

"What do you mean there are no tickets left? They can't fit one extra kid in?" Mason frowned. "Did you ask at school?"

Ty sighed. "Yes I asked and no they can't fit one more kid in. It doesn't matter. I don't want to go anyway." Ty put his second slice of pizza down. "Now can we drop this?"

"Is there a waitlist?" Mason asked, ignoring Ty's stormy expression. "A few kids are bound to drop out. We should get you measured anyway."

"No, there's not a waitlist. And no I don't want to get a suit for a dance I'm not going to. It's fine," Ty said, his teeth gritted. "It's just a shitty dance anyway."

"What about that girl?"

Ty's jaw twitched. "I guess she'll go with somebody else. Whatever." Stuffing the rest of his pizza slice into his mouth, Ty barely chewed it before swallowing it down and chasing it with a glass of water. "I need to do my homework. Thanks for dinner."

He stood, and Mason watched him, his chest tight. He felt angry for him, disappointed, too. This dance was the first thing Ty had shown any enthusiasm over in months and he'd received a knockback. Sure, it wasn't a big deal. Or it shouldn't be.

But it was clearly a big deal for Ty.

What kind of school wouldn't find space for a new kid? Surely one more person couldn't make any difference. It was no skin off their nose, but it would dent Ty's confidence.

And each little dent added up into a chasm. Mason remembered his own dents. A visit from an angry father telling him to stay away from his daughter. The lack of invitations to parties because he was a foster kid and not welcome in nice middle class homes.

Feeling that he'd never be good enough, and deciding to act as though he didn't care.

"Okay," Mason agreed, watching Ty wash his plate and put it on the drying rack. That proved he was upset, Ty never cleaned without nagging. "Hey, you want me to bring you in a hot chocolate to help you concentrate?"

Ty finally looked at him. "I'm not a kid," he said, shaking his head.

Yeah, and that was the problem. He wasn't a kid but he wasn't an adult either. He was in that wasteland where he needed support but wouldn't accept it. Where he thought that wanting to be loved meant he was weak.

Mason remembered it all too well. "Well if you change your mind..."

"I won't."

Picking up his own half-eaten plate of pizza, Mason emptied the remains in the trash as Ty pushed past him.

"I'm going to do more work in the bathroom while you're studying," Mason said.

"Uh huh." Ty looked supremely uninterested.

"It'll be ready for use before you go to bed though."

"Sure." Ty walked into his room, slamming his door behind him.

That went well.

18

Alaska was sitting on her sofa, cuddling with Leo when her phone rang. She reached over his fluffy head to pick it up, and Leo gave a low growl, grumbling at being moved.

"Live with it," she whispered, smiling at his sleepy eyes.

Her smile widened when she saw Mason's name on her phone screen.

"Hey," she said after she slid her finger to accept the call. "You okay?"

"Yeah. Just finished up in the bathroom. Ty's taking a shower so I thought I'd check in on you."

"I was going to call you actually," she said, the smile still in her voice. "I hear you had a visitor earlier."

"Why am I not surprised that you know about North coming here?"

She grinned. "Want to hear the chain of information? North got back to the Christmas Tree Farm and told his co-owner, Amber, that he'd seen you. But Everley's father-in-law over heard and then—"

"Told Everley, who told you?"

"Nope." Alaska smiled because damn there were so many networks of gossip in this town. "I mean, she probably would have except she's performing right now. But Charlie – that's Everley's father-in-law – told Dolores who runs the coffee shop."

"I know who Dolores is," Mason pointed out.

"And Dolores told my cousin's wife, Nicole, who told me."

"Jesus how many degrees of separation is that?" Mason asked. "Six, seven?"

Alaska counted in her head. "Maybe five? If you count Amber as a degree."

"So we're pretty safe in the knowledge that the whole town knows."

"Yep, pretty much. Sorry. So how did it go? Did you and North decide to make nice?"

"It was fine," Mason told her. "He apologized for being a dick and I accepted. Done."

"Well that'll disappoint the gossips," Alaska mused. "I guess they'll just have to talk about something else."

"Maybe they can talk about how Ty can get a ticket to the damn winter formal," Mason said, his voice low.

"Why?" She frowned. "Hasn't he bought his yet?"

"He tried and they said they were sold out. Kid looks fucking disappointed." Mason let out a breath.

"Oh no. Do they have a waitlist?" she asked. Poor Ty. She hated the thought of him being left out.

"Apparently not."

"Is he really upset?" Her chest clenched.

"He says it's no big deal but he's also not talked to me since dinner. Just hid in his room until five minutes ago when he stomped into the bathroom and slammed the door."

"Sounds like a typical teenager," she said.

"Right?"

"Maybe the two of you could do something nice on the night of the dance," she suggested.

"Maybe." He sounded pissed, too.

"That sucks. I'm sorry."

"Yeah, well I feel better now that I've heard your voice."

That made her smile. "Glad I can be of help."

"Baby, you're always of help. Always."

"I'm not much help now. Maybe I can ask the kids at the Inn to find out if somebody has a spare ticket to the formal."

"I don't know if Ty'll go," Mason admitted. "He was pissed and doesn't want to look for a suit. So even if we got a ticket, he won't have the clothes. It's a catch-22."

"So make him get the clothes. What can it hurt?"

Mason started to laugh.

"What?" she asked, perplexed.

"I thought you knew how to deal with teenagers. You think I can persuade him to get fitted for a suit when he's decided against it?"

"I do know how to deal with teenagers," she said, letting out a huff. "And I think you could persuade him to do anything if you wanted to."

"How would I do that?" He sounded interested now.

"I don't know. You're just very... persuasive."

"You got me intrigued," he said. "How am I persuasive? Give me an example."

"You took over starting my generator when I told you I had it covered," she pointed out.

"Yeah, but that's because you needed me." He sounded like he was teasing her. That was new. And she liked it. A lot.

"I didn't need you. I humored you. I can start my own generator. But I knew that if I let you go all caveman on me I might enjoy the benefits, too."

"What kind of benefits would those be?" he asked, his voice low.

"The kind that involved taking your top off and kissing you all over."

He let out a low groan. "Jesus, Alaska."

"You want me to stop?" she asked softly.

"No. I want to stomp over to your house and throw you on the bed."

An image of him slamming through her door and throwing her over his shoulder flashed through her brain. "That would be hot."

"Yeah," he agreed. "It would. And if Ty wasn't here right now..."

"You wouldn't be here either."

He ignored her reply. "What are you wearing?"

"Mostly a dog," she said, ruffling Leo's fur.

"And under the dog?"

"Pajamas." Her lips curled.

"And under those?"

"You know what's under those." She felt her skin warm at his questions.

"Yeah, I do. And I wish I was there right now. Are you blushing?"

"All over."

"Fuck." She imagined him raking his hand through his hair. His eyes darkening the way they did when he touched her soft curves. "Baby, you're killing me."

"That's not the plan. I like you alive and kicking."

"I'm about two seconds away from running over to your place and showing you exactly how alive I feel."

"Come over tomorrow," she suggested. "I'll call you with an emergency. A broken fuse or something."

He laughed. "Ty'll never believe it."

"Ty probably already knows what's going on. That's what teenagers do. Our job as adults is to pretend we're wiser and he has no idea what's happening."

"I take it all back," Mason said. "You do know teenagers."

"Yeah," she agreed. "I do. Now get some sleep and I'll do the same. That fuse is going to need a lot of tender loving care tomorrow."

He laughed. "Good night, baby."

"Good night."

"And Alaska?" he said. "That fuse is going to explode. At least three times."

"Hi," Alaska said to the school receptionist. She'd driven to Marshall High School on her break at the Inn. And yeah, she knew Mason would probably be pissed, but she liked Ty and she was pretty good at persuading people to do the right thing. "I was just wondering if you had any tickets available for the winter formal. For my... godson."

The school receptionist looked up from her computer. "You're the second person who's asked in two days. No, I'm sorry, we don't. We sold out weeks ago."

"What about a waitlist?" she asked. "Somebody's bound to drop out, right?"

"We don't have a waitlist. Once you buy the ticket it's yours."

"But that's silly. Somebody's bound to drop out."

The receptionist didn't look impressed. "Those are the rules the PTA made."

"The PTA?" Alaska asked.

"The dance is being run by the events committee of the Parent Teacher Association. They make the rules, we sell the tickets," the receptionist said, sounding bored. "Or we sold them," she corrected.

"And who runs the events committee?" Alaska asked.

"I'm afraid I can't tell you that." The receptionist gave her a sickly smile. "I have to respect the confidentiality of our volunteers."

"Seriously?" Ugh, no wonder Ty hadn't bothered to fight this. She was losing the will herself.

"We take data protection very seriously."

"Okay," Alaska said, her annoyance rising. "So, if I pull up the school website and look at the PTA section, I won't be able to see who runs the committee?"

"Um..." The receptionist blinked, flustered. "I suppose you will."

"So it's public knowledge but you won't tell me." Alaska let out a frustrated sigh. "Okay then." She pulled her phone from her bag with an exaggerated flourish, then quickly tapped in the school's name. The website loaded, and she clicked on the menu, navigating to the PTA page.

And there it was. The events sub-committee. Chaired by...

Oh shit.

"Lisa Gaughran." The receptionist finally smiled. It almost looked genuine.

"I can see that," Alaska replied testily, looking up from her phone. Of all the people in the town who could chair that damn committee it had to be the one woman she'd embarrassed publicly. Lisa Gaughran.

And then because life wasn't being enough of a bitch she heard footsteps approaching. She didn't have to turn to see who it was. The cloud of Coco Mademoiselle wafting through the hallway was enough to tell her who was walking toward her right now.

"Lisa, how lovely to see you," the receptionist said, pointedly ignoring the fact that Alaska was right in front of her. "Principal Tasker will be here in just one moment. She's looking forward to your update."

"That's wonderful," Lisa said. Her footsteps stopped.

Alaska finally glanced over her shoulder to see Lisa looking directly at her. "What are you doing here?" Lisa asked, the sweetness in her voice disappearing. "You don't have children at this school."

"Actually," the receptionist said. "Alaska was asking about winter formal tickets. I was just explaining you've been sold out for weeks. She wouldn't take no for an answer."

Lisa rolled her eyes. "Aren't you a little old for school dances?" she asked Alaska.

Alaska told herself to keep calm. "I'm asking for a friend's son."

"Tyler Parker," Lisa said. "I heard he was looking for a ticket."

"Yes, he is. He joined the school late but would still like to go to the dance. I was hoping there was a waitlist he could be put on."

"No waitlist. We're at capacity." Lisa looked delighted. "If we have any more students coming we'd need an extra adult chaperone and we're all out of them."

"I'll volunteer," Alaska blurted out.

Lisa laughed, but there was no humor in it. "No dear, we don't accept just any volunteers. You'd need to be a parent or guardian and you aren't either, are you?"

"No," Alaska admitted.

"Then that's it. I'm afraid Tyler is out of luck. Too bad."

"That's it?" Alaska said, shaking her head. "You're gonna let one kid miss out just because of one volunteer? When you know at least one or two other kids won't show?"

Lisa flicked her blonde hair over her shoulder. "I'm sorry," she said, sounding completely unapologetic. "But those are my rules and I'm sticking to them."

Alaska was still quietly fuming that afternoon as she checked guests in at reception. Sure, she smiled and made them all feel welcome, but inside she was imagining all the ways she could get her revenge on Lisa Gaughran. Maybe that's why she didn't hear the heavy stomps of a pair of size thirteen work boots as Mason walked up to the Inn's reception desk. She looked over the shoulder of the guest she'd just handed a key to, her gaze clashing with Mason's stormy dark eyes.

Oh he looked mad. Had he heard about her talking to Lisa? He probably thought she was an interfering bitch.

"Um, take the elevator to the third floor," she said, dragging her eyes back to the guests in front of her. "Go through the right hand door and your room is the third on the left. You're booked for dinner at six, and breakfast at nine."

"Thank you." The wife of the lovely middle-aged couple gave her a big smile.

"No problem."

She let out a long breath and brought her gaze back to Mason's. "Can I help you?" she asked, trying to keep her voice professional. He really did look annoyed. What had she done now?

"I need a word. In private." His jaw was ticking. Oh boy, she was in for it.

Her gaze flickered behind him. There was only one more guest waiting in line. "Give me one minute."

He nodded, saying nothing. He stood still as a statue as she smiled at the guest and took their details, taking their payment, and giving them a room card. His eyes never leaving her face.

And once she'd given them a recommendation for dinner outside the inn, and typed in their allergies, they left and she was standing alone with the grumpiest man in Winterville.

"Okay then," she said. "You want to do this in the office?"

He nodded and she pointed at the door, feeling his eyes boring into her back as he followed her into her office.

Alaska didn't use this room much. She disliked being away from the hustle and bustle of the reception. If she had work to do she'd usually do it at the reception desk, unless for some reason it was busy. She walked over to her desk, hearing Mason close the door behind him. She turned and leaned against the oak edge, pulling her lip between her teeth.

"Okay, just let me explain. I didn't mean to cause any problems..."

"So you did talk to Lisa about the school dance?" His voice was low and gritty.

"Um, yeah. But I was only trying to help," she told him. "I think I made everything worse though." She ran her tongue over her dry bottom lip. "How did you find out?"

"I got a phone call from Lisa. Told me you tried to volunteer as a chaperone."

Alaska swallowed. "I did. But it doesn't matter because they won't accept me since I'm not a parent."

"But you tried." His eyes were still dark. "You fucking tried, Alaska." He exhaled raggedly. "Do you know how that makes me feel?"

"Angry by the look of it."

He shook his head. "It makes me feel... I don't know. It makes me feel weird. Nobody fights for Ty. Nobody fought for me. And you went there and tried and, goddamn it!" Without breaking their gaze, he stalked toward her, his jaw tight. She curled her fingers around her desk top, not moving an inch as he stopped dead in front of her and cupped her chin with his warm, rough hand.

"You slay me, you know that?" he whispered gruffly, tilting her head gently with his hand. Her breath caught at the intensity of his expression. "You're a good person, Alaska. All I want to do is kiss the hell out of you right now."

"You're not mad?"

"Not at you." He shook his head. "Not at all."

"You looked so pissed."

"I wasn't pissed. I was trying to find some restraint. It took everything I had not to haul you over the reception desk and ravish you on the goddamn floor."

She started to laugh, but he cut off the sound with his demanding mouth, pressing it hard against hers. A shiver wracked through her as he kissed her hard and deep, leaning down and holding her tight as she reached to slide her fingers into his hair.

"Need you closer," he muttered, lifting her onto the desk. Then he kissed her again, one hand sliding down her back, the other curled around her neck. Damn, the man knew how to heat her up. How to chase everything out of her mind until it was full of him and need and nothing else.

"Alaska... oh shit."

The two of them jumped at the sudden interruption. Mason released his hold on her back, and she peeped around his shoulder to see Eloise standing there, her mouth hanging open.

"Um, I just wanted to request a day off, but I can come back later," Eloise said hurriedly.

"Hi Eloise," Alaska managed, lifting an eyebrow at Mason so he knew who'd interrupted them.

"You're Eloise?" he asked.

Eloise shifted her feet. "Um, yeah."

"This is Ty's brother," Alaska told her, embarrassment suffusing her. "Mason Parker."

Eloise couldn't meet either of their eyes. "Um, hi, Mr. Parker."

"It's Mason," he told her.

She nodded quickly. "Hello, Mason," she squeaked.

"I'll leave you to get back to work," he said, looking from

Eloise back to Alaska. "I hope I managed to, ah, help with that sore throat. Those tonsils are definitely swollen."

It was all she could do not to burst out laughing as he high tailed it out of there, giving Eloise a quick nod.

"I'll call you later," Alaska said as he yanked the door open. "Give you an update on those tonsils."

He didn't reply back.

19

"There you go," Mason said, passing a piece of paper to Ty a few days later.

"What's this?" Ty asked, his brows pinching as he took the paper.

"A ticket to the winter formal. With your name on it."

"How'd you get this? Is it bootleg or something?" Ty turned it over in his hands suspiciously.

"I spoke with the PTA. They agreed to release some more tickets."

"How'd you manage to get them to do that?" Ty asked.

"I volunteered to be a chaperone." He'd done more than that. Apparently, chaperones had to be on the PTA itself.

So, yeah, now he was on the PTA. Fuck his life.

"You what?" Ty's voice rose half an octave.

Mason lifted his hands up in reassurance. "It's okay. I won't cramp your style. I've told them I'll man the entrance. You can get up to what you'd like inside and I won't be there to watch you."

Ty wrinkled his nose. "Do you have to go?"

"If you want to go, yeah. I don't like this any more than

you do." In fact, he liked it a hell of a lot less. "But either I chaperone or you stay home. Your choice."

Ty opened his mouth to answer, but Mason thought better of it.

"Actually, you have to go," he told his brother. "Because I do. So yeah, no choice."

"You promise not to embarrass me?" Ty asked, still frowning.

"I'll do my very best."

"And you'll stay away from the gym?"

"Again, I'll do my best."

Ty tipped his head to the side, his eyes hooded. "And you promise whatever happens you won't dance."

"That you can bet your life on," Mason said.

"Will I have to go there with you?" Ty asked him. "Because I was hoping to go with some of the others. They're talking about splitting the cost of a limo and getting reservations at a restaurant first.

"That's fine. It'll be like we're not related. You won't even know I'm there."

Ty gave a half-nod. "Well, okay, I guess."

"You're welcome," Mason said pointedly.

Ty had the good grace to look embarrassed. "Ah yeah, thanks. I appreciate it."

"So now you can call that girl and ask her, right?"

"Yeah, right."

"And I'll call the formalwear shop and see when they can fit us in," Mason told him.

"That sounds good," Ty said. "Thank you."

"You're welcome."

There was an uncomfortable silence. Neither of them knew what to say. So Ty walked over and punched Mason in the arm. Hard.

"Shit." Mason rubbed his bicep. When did his brother's

knuckles become like iron?

Ty grinned at the pained expression on his brother's face. "I'm gonna do my homework," he told Mason. "And talk to my friends."

"Sounds like a good idea. I... ah... promised I'd take a look at Alaska's fuse box. She called me earlier, she's having some problems with it."

"Sure." Ty pulled his bedroom door open. "Talk later."

He hadn't even heard him. And that was fine. The more Ty was distracted by the thought of dances and girls the less he'd notice what Mason and Alaska were up to.

He waited until he could hear silence from Ty's bedroom – meaning his ear pods were in and his laptop was booting up, then grabbed his coat and work boots, putting them on quickly because he needed to see her again.

This time preferably uninterrupted.

"I'm goin'," he yelled. Ty yelled back something incomprehensible and Mason walked out of the door.

It was icy cold out here. Snow covered the grass, but the pathways and roads were clear. He'd heard talk in town about another storm coming, but he'd learned here in Winterville people either talked about the weather or gossiped.

He preferred the weather.

His feet crunched in the snow as he took the shortest route to Alaska's house. The lights were glowing softly through her curtains, a curl of smoke escaping from her chimney telling him she'd built a fire.

She hadn't closed the curtains in her kitchen yet, and he caught a glimpse of her leaning over to pet Leo. The dog was staring up at her in adoration as she passed him a piece of cooked chicken.

Mason wondered if he had the same expression when he looked at her.

He suspected he probably did.

He rapped on her back door and she looked up, her eyes widening when she saw him standing there. A huge smile pulled at her lips and he felt something weird in his chest. Like a heart attack but less painful.

Or he hoped so.

"Hey." Her grin still lit her face as she opened the door and welcomed him inside. "I was about to turn all the lights off and call you about my fuses."

"I'm pretty sure it's too late for all that." He pressed his lips against hers. "How are the tonsils?"

"Better than your attempts at lying," she said.

"I was trying to protect your virtue," he protested, smiling when he smelled the sweet aroma filling the kitchen. His crappy lying forgotten, he walked over to the stove and tried to peer in. "What are you cooking?"

"Don't open that door," she warned him. "The muffins won't rise properly."

"You're making muffins?" His grin widened.

"White chocolate chip and raspberry ones."

"Do people usually bake this late at night?" he asked, still distracted by the oven.

"Bakers do. And I do when I'm anxious."

That got his attention. He turned to look at her. "Why are you anxious?" he asked her.

"Because I had to ask Eloise to keep a secret and I don't like asking my staff to do that. Among other things."

He turned to look at her. She'd twisted her blonde hair into a topknot, little locks falling out of it around her neck and cheeks. On her bottom half she was wearing yoga pants – the kind that made her already-perfect behind look even more peachy – and a little sweater with a slogan across her chest.

Express Your Elf.

"Cute sweater," he said. "And why does Eloise need to lie?"

"Because we don't want people knowing our business," Alaska said.

He reluctantly pulled his eyes away from her chest. "They'll know. Or they'll gossip. Who cares?"

"You will when North comes over and hits you again," she pointed out.

"North and I have come to an understanding," Mason told her. "And let's face it, nothing stays a secret long around here. Let them talk."

She blinked. "I thought..."

"Thought what?"

Alaska paused, then shook her head. "You're confusing me. You don't like people all up in your business yet you don't mind them knowing your business?"

His lip quirked. "I don't care. That's the difference. As long as they don't bother me, let them talk."

"And Ty? Aren't you bothered if he knows?"

"I'm bothered if it bothers him," Mason clarified. "And I'm pretty sure it doesn't. I told him I was coming over to look at your fuses and he didn't even raise an eyebrow. He's too busy thinking about girls to care what's going on here." He reached for her, pulling her close because he couldn't bear to not touch her any longer. "You said among other things. What are the other things?"

"We're busy at the Inn. I thought you were annoyed at me. And my parents are coming for Christmas."

She stared up at him, wide-eyed, and he felt his chest do that weird flip thing again. Smoothing the stray locks of hair from her face, he cupped her jaw with his hand and gently kissed her brow. "Let's hit them one by one," he suggested. "You're busy at the Inn. Is it anything you can't handle?"

"No," she admitted, leaning against him. "But there are always upset guests. Things go wrong."

"And you make them right. I've seen you in action. You're

good at what you do. So let's talk about me being annoyed at you. I thought we'd talked that through."

"We did. Until we were interrupted."

"Yeah, well we're not getting interrupted now. So let me tell you again, I'm not mad at you, Alaska. I'm very fucking far from being mad at you. I'm grateful. I'm in awe, and I'm wondering how the hell I'll ever repay you for having Ty's back." He kissed the tip of her nose and then her soft lips. She let out a sigh, her breath warm.

"I shouldn't have interfered," she said, her eyes wide and trusting. "I know you hate that."

"I don't hate it so much when you do it." It was a surprise to him, too. He'd spent his life hating when people meddled. Mostly because meddling meant his life would be worse somehow.

But with Alaska it felt better. Like he was being covered with a warm blanket.

"In fact, I like it," he whispered, kissing the sharp line of her jaw. She let out a strangled sigh and fisted his shirt in her fingers.

"Remind me what else is making you anxious," he said, sliding his lips down her neck. He could feel the sharp intake of her breath as she arched against him. Christ, he was as hard as a rock.

"My parents..."

"Are coming for Christmas," he said against her throat. "That's nice."

"No it's...ah...not..." Her breath caught as he slid his hand inside her sweater, his fingers tracing a lazy line up her spine.

"Christmas is for family, right?" He moved back to her lips, kissing the corner of them, before yanking the sweater over her head.

She was wearing a red bra. Was she trying to kill him?

"It's... they're..."

He dropped to his knees, kissing her smooth stomach. He'd never get used to how soft her skin was. Reaching around her back he unclasped her bra, kissing his way up to her oh-so-perfect breasts.

"Are you feeling less anxious?" he asked her.

She tangled her fingers in his hair. "No. I'm worried the muffins will burn."

He smiled against her stomach. "Not gonna happen. I got this." He threw her bra on the floor behind him, then kissed his way to the gentle swell of her breast. "Maybe this will help," he muttered, using his tongue to flick at her nipple.

She let out a strangled groan. Yeah, that was working.

Then he closed his mouth around it, sucking until she let out a cry.

"These need to go, too," he murmured, pulling at her yoga pants. He smiled when he saw her matching red thong. He'd have to ask her to put them on again later, just so he could enjoy the effect. But for now it was surplus to requirements, so he slid them down her thighs, taking the time to enjoy the suppleness of her legs.

And then he lifted her onto the counter.

"Here?" she asked, her voice lifting.

"Here," he agreed, parting her legs, his body tightening at the sight of her in front of him.

"I'm going to have to disinfect this afterward," she said as he knelt in front of her, ready to worship at the altar of Alaska Winter.

"It'll be worth it," he murmured, kissing his way along her inner thigh. "I promise." Curling his fingers around her legs, he pulled them further apart to give himself more access. He leaned in, the scent of her intoxicating, then pressed the softest of kisses where she needed it the most.

"Mason..." She dug her fingers into his scalp as he dragged

his tongue along her, and when he reached her most sensitive part she let out a ragged breath.

He needed this. She did, too. He wanted to give the way she gave. Wanted to make her see stars and forget every damn worry she had.

He wanted to take her to the peak and keep her there with him.

And when he slid his finger inside her, she almost got there within seconds.

"Oh God!" Her nails dug in deeper. It was such sweet pain.

He loved this. Tasting her, teasing her. Loved the little pants of her breath and the scrape of her fingers. Loved the way her thighs tensed against his cheeks and her ass gyrated on the counter.

He steadied her with his free hand, using the other to slide inside of her, matching the rhythm of his tongue as he took her higher still. She was so damn tight, like a vice around his fingers, and he loved that.

And then he felt it. The calm before the storm. The cliff edge she teetered on, her hips rocking against him as he helped push her over, her body convulsing around his fingers as she let out a long, aching groan.

"Mason, I'm..."

"I know." He smiled against her, holding her gently as pleasure wracked through her, squeezing his fingers until they were almost numb in the best fucking way.

If he lost them he lost them. He didn't need them that much anyway.

And then when she caught her breath she propped herself up on the counter, giving him the sweetest smile. It pretty much ripped his heart out.

"Feeling better?" he asked her, the taste of her still on his lips.

"So much." She cupped his jaw, her gaze intense. "But now I need you inside of me."

Yeah, he needed that, too. As much as he needed oxygen. He stood and pulled her against him, feeling her naked body against his fully-clothed one.

The oven started to beep and they both laughed. "I'd forgotten about those," she said.

"I hadn't," he said, because he needed her muffins inside of him, too. But later. Because now, all he wanted was to take the muffins out of the oven then take his woman to bed.

20

"Well hello everybody!" Lisa Gaughran smiled from her position on the podium in the center of the high school gym. She'd actually walked onto the stage to a song, he assumed of her choosing. He looked around as Alicia Keys belted out "Girl on Fire", wondering if anybody else found this as weird as he did.

Apparently not, because the rest of the PTA events team – all twenty of them – jumped to their feet and started applauding like Lisa was coming out to inform them of the second coming.

"Oh, I like this even better than last month's song," the woman next to him said breathlessly.

"What was that again?" her companion asked.

"Chaka Khan's "I'm Every Woman"."

Of course it was.

He'd imagined the PTA events sub-committee meeting to be a little more sedate. Sitting around the school cafeteria with a cup of badly brewed coffee while he agreed to man the door and then got the hell out of there.

Instead he was in some kind of cultish nightmare.

"We have a new member," Lisa yelled over the song. "Give it up for Mason Parker, everybody."

And yeah, all twenty of them turned to look at him, still dancing in front of their seats, clapping.

He gave a little wave.

"Come on up here, Mason," Lisa yelled. "And tell everybody about yourself."

Oh hell no. He shook his head.

"Oh come on. This isn't the library sub-committee, it's the events team. We make every meeting an event," Lisa shouted. "Now get your sweet behind up here."

Fuck his life. He gritted his teeth, reminding himself he was doing this for Ty. His brother had better remember this. When Mason was old and incontinent he fully expected Ty to step up to the mark and wipe his damn ass.

The music changed as he stepped onto the stage. Alicia's vocals melted into the air, replaced by Tammy Wynette's "Stand by Your Man".

Mason winced. He really didn't like Ty enough to endure this.

"Mason Parker!" Lisa shouted. Did she have to keep repeating his name? "Welcome to the team. Please tell us a little about yourself."

He realized what this reminded him of. One of those MLM conferences they showed on reality TV. Or maybe some kind of cult.

"Hi. I'm Mason. Thanks for having me." He waved and went to walk off, but Lisa grabbed his arm.

Her eyes widened as he tried to pull away again and she felt the steel of his bicep. "You get to sit with me," she told him. "As our newest attendee." She pointed to a chair on the left hand side of the stage.

"It's fine. I get... ah... vertigo when I'm on stages. But thank you anyway." Before she could protest, he hightailed it back to his seat, trying to ignore the way every woman he passed gave him what could only be classed as a Stepford Smile.

Then he spotted another guy in the corner. A cap was pulled down over his eyes, his glasses pulled tightly up to his eyes like a force field protecting him.

He gave Mason a nod as though acknowledging a fellow sufferer and then looked away. He'd clearly learned the art of disappearing into the background.

They were twenty minutes into the meeting before he felt safe enough to pull out his phone. There was one message.

How's the Marshall's Gap PTA going? – Alaska

Like hell. But worse. Did you know Lisa has an entrance song? – Mason

OMG! I need details. What song is it? – Alaska

It changes every week apparently. I also was given an entrance song, in case you were wondering. – Mason

I wasn't BUT NOW I AM!! This is too delicious for words. Please tell me it's "Eye of the Tiger" and you walked in punching the air. – Alaska

Nope. – Mason

. . .

So? – Alaska

What? – Mason

What's your song? We need to know. – Alaska

Who's we? – Mason

Everley, Nicole, Holly, and me. We have a group chat. They'll want to make it our theme tune. – Alaska

There's something very, very wrong with you. All of you. I feel like I'm in some romance writer's idea of Deliverance. – Mason

Out with it, Parker. – Alaska

Standbyyourman. – Mason

I AM IN HEAVEN!! – Alaska

"Don't you agree, Mason?"

Mason looked up from his phone. Twenty pairs of eyes were trained on him. He cleared his throat.

"Um, yeah?"

"Wonderful." Lisa clapped her hands together. "How easy was that? Thank you, Mason, having you helping us set up will help so much. You have the height and the muscle." She lifted a brow. "Okay then. Let's go on to security and purity."

He opened his mouth to protest, but closed it because seriously, how much worse could setting up be than sitting here?

"We have the boys' bathrooms covered thanks to Bob," she said, smiling at the man who was trying to disappear into the wall.

Mason tried not to imagine what Bob would be doing to promote security and purity.

"And for the girls' bathroom, I'd like to suggest Monica." She smiled at a small woman in the front row. "All you need to do is make sure there's only one person per stall. And that nothing," she lowered her voice, "profane happens in these hallowed halls."

"Sure thing." Monica said, crossing her arms in front of her. She looked like she was getting ready for a fight. "These kids will all leave with their virtues intact. I'll make sure of it."

"Rita, as always, will be on drinks duties," Lisa said. "All alcohol to be confiscated and anybody who brings it to be thrown out."

Mason winced. The only good things about school dances when he was in high school were the alcohol and profanity.

"And we'll have Mason on the front door because he's our muscle man." Lisa smiled knowingly at him. "Nobody will mess with him."

His phone screen lit up again. Thankfully, Lisa moved on to the banned music list, which was completely out of his domain. He looked down at his phone, shaking his head as he read his latest message.

. . .

Can we have sex to Tammy Wynette tonight? – Alaska

No. – Mason

Alicia Keys? – Alaska

Definitely not. Unless you want me to suffer from a severe case of non-performance. – Mason

Somehow I don't see that as a problem you'd ever suffer from. ;) – Alaska

Yeah well, he never had before. But all this talk of purity was getting to him.

Maybe Tammy Wynette could work after all.

"So, Mom and Dad arrive on the nineteenth," Everley said, looking at the lined sheet of paper in front of her.

They were sitting around a table in the Inn's dining room. It was between services so nobody would disturb them. Along with Alaska and Everley, Holly and North had joined them to talk parent strategy. Or more precisely, how to stop their parents from driving them all mad while they were in Winterville.

"I'll be picking them up from the airport," Holly said. "And I'll drive them to my mom's for their first night. She'll put them up and give them dinner, then bring them to your place in the morning, Everley."

Everley nodded. "I'm hoping they'll be hungover enough to want to chill for the morning. Then they can come with me to the theater. That should keep them busy for the twentieth."

"And then on the twenty-first, I'll have them over for dinner," Alaska said, her eyes meeting Everley's. She knew it was going to be painful. They'd hate seeing how secluded her house was. They'd never let her hear the end of it.

"And on the twenty-second, we've booked them in at the ski resort for a spa day," Holly said. "Josh has it all covered." Her husband, along with their cousin, Gabe, co-owned the ski resort and spa on the outskirts of Winterville.

"Will Gabe be there?" North asked.

Holly shook her head. "He and Nicole are planning to visit her parents on the twenty-second and twenty-third. So they'll be in Washington DC."

"Good."

There was no love lost between Gabe and Alaska and Everley's parents. It was completely understandable. They'd treated Gabe badly when he was a kid, practically accusing him of being involved in Alaska's disappearance. Gabe had never forgotten it and neither had North.

"They're seeing friends on the twenty-third for the day, so that brings us to Christmas Eve," Alaska said. "We have a full day of events planned at the Inn, so I've booked them in. There's a Christmas singalong and quiz in the morning, then horse and sleigh rides after lunch. In the evening, we have a screening of *It's a Wonderful Life* for those who aren't going to the revue, followed by singing around the tree." She smiled at that. Christmas Eve had always been her favorite day. All that anticipation. "Oh, and we'll be having a visit from Santa, of course." She winked at North.

He rolled his eyes.

"It's your turn," she pointed out.

"I know. Doesn't mean I have to like it."

"And Christmas Day they'll have to muck in with the rest of us," Everley said gleefully. "Then we'll feed them in the evening, spike mom's eggnog, and hope they sleep soundly until it's time to leave for the airport the next morning." She'd folded up her paper with notes. "Dylan comes home a few days after they arrive. He's agreed to fill in any gaps by dragging them around with him." She lifted a brow. "I suspect he hasn't bought my Christmas gift yet."

"Have you bought his?" Alaska asked her.

"Of course." Everley smiled smugly. "I've got all my gifts."

"Have you?" Alaska asked Holly.

"I had to. Last minute Christmas shopping with a toddler isn't exactly my idea of fun."

"So it's just you and me who are lacking," Alaska said, wrinkling her nose at North. He slowly shook his head.

"Got all mine, too."

"What?"

He lifted a brow. "You're always telling me I leave things until the last minute. So I decided not to this year."

"I have my day off this week. I can do it then," she told him. And it was only family gifts she was missing. She'd already organized staff gifts.

Oh, and she'd need to get something for Mason and Ty, too.

"You and half of West Virginia will be in that mall," North said. "Good luck with that."

"You could always try Marshall's Gap," Holly suggested helpfully. "They have some nice stores."

Yeah, all fifteen of them. Marshall's Gap was bigger than Winterville, but it was still a small town. There was no other option, she'd have to spend her day off shopping.

Which was annoying, because she'd really wanted to spend the day with Mason.

"Can we get back to the parent planning?" she asked. "Who's taking them back to the airport on the twenty-sixth? I can do it if you like?"

"Dylan said he would," Everley told her. "Because the rest of us will be at work."

"Speaking of work," North said, standing. "Unless you need anything else from me, I have some deliveries to make."

"Do people really leave buying their Christmas trees until now?" Everley asked. "I don't understand it. My place gets decorated the day after Thanksgiving."

"Mine, too," Holly agreed.

North shrugged. "Not everybody is as prepared as you two. And there are still two weeks until Christmas." He kissed their cheeks and then leaned down to kiss Alaska's. "By the way, I made my peace with your neighbor."

Alaska tried to look surprised. "You did?"

Unfortunately, at the same time as she feigned innocence, Holly chimed in. "I already told her."

He looked at Alaska for a moment. "You all right with that?"

"I'm fine. Thank you for making things right." Ugh, she really didn't want to talk about Mason with North. "Now go deliver your trees."

He winked. "Good luck with the shopping."

Leaving the three of them sitting at the table, he ambled out of the dining room. "He seems in a better mood," Alaska said.

"Yeah he does," Holly agreed. "It's nice to see."

"On the subject of good moods, how's Mr. Grumpy?" Everley asked.

"I bet he was all hot and delicious after that PTA meeting." Holly grinned. "Did you have moody sex?"

"Did he let you play his entrance song?" Everley joined in.

"As he made an entrance..." Holly wiggled her brows.

"Can you both shut up, please?" Alaska sighed.

"Come on, we spilled the beans to you," Everley pointed out.

"No, you didn't," Alaska told her. "You both hid your relationships when they were new. And now I know why."

"I'm your big sister. I just want to make sure you're okay," Everley said. "And also with Dylan away I need to live vicariously through you."

"Like you don't have phone sex every night." Holly shook her head.

Everley said nothing, but her big grin told them she definitely did.

"Are you worried about talking about it in case you might jinx things between you and Mason?" Holly asked Alaska.

Alaska blinked. "I don't know. It's just all so new. And he's such a private person. I really don't think he'd like me talking about him."

"But we're not asking about him. We're asking about you," Everley said softly. "How you're feeling about it all."

A smile pulled at her lips. "I'm feeling good," she told them. "Very, very good."

Everley clapped her hands. "I love it. I'm so happy for you. So, when do we get to meet him officially?"

"Oh, we're not there yet."

"Why not? Don't you want him to come to the Inn for Christmas dinner?" Holly asked. "I may be wrong, but I can't imagine he and Ty are going to have a great Christmas in their cabin."

"I don't know what they have planned," Alaska admitted. "We haven't talked about Christmas." But maybe they should. Ty would love spending time at the Inn for Christmas. It was always so much fun.

"You don't have to make it a big thing," Everley suggested. "Just invite him as a friend. I have a lot of them who come."

"True." Alaska nodded. "I'll think about it."

"I guess you won't be introducing him to your parents then," Holly asked her.

Alaska winced. "Ugh, no. Not unless I want him to run screaming."

"Somehow I can't picture him screaming," Holly said, amused. "Growling, yeah. But not screaming."

"Either way, I'm definitely not introducing them," Alaska told her sister and cousin.

"So then Christmas is out." Everley caught Alaska's eye. "Because they'll be here for dinner, too."

"Ugh. I'd forgotten about that." Alaska rubbed her eyes. The last thing she needed was for her parents to meet Mason and ask him one too many questions. It was asking for trouble. "I'll work something out."

"Of course you will," Holly said warmly. "You always do."

"And in the meantime, you can keep having hot sex to the sound of Tammy Wynette,'" Everley said.

"'Stand by Your Man'," Holly mused. "I'm not sure that's very hot."

"Sit on Your Man. That's hot." Everley grinned.

"Lay Under Your Man," Holly added.

"Ride Your Man Like You're His Favorite Cowgirl." Everley's eyes sparkled. She was enjoying this way too much.

"Shut up both of you." Alaska shook her head.

"Oh, but I have more," Everley protested.

Alaska put her hand up. "I don't want to hear them."

Everley looked at Holly. "Shall we take it to the group chat?"

"No," Alaska said firmly.

"Definitely," Holly said, ignoring her. "We wouldn't want Nicole to miss out on this."

21

"You don't need to do this with me," Alaska told Mason as he pulled into the parking lot of the Allegheny Mall. It was packed with cars and he had to drive around three times before he could find a space to pull into. A man driving the wrong way up the aisle gave them a honk of his horn, annoyed he'd been beaten to it.

"Asshole," Mason muttered.

"Honestly, it's not too late to turn back," she told him. "It's only going to be worse in the mall."

"You need to get your gifts," he said. "So we're going in."

Well okay then. Him offering to go shopping with her had come as a surprise. She still wasn't sure he was going to survive it. "This means you're going shopping twice this week," she told him.

"Twice?"

"Don't you have your appointment for fittings with Ty tomorrow?"

"Yeah. But that's not shopping. That's sitting and watching Ty moan about having to wear a suit." He shrugged. "Not the same."

He walked around and opened her door, taking her hand to help her down from the cab of his truck. "Maybe we should have a safe word," she suggested.

"A what?"

"You know, like with doms and submissives. If it all gets to be too much you just say a word and we'll leave."

"How about 'let's leave'?" he said, giving her a strange look.

"Now?"

He almost laughed. "No, I mean 'Let's Leave' can be the safe word."

"It's not a great safe word." She wrinkled her nose, pulling her purse over her shoulder. "How about yellow? Or purple?"

"Why would I say purple if I want to leave?"

"Because... oh!" She stepped back as a speeding car almost hit her. Mason groaned and pulled her close.

"Jesus," he muttered. "People are crazy here."

"I told you." She lifted a brow. "It's dog eat dog." They made it across the road to the entrance of the mall without any more risk to their lives. Christmas music spilled out into the cold air as they pushed their way in.

"And to think we could have been curled up in your bed right now," he said, looking regretful.

"Later. If we get everything quickly," she promised.

"Ty will be back by the time we get home."

"Who said we'd be going home? Your truck has heat, doesn't it?"

He laughed. "And where do you propose we park?"

"There's a place on the way back to Winterville. In the middle of nowhere." She grinned up at him. "You park, and I'll climb on and make sure you stay warm, baby."

He grabbed her arm. "Yellow. Or purple. Whatever."

"You can't use your safe word before we're even in the mall." She lifted a brow.

"Let's just leave and find this place. I like the sound of it better."

She laughed. "Have patience. I need to get some gifts first. And I have no idea what to get my mom. I mean, what do you get a woman who has everything? And who lives in kaftans in her Florida retirement village?"

"Another kaftan?"

"I mean, that's a good idea." She nodded. "We should go to the swim shop."

"Are you all ready for their visit?" he asked her. There was a softness to his voice.

"As ready as I'll ever be."

"It'll be fine, Alaska. They're coming to see you. They love you. Try to not worry."

"I wish it was that easy. They haven't really forgiven us since we went behind their backs and stopped them from selling the town."

"So why are they coming?"

She blinked. "I don't know. Mom just says she wants to see us."

"Maybe it's as simple as that," he said, sliding his hand into hers. She liked the way it felt. "I don't know your parents, but I know what it's like to not have any."

Her heart clenched. Of course he did. "I'm sorry."

"No need to be. I'm just saying that life is complicated. And short."

She nodded. "You're right. It'll be fine. Between us all we'll keep them busy for the whole time they're here. And on the plus side, the only time I have to entertain them is on the twenty-first."

"The day of the Winter Formal."

"Right? It works out perfectly." She grinned at him. "You'll be able to avoid them completely. No chance of bumping into them when you'll be doing your security duties outside Marshall High."

"I would have met them if you wanted me to."

She looked up at him to see if he was joking. But the serious expression on his face told her otherwise. "You would?"

"I mean, meeting parents isn't exactly my strong point. But if you asked I would say yes."

"I wouldn't put you through that. But that's sweet of you."

He gave her a strange look. One she couldn't quite place.

"Do you *want* to meet them?" she asked, trying to work out what was going on in his mind.

"Not particularly." He shrugged. "Come on, we need to get going if we want to get out of here before sundown." They stopped in front of a pharmacy. "We should start here," he told her.

She checked the list she'd written out. "I don't need anything from here."

"Yeah, but I do, if we're planning to stop on the way home."

"Oh!" She started to smile. "I have some in my bag."

"Of course you do." He kissed her brow. "My goddamned girl scout. Always prepared."

"You know it." Their eyes caught and she felt the heat between them. Maybe she didn't need to get gifts after all.

She could make a donation to charity on her whole family's behalf. The thought of it made her lips twitch.

"Speaking of safe sex," she said, when they reached their first stop, Ocean Air, where she hoped to at least get her mom's gift. "Have you had that talk with Ty yet?"

"What?" Mason frowned. "Why would I do that?"

"Because he's taking a girl to a dance. And things tend to happen between girls and guys." Alaska shrugged.

"He's only seventeen," Mason protested.

"And what age were you when you first started experimenting with girls?" she asked him.

Mason blinked. "Fuck." A look of horror came over his face. "Jesus, I'm not built for this parenting crap."

Alaska grinned. "Maybe you'd better go back to the pharmacy after all."

Ty stared at his reflection, pulling at the bowtie the shop owner had patiently shown him how to knot.

"I think you look very snazzy," the owner said. He was a man in his late sixties, by Mason's guess. The sign over the door said the shop had been established in 1973 and it was obvious the décor had been changed since.

But still, it had suits and Ty needed one. They'd go with that.

"And how do you like the suit?" the owner asked Ty.

Ty grimaced and pulled at the lapel. "Ah, the suit is a little... boring."

Mason blinked. "It's a black suit. I thought you wanted something understated." He'd never understand teenagers.

"Yeah, I do. But I don't want to look like everybody else either. Eloise says she likes guys who show their personality."

"What kind of suit were you thinking of?" the owner asked.

"I don't know," Ty admitted. "Just something different."

"Leave it to me. I'll see what we have in the stock room." The owner didn't look perturbed at all. "Thirty waist, thirty four legs," he muttered to himself. "We should have plenty of those."

Ty collapsed on the sofa next to Mason. There was a table with old magazines in front of them, along with an arrangement of dried flowers that had seen better days. The whole place smelled of mothballs.

He couldn't quite believe the place was still making money.

"Maybe you should send a picture of your suit to Eloise," Mason suggested, hoping they could get out of here some time before Christmas Day.

"I did. She said it was nice."

"Oh." Mason bit down a smile. "The kiss of death."

"Right? I want something that's fucking amazing. Not nice."

"Watch your language," Mason warned him.

"You swear," Ty protested.

"Yeah, but not in a store. And not in front of ladies."

"You're telling me you don't cuss in front of Alaska?" Ty asked, tipping his head to the side.

Mason blinked. Did he swear in front of her? He might have sworn when they pulled into that small rest area and she'd made him see stars within five minutes.

He certainly wasn't going to ask Ty what he knew about Mason and Alaska. Better to hope he still thought they were just friends.

"Nope," Mason said confidently. "I never swear in front of any ladies."

"Liar."

"I'm just telling you how it is. Keep the swearing down. Girls don't like it."

Ty grinned. "How do you know what girls like? You're thirty-four years old and single. Never been engaged never been married. Taking dating advice from you would be like asking a dinosaur the best way to avoid a meteor shower."

"Thanks for that comparison," Mason told his brother.

"Yeah, well maybe I'm the one who should be giving you advice."

Mason rubbed his face with the heels of his hands. Lord save him from the all-knowing teenager. "Now that you mentioned advice, there is something I need to ask you."

Ty blinked. "You really want my advice?"

"No. I want to ask you something." Except he didn't want to ask it. The only reason he was even opening his mouth was because Alaska would kill him if he didn't.

"What do you want to ask?" Ty asked, his brows dipping.

"Did Dad ever have the sex talk with you?" Mason had to force the words out. He'd avoided this conversation for as long as he could, but it had to be done.

"Oh God, no. I mean yes. He talked, I listened, and I never want to talk about it with you."

"Yeah, well the feeling's mutual," Mason told him. "But as your guardian it's my job to make sure you're being responsible."

"What does that mean?" Ty asked.

"It means you're only seventeen. So you shouldn't even be thinking about sex. But if you do, you need to be protected."

"Oh no. Oh no, no, no." Ty shook his head, appalled. "We're definitely not doing this."

"We definitely are. You're the man. It's your responsibility to take care of the women you care about. That includes their sexual health."

"Can you stop saying the word sex?"

Mason tried not to laugh. "A minute ago you told me it was okay to swear."

"I said it was okay for me to swear. I never said about you saying the 's' word."

"Just tell me you understand and I'll never say anything again."

Ty caught his eye. "I understand."

"And do you have protection?" Mason asked. Mostly

because he knew Alaska would be giving him hell about that, too.

"How about blue?" the owner asked, carrying a powder blue suit zipped into a yellowing plastic cover.

"No," Mason and Ty both said at once.

"Okay, I may have a white one."

When he disappeared again, Mason turned back to his brother. "So do you have protection?" he asked again.

"No. Because nothing's going to happen."

"Well I'm glad to hear that. But you need condoms just in case."

"Mason! Jeez."

"Is there something wrong with the word condom?" Mason asked. Maybe there was some fun to be had in this talk.

"There is when you say it."

"So that's sex and condoms out." Mason grinned at his brother.

"If I get some do you promise to never say those words to me again?"

"It's okay, I already picked you some up. They're in the bathroom closet."

Ty eyed him carefully. "I could've just stolen some from the drawer beside your bed."

"You know about those?"

"Of course, I know about those. I also noticed there were a few missing the last time I checked."

Okay, so this wasn't fun anymore. Mason swallowed hard. "You shouldn't go through my things."

"I was looking for a pair of socks for gym class. I thought you might have put them in your drawer."

He didn't have an answer for that. But he didn't like it anyway. "Next time ask."

"You weren't there."

"Then call me."

"Okay." Ty grinned. "So are we done with this conversation?"

Mason nodded. "Absolutely."

"And we'll never have it again?"

"If you promise me you'll wait until you're eighteen and in an established relationship, then you'll never again hear those words from my mouth."

Ty shrugged. "I promise. I wasn't going to have sex, anyway. I'll wait until I'm in love, thank you very much." He lifted a brow at Mason.

"Good plan."

"Okay we have white, silver, and pink," the owner said, carrying in more suits. "If you'd like to come to the changing room, I'm sure one of these will do the trick."

22

"You have knots in your knots, sweetheart," Mason told her, his fingers digging into the muscles on her back. She wasn't sure where the man had learned to massage like this, but she was so damn glad he had.

"That's because my parents are in town," Alaska said, letting out a low groan when he hit a painful spot just above her right shoulder blade. "My body feels like it's preparing for battle."

"So they landed okay?"

"Mmmhmm. Oh God there. *Right there*." Damn her muscles were sore. But the release was pure pleasure. She really thought she was over this anxiety whenever they were around.

But yeah. She was wrong. "And yep, they landed on time. Holly picked them up and took them straight to her mom's place. She said they kept asking to swing by my place first. She had to lie and tell them Aunt Susannah was making an early dinner for them. But then they arrived and of course there was no food."

"Susannah is Holly's mom?" Mason clarified.

"Yes. My dad has an older brother, Noel, and a younger sister, Susannah. Noel lives in Florida, too."

"But he didn't come up for Christmas?" Mason leaned in to kiss her neck. It sent a shiver down her spine. Ty was out – having dinner with Eloise and her parents. It was his first time meeting them and according to Mason he was as skittish as Alaska was.

Thank God Mason was always calm.

"No. And my parents don't usually either. I still don't know why they bothered."

"Maybe they miss you."

"They barely talk to us." And to be honest, that was how she liked it. But she didn't need to tell Mason that. "Anyway, if it means I get a massage every time they're in town, maybe I'll encourage them to visit more often."

"Maybe you should," Mason said, a smile in his voice. "Although I'd massage you even if they weren't here. Just say the word."

"Oh I will." She finally felt herself relax. Mason moved his hands from her back and leaned over her, passing her a glass of red wine. They were at his place. She'd wanted to see the bathroom now that it was up and running. It looked amazing; simple yet perfect. She loved how good he was with his hands.

In every way.

"Talking about parents, how was Ty feeling about meeting Eloise's?" Alaska asked, because she didn't want to talk about her own anymore. Especially since the ache in her shoulders had finally eased up.

"Nervous but brazening it out in a typical Ty way. I asked him if I should invite Eloise around to meet me and he gave me a withering look." Mason didn't sound too unhappy about it.

"What a shame. You could have cooked her your world famous canned chili."

"Hey, I can cook other things, too."

"You can?" She turned her head to look at him. His lip was quirked as he stared at her with amusement. "Like what?"

"I make a mean breakfast."

"For dinner?"

"If necessary. Anyway, it doesn't matter because he doesn't want to invite her over." Mason shrugged.

"Well she's a nice girl. If she does visit she'll pretend to love your cooking."

Mason frowned. "I resent that."

"Well at least you know I'm not with you for your culinary skills," she told him, climbing onto her knees on the sofa. The movement made her wobble, and he caught her, his hands curling around her waist. She leaned forward to softly kiss him.

"I'm glad to hear it," he told her. "You'd be running screaming."

"And yet here I am. Not screaming." She pouted.

"Plenty of time to change that." He winked.

"I thought Ty would be home in an hour."

"As I said, plenty of time."

She was about to tell him it was a challenge when Leo came bounding up to the sofa. She hated to admit it, but she hadn't even realized he'd gone. So much for being a good doggy mom. She reached down to pet him then saw something in his mouth.

A little toy rabbit.

"Man, he's been going through the trash." Mason grimaced. "What the hell else did you find?" he asked Leo, shaking his head.

"Oh my God." Alaska reached down to take the rabbit from Leo. "Why was this in the trash?"

"Because it's garbage." Mason looked at her strangely. "I've been meaning to burn that stuff for weeks. Just haven't gotten around to it."

"It's mine," she said, turning the toy over in her hands. "Oh God, he's mine." She looked up at him. "This is so weird. I remember thinking about him last summer. I found a stuffie some kid had lost at the Inn and it reminded me of him." She blinked. "And now here he is."

"What?" Mason shook his head. "How can it be yours? I found it beneath the bathroom floor when I was doing the renovations."

Her heart started to hammer against her chest. "I lost it," she told him, her voice low. "When I went missing."

It took a moment for her words to sink into his brain. Slowly he looked at her, his brows pulled tight. "Are you certain it's the same one?" he asked, staring at the rabbit. "How can you tell?"

"I remember his wonky eye." She nodded. "It was my favorite stuffie." She ran her tongue over her dry lips. "Where exactly did you find it?"

"Beneath the floorboards." He shook his head. "But you couldn't have put it there. I mean there are holes now, but there weren't then." He was still staring at it, as though it held all the answers.

"Is there a crawl space?" she asked him.

"Yeah, but only something or someone tiny could get in there."

"Like a small for her age eight-year-old girl?" she asked him.

He brought his gaze up to hers. "You think you put it there?"

"I don't know. I guess I never will. But it seems as good an explanation as any. Maybe I hid it there and crawled out when you two came back from hunting."

"You want to take a look under there now? See if you remember?" he asked her.

"No. I don't want you taking those beautiful floorboards up. Not after all the effort you've gone to."

"I'd take those damn floorboards up in a second if it'd help," he told her. "But there's another way. We can look under the porch and shine a flashlight. We won't be able to get in there, but we might see something." He glanced at his watch. "We should probably wait until morning, though. It's too dark now."

"I have to work in the morning," she reminded him.

"Then do you trust me to look without you? If I find anything I'll let you know right away."

She nodded, her gaze connecting with his. "I trust you," she whispered. And she meant it. She hadn't met anybody she trusted more. Not even her cousins, even though she knew they'd kill for her.

"I wish I could remember more," he told her. "I keep thinking about it. Every moment we were here."

He looked so sincere it made her heart clench. "I know you do. But it doesn't matter. The past is the past, I'm over it. I'm just curious about the crawl space."

"After tomorrow hopefully you won't have to be curious. Either I'll find something else or I won't." He gently took the rabbit from her. "What's his name?" he asked.

"Mr. Bunny." She grinned. "Original, right?"

"I'll clean him up for you," he told her. "It stinks."

"No." She shook her head. "It's fine. Anyway, I kind of like him like this."

"Dirty and battered?" he asked, his brows lifted.

"Yeah, but not broken. He survived all these years. Just like we did." She smiled at him. "It's weird but having him back feels like we've gone a full circle. Maybe it's a sign we're exactly where we're meant to be."

"Karma, huh?"

"You don't believe in that?" she asked him.

"Nope." He kissed the tip of her nose. "But if you do, that's good enough for both of us."

Eloise picked Ty up in her little red Fiat the next morning, but he forbade Mason to come out and say hi.

"Isn't that what I'm supposed to do?" Mason asked. "Check that she's a responsible driver? I'm still your guardian, after all."

"She's been driving for almost a year. She's had the car for longer. She can drive better than you." Ty slung his backpack over his shoulder.

"So when am I going to meet her?"

"You already met her," Ty pointed out. "You were just a bit distracted at the time."

Damn. He'd forgotten about her walking in on him and Alaska. So she hadn't believed the tonsils story. He assumed she'd told Ty exactly what he and Alaska had been doing.

But Ty clearly didn't want to talk about it.

"I'll introduce you to her at the formal." Ty offered.

"Because you won't be able to avoid me then." Mason half-smiled. He understood it. This was new and Ty didn't want anything to jinx it. But he also wanted to show Ty his support. He'd never had that kind of backing when he was a kid and he'd wanted it.

Once Ty was safely in Eloise's car and it was disappearing into the distance, Mason pulled on his old work boots and thick coat, grabbing a flashlight and a crowbar before walking down the steps. Alaska had left for work at five that morning, and her house was dark. He didn't like it.

He preferred it when smoke was rising from her chimney

and her windows were glowing yellow from the lights and candles she always had going. Preferred when he could hear Leo yapping to be let outside before he'd see the door open and Alaska step out while he drank his morning coffee.

Yeah, well he'd have that again tomorrow. It was something to look forward to. And in the meantime, he had some investigating to do. He crouched down and inspected the boards covering the gap between the ground and the floor of the cabin.

Just as he'd suspected, there was a gap in the wood. Not big enough for a man like him, but probably big enough for a small child to crawl under the house. He tried to imagine it, a tiny Alaska holding her rabbit, looking for somewhere to keep safe.

Jesus, she must have been brave to crawl into a hole like this.

Flicking the flashlight on, he aimed the beam in the hole. If any snow had gotten through the hole during the last storm, it had long since melted thanks to the heat of the cabin above. All he could see were cobwebs and earth, and... what was that? He moved the flashlight around but it was no good. He couldn't angle it right.

Grabbing the crowbar, he slid the end between the two planks next to the hole, using his muscles to lever them until the first plank popped out. He put it on the ground – he'd replace it later, along with more planks to cover up the hole so nobody else could ever get under there.

He had to lay on his stomach to be able to peer in properly. Stretching his arm out, he put it through the enlarged gap and swung the beam of the flashlight around until he could see a little better.

And there it was. What looked like a blanket. Putting his flashlight on the ground so the beam was still lighting it up, he grabbed the crowbar and used the hook to try to get to it, but he was a couple of inches short.

Exhaling in annoyance, he scooted closer, until his shoulder hit the edge of the hole and he couldn't see inside. He moved the crowbar around again, feeling it hook something, then with gritted teeth slowly dragged it toward him. Scooting out, he took a look. The blanket was closer now. Enough for him to reach out and grab it.

Christ, it was filthy. Covered in dirt and dust and cobwebs. Wet as anything, too. But yeah, it was a blanket. The kind you'd put in a child's crib. He pulled it out from beneath the cabin and laid it out.

Inside it was a box. Or what remained of one. Most of the cardboard had rotted away but he could make out three letters.

TWI. In red letters.

And he knew without having to look twice what it was. A box of Twinkies. Or at least it used to be before it spent almost twenty-two years underneath an empty cabin.

Another thought occurred to him. He picked his flashlight up again, training it on the hole where she must have crawled through. And sure enough, there was a piece of wood just inside it, hanging down from the cabin.

At exactly the height a kid's head could hit if they crawled inside.

Jesus.

He needed to go to her. Tell her what he'd found. It couldn't wait for tonight. He wasn't sure he could wait the twenty minutes it would take for him to drive into Winterville.

Because he needed to see Alaska right now.

23

From the moment the Inn door opened, Alaska knew it would be Mason walking in. Call it a sixth sense or a deep connection or whatever you wanted. There was a half-smile on his face as his soft blue eyes caught hers and she felt it down to her toes.

It was only when he reached the desk that she realized he was carrying a white plastic bag. And he was covered in mud. It was down the front of his coat and clinging to the denim of his jeans. She wanted to laugh because he looked like he had no idea.

"I found something," he told her gruffly.

She was on her own at reception thanks to three people calling in sick today. She'd had to rearrange the rota to cover the restaurant and housekeeping. Luckily they had very few checkouts today, so it was quiet.

And they were alone.

"What is it?" she asked as he put the white bag onto the counter. He nodded and she looked inside, her brows raised as she saw the dirt-ridden heap of fabric. "Eep, that's dirty."

"It's a blanket. The kind a little kid would have." He

looked at her carefully. "Did you have a blankie when you were a kid?"

"I don't know." She shook her head. "Maybe."

"How about Twinkies?" he asked her. "Did you like them?"

What a weird question. But she knew the answer anyway. "I had the biggest sweet tooth. My mom refused to buy them, but Candy – my grandmother – always used to sneak them to me."

"Maybe she gave some to you the night you left. You were camping here, right?"

Alaska nodded. "Right. But why do you ask?"

"Look." He picked a piece of thin cardboard up. Sure enough it was the edge of a Twinkies box. "I think you must have had these with you when you got to the cabin. And here." He grabbed his phone, bringing up a photo of a jagged plank on his screen. "I think you banged your head on this when you went down into the crawl space. I think you were there all that time. Must have walked for hours from your tent to the cabin. Maybe you got lost, maybe you were half asleep. I don't know."

"You think I was there on my own?" she asked him, blinking. "That nobody took me?"

"It's a strong possibility. I think you could have been beneath that cabin all night while we slept inside and didn't know." He winced. "I wish we'd known. But instead we left for hunting and you were there and when we got back..."

"I'd crawled out and was asleep on the porch."

"You were probably starving." He looked at the rotted cardboard. "You probably ate all the Twinkies and you needed more food."

"So nobody hurt me."

"I don't think so." He shook his head. "I think you banged your head and stayed in one place. You found shelter.

The most important thing. And you knew to stay close to it."

She didn't know what to say. It felt like a weight was lifting off of her. It was the loss of memory that had always killed her. But maybe that knock on the head – or the horror of being alone – was what caused it. But this felt right. She'd found somewhere safe and she'd stayed there until she found people.

And they took her to Winterville and made sure she was secure.

"I feel like you've saved me twice now," she said. A wave of emotion washed over her. She'd always hated being taken care of, but not by this man. His care felt hard won. That made it so special.

God, she cared for him, too. And she was trying to let it all sink in. She probably hadn't been taken. She'd wandered to the cabin and found somewhere to hide.

"No, sweetheart. You saved yourself."

He was right. She wanted to hug the little girl she'd been. She was smart. Resourceful. She'd taken care of herself.

The way he was looking at her made her breath catch in her throat. If they weren't in public – in her Inn no less – she'd probably be throwing herself at him right now and wrapping herself around him like it was Christmas morning. Instead, there was a counter between them, along with a wet, smelly blanket.

"Can I see you tonight?" she asked him.

"Definitely."

They both smiled again. She was falling for this man. Or maybe she'd already fallen.

He knew she wasn't fragile. That she didn't need protecting. When they were together she was his equal in every way.

"Alaska!"

The familiar female voice made her stomach twist. Her

parents walked into the Inn, followed by Everley who shot her a wide-eyed apologetic glance.

"That's my mom." She brought her panicked gaze back to Mason's. "My parents are here."

He nodded, looking strangely composed. "Okay."

Then she realized the blanket was still on the counter. She grabbed it and stuffed it beneath the counter next to her feet, wiping her hands on a paper towel. She couldn't bear for them to see that right now.

"Darling!" Her mom was wearing a cream wool coat and a brown fur hat. Her legs were covered in matching fur boots. "Dolores told us you were here this morning, and we couldn't pass by without saying hello." She swept toward them in a cloud of Chanel No. 5, Alaska's dad close behind. "Silly Everley said we shouldn't disturb you."

"I said she was busy working, Mom." Everley gritted her teeth.

"But of course she wants to see us. Come around the counter and let me look at you."

"I was just..." Alaska gestured at Mason. Her mom grimaced when she saw the mud caked on his coat and jeans.

"Oh my." She stepped back as though the mud could fly from Mason to her. "I'll let you finish with the staff."

"He's not—"

Mason put his hand on hers. "I'll go."

She frowned, her eyes full of questions.

"It's okay. We can talk about it later."

"Okay." She nodded. "Thank you for the... ah... things you brought."

"No problem." He gave her a half smile. "Mrs. Winter. Mr. Winter." He nodded at them as he turned to walk toward the door. "Everley."

"Mason." She smiled at him. "It's good to see you."

Alaska watched him walk away, her heart tight in her chest.

"Is he new?" her mom asked. "You should probably tell him to keep himself clean while in the Inn. It's not good for the ambiance."

She ignored her mom's suggestion. "He just moved here a few weeks ago."

"Ah well." Her mom wrinkled her nose. "Maybe he'll learn. Now come here, darling. We didn't come all this way just to talk to you over the counter."

Forcing a smile on her face, Alaska lifted the counter top and submitted to her mom's fragrance filled hug. Then she kissed her dad's cheek. He said nothing, just nodding at her. The fences between them had never been mended since he and his siblings tried to sell Winterville to the highest bidder. But she could be civil for a few days.

"So we're going to head over to the theater now," Everley said. "Mom and Dad are going to watch the matinee performance, and then they are meeting some old friends at the Tavern for dinner."

"And tomorrow we're coming to your place," her mom said to Alaska, as though she'd forgotten. "We can't wait to see your new house," she looked at her husband. "Can we, darling?"

"Oh it's a beautiful house," Everley enthused. "In such a great location. And with beautiful views. You're going to love it."

Her mom nodded. "I'm sure we will."

"But now we need to leave." Everley put her arms out, hustling her parents away. "I can't be late for the theater."

"But it's not even twelve," her dad said, frowning.

"I know. But you know me, I love to be early." Everley's voice was too high. And Alaska had to bite down a smile because Everley hated to be early. "Oh, are you okay to look after Leo today?" Everley asked her.

"Yep. He's sleeping in the office. Want to see him?"

Everley grinned, their parents forgotten. "Of course I do." She leaned closer to Alaska. "I'm so sorry about this. Let me get them out of here and then I'll come give him all the hugs."

"It's okay," Alaska told her. "I can deal with them. I'm not afraid." The truth was, she'd never felt stronger. Never felt more in charge of her own life, her own destiny.

A visit from her parents wasn't going to change that. She wouldn't let it.

"How about I get you both a cup of coffee," she suggested to her parents. "And Everley can introduce you to Leo."

"Coffee would be lovely." Her mom gave what looked like a genuine smile. "Thank you, darling. It's so good to see you again."

24

"How do I look?" Ty walked out of the bathroom, pulling at the bow tie knotted around his collar. He'd gone for the white suit in the end, and it actually looked amazing.

"You look good. Real good." Mason nodded, his throat tight. "You got the flowers for Eloise?"

"Yep. And put one in my buttonhole like you suggested." Ty gestured at his jacket, where a pink rose was fixed to his lapel. "Does it look stupid?"

"Nope. Not at all." Mason wanted to say more. To say that Ty looked like a guy who finally knew who he was and where he was going. That he deserved all the good things in life, even if he could be a pain in the ass.

That he was proud as hell of him.

But they weren't the words you said to your almost-eighteen-year-old brother. Instead, Mason swallowed the tightness away and gave his brother what he hoped was a normal smile. "Dad would have been proud."

Ty glanced down at his freshly polished shoes. "Yeah, maybe."

"And we need to take a photo for your mom."

"Sure."

"Oh, and Alaska asked if she could come over and see you all dolled up." Mason lifted a brow. "You okay if she does?"

"Yeah, but I gotta leave in ten minutes. The limo will be here soon."

"I guarantee she'll be here in five," Mason told him. "Let me send her a quick text."

In fact, she made it in two. She was all messy bun and pink cheeks when Mason opened the door for her, her breath coming in little steamy huffs after she'd run from her place to his.

"Don't worry," she told Ty. "I can only stay for two minutes. I need to finish the lasagna before my parents arrive." Then she took him in and her smile widened. "Oh my, look at you. Eloise is going to love that suit."

"You think so?" Ty's expression was pleased.

"I know so. You look like James Bond or whatever the cool kid equivalent is. Seriously, Ty, you should always wear a tux."

She always knew the right thing to say. Mason smiled at her and she grinned back.

"And by the way, Mr. Parker. You look pretty hot yourself."

Mason rolled his eyes. He was wearing a dark suit and an open-collared white shirt. He'd be standing outside the school all night, so no need to go too overboard.

"Let me take a picture of you both," Alaska said.

"Do we have to?" Ty wrinkled his nose.

"Took the words right out of my mouth," Mason grumbled.

She shook her head at them. "Yes you have to," she said. "Because you both look amazing and handsome and I want to remember it. Let's go out on the porch, it'll be better out there.

After some grumbling they followed her out, and Alaska fussed over them, making them stand in exactly the right place, as she walked backward until she'd gotten them into the right pose on her phone screen.

"Okay," she called out. "Think happy thoughts."

Mason lifted a brow and Ty shook his head.

"Damn, that was terrible. I'm gonna take another one. This time try to smile, okay?"

She must have been satisfied with the second because she didn't make them take a third. Instead, she took some pictures of Ty, then made him promise to send her one of him and Eloise once he'd gotten to her house in the limo.

"Can you send me that picture?" Mason asked her. "The one of Ty? I promised his mom I'd text one over to her."

"Of course." She smiled. "That's a lovely thing to do."

In the distance, he saw the limo approaching the cabin. When he looked over at Ty, he could see the tightness in his jaw, as though he was suddenly nervous.

"You're gonna have a good time," he told Ty.

"Yeah, I know."

"And if you need me I'll be at the school, okay?"

"I won't need you."

Mason nodded. "I know. But just in case."

Two minutes later, the limo pulled up and two of Ty's guy friends got out. They'd paid for the ride between them, pooling their money from working at the Inn. Next they'd go to pick up the girls – who were getting ready at Eloise's house, before having their photos taken and heading to Marshall's Gap for a pre-dance dinner.

And Mason would head over to the high school in ten minutes, ready to help finish the set up.

"You guys look like gangsters!" Alaska shouted, grinning,

as Ty and his friends fist bumped each other. "I gotta get a photo of this."

Not one of them complained. In fact, they were all smiling at Alaska. She had that effect on people. She took their picture in front of the limo, then gave each of them a hug, and Mason watched, appreciating that she was here.

That she was making Ty's send off a *thing*. Not just a muttered goodbye but a happy event. Ty was all smiles and nods as the guys got into the limo and pulled away from the house.

Alaska turned and looked at him, the smile still playing on her lips. "I meant what I said. You look great."

"You look pretty hot yourself."

She rolled her eyes. "I'm wearing an old t-shirt and yoga pants."

"Exactly."

She ran her tongue over her bottom lip, her eyes assessing him. "I guess we don't have time, huh?"

"Not for what I want to do to you."

"Then I guess we'll have to save it for later. Come over when you're back."

"Your parents will be here," he reminded her.

"They're staying at Everley's tonight. They'll probably be gone before you even get home."

"Call me once they've left and I'll be there," he promised her.

"And Ty?"

"Ty knows there's something going on."

"And he's okay with that?"

"As long as I don't give him the safe sex talk again, yeah he's fine."

She grinned and he smiled back. His little ray of goddamned sunshine. Damn, she was beautiful.

She glanced down at the hole beneath the porch, blinking

when she saw the crawl space inside. "I can't believe I got in through there."

"It was smaller, too. I took a panel off to get the blanket. I'll close it all up tomorrow. Unless you want to look at it?"

"No." She shook her head. "I'm good."

"Are you?" He looked at her carefully.

"Yes." She nodded. "I know it's weird but I feel better knowing I was here. Knowing I was safe all along. Even knowing for part of the time you were here with me. It feels... I don't know. Just so much better."

"I'm glad I was there." His voice was gritty.

"Me, too."

He reached for her and she walked toward him. He leaned down to kiss those perfectly pink lips, his hand tangling into her hair as she kissed him back, achingly sweet.

And she was right. Everything felt better. Especially when she was in his arms. He wanted to tell her that, but the thought of admitting his feelings made his muscles tense. So instead he kissed her harder, hoping she'd know.

"You'd better go before I drag you inside," he told her when they parted, feeling the familiar need rush through him.

She looked up at him, and he could see the need in her eyes, too. "But I'll see you tonight, right?"

"Yes you will." Wild damn horses couldn't keep him away.

"Well that was very lovely, darling." Alaska's mom smiled and put her silverware down on her barely touched plate. "I never knew you were such a good cook."

Her dad was still eating. He'd spent most of the evening either wandering around the house, flushing toilets, and flicking light switches as though he couldn't quite believe everything worked in here, or on his phone because some stock he was following in Japan was starting to take off.

Or something like that.

"It was just a lasagna."

Her dad was still shoveling it into his mouth with one hand, the other holding his phone up.

"But the ragu was delicious. I'm so sorry I couldn't eat the pasta, but I have to watch my weight." Her mom patted her completely flat stomach.

"I'll eat it," her dad said, not looking up from his screen.

"You need to watch your weight, too," her mom told him, smiling indulgently. "Don't forget what your doctor said. Thirty pounds off and you'll feel like a whole new man."

"Hmmph."

Her mom brought her gaze back to Alaska. "Seriously, darling, I'm so pleased you're settled. I was worried when I heard you were living so far out of town."

"It's only twenty minutes away," Alaska pointed out. "It's hardly in the wilderness."

"I'd still feel better if you were in Winterville." Her mom glanced at her dad. "We both would, wouldn't we, Joe?"

He blinked and looked up. "What?"

"We'd both feel better if Alaska was living in Winterville." She tipped her head to the side. "Didn't you like living in the Inn? You had a lovely apartment there."

"Not really, no." Alaska shook her head. "I couldn't get away from work. Whenever there was a problem I was the first one who got called, even when I was sleeping. And the same thing would happen if I was in Winterville. I don't want to bump into guests on my day off and listen to all their problems. I want to relax. Spend time in the mountains. Enjoy the silence."

"Maybe you should install a panic alarm," her mom

suggested, her face lighting at the thought. "That way you could get help as soon as something bad happened."

"Nothing bad is going to happen, Mom." She managed to stop herself from rolling her eyes.

"That's what we thought. Until it did." The smile slipped from her mom's face. Her dad finally put his phone down and looked up at them both.

"That was a long time ago," Alaska said softly. "I'm safe. I'm happy. Isn't that enough?"

Her mom took a deep breath. "Actually, it isn't. I'd like us all to go for family counseling."

"What?" Alaska frowned. What a weird thing to say. "Why would we do that?"

"My therapist suggested it. We have unresolved issues. You barely talk to us, both of you girls."

"That's because you're in Florida and always out and about."

"You could come visit," her mom said. "Or at least call more regularly. Our neighbor's daughter calls every Sunday at eight."

"I work some Sundays." And the thought of having to make small talk with her parents sent a shiver down her spine. "We keep in touch. That's good enough."

"But it isn't. I'm not happy. We all need therapy. Look at you, living out here all alone. It's not right. You're not right. Honey, you need help."

Alaska looked up at them. "I don't need help. I'm absolutely fine." She tried to keep the anger from her voice. How dare they come here and tell her there was something wrong with her? They barely knew her.

"Your mom can't sleep," her dad said, suddenly interested in the conversation. "Her doctor thinks it's because of you."

Oh boy. She let out a long breath. "So let me get this straight," she said, every muscle in her body tensing. "You've come to visit not because it's Christmas but because you're both unhappy and you expect me to solve it?"

"No!" Her mom shook her head. "We wanted to see you and your sister. Make sure you're okay. Maybe try to mend some bridges." She looked pointedly at Alaska. "The ones you tried to burn when you and your cousins messed with your father's inheritance."

"We didn't mess with anything. We just didn't want him selling Grandma's town to the highest bidder."

"You interfered where you had no right to," her dad said, frowning. "I could have lost everything."

Alaska took another mouthful of wine. She'd already drunk three glasses just to get through the evening. This should be her last. If she had anymore she might tell them what she really thought.

"Please, sweetheart." Her mom reached for her hand. "I can't tell you how many nightmares I've had about what happened to you."

"Nothing happened. I'm here and I'm good." Okay, one more sip. "Seriously, it's great you're going to therapy. I'm pleased for you. But I don't want to join you, okay?"

"So that's it?" her dad asked.

"I don't know what else you want from me. We barely talk. You haven't been here since you tried to sell the town and the Inn. And the first thing you say is I need to solve all your problems."

"Maybe you'd solve all your problems, too," her mom said.

"I don't have any problems. Not like that. Can't you just accept that I'm happy?" She glanced at her watch. It was almost nine. Surely they'd want to drive back to Everley's soon.

"Not when I know you're not. Not deep inside. You disappeared, Alaska. You were a child. You could have been hurt or molested and you don't even remember. Do you know what that does to a parent? Knowing their child has suffered and they can't do anything about it?"

Goddammit. Now she was feeling sorry for her mom. And she really didn't want to.

"I can't imagine," she said softly.

"Well you'll know when you're a mom. It kills you from the inside out." It was her Mom's turn to take a huge mouthful of wine. When she'd swallowed it down she looked at Alaska with teary eyes. "I let you down. We all did."

"You didn't." Alaska's chest tightened. "It wasn't anybody's fault."

"I'll always think it was mine. When I walked into that police station and saw you, all dirty and scratched up with that huge bump on your head I knew how much you'd suffered. And we don't know who did that to you."

"Nobody did it to me." Her heart went out to her mom. She knew she'd blamed herself. And yes, everything between them had changed. It was like her mom had built a wall between them, one neither of them could tear down.

Maybe neither of them wanted to. Because they weren't sure they'd like what they'd find behind it.

"Mom, believe me when I tell you nobody did it to me. I bumped my own head."

Her mom's face crumpled. "I wish that was true."

"It is. I promise. I was alone, I found shelter, and I bumped my own head. Nobody hurt me."

Her mom blinked away her tears. "Are you starting to remember things?"

"I..."

"Answer your mom. Do you remember? How long have you remembered?" Her dad leaned forward, his face red. "Why didn't you tell us?"

"I don't remember exactly. I've just... pieced it together."

A look of disappointment washed over her mom's face. And she hated that. Alaska took a deep breath.

"Seriously, Mom. I know where I was. And I have corroborating evidence."

"What evidence?"

Okay, so this was it. She could either pull back and let her mom suffer or tell her some of the truth. Enough to allay her fears. Maybe enough to let her sleep properly.

She had to choose between peace and anguish for her mom who she still loved. And she chose peace.

"Just a minute." She walked across the kitchen and opened the cupboard where she kept her cleaning supplies. Scooting down she pulled at the soft fabric, then turned to show them.

"Remember Mr. Bunny?"

"That's Mr. Bunny?" Her mom frowned.

"Who's Mr. Bunny?" her dad asked.

"Alaska's lovey," her mom told him. "She used to take him everywhere. You must remember..."

"I lost him when I was eight." Alaska swallowed. "I never saw him again after that night. Until a few days ago."

"Where did you find him?"

She took a deep breath. "He was under a cabin. Along with my old blanket and a Twinkies box."

"What?" Her mom shook her head. "I don't understand."

"What cabin?" her dad asked. "Whose was it?"

"We think I must have gotten lost when I crawled out of the tent. Maybe wandered for a few hours until I found shelter. It was warm then, because it was summer, so I wouldn't have suffered too much. But eventually I must have found a cabin and gotten into the crawlspace until they found me."

"Wait." Her dad put his hand up in front of him. His stocks were well and truly forgotten. "Who's we? Who's they?"

"The people who lived in the cabin." Damn, she was sailing too close to the truth. "I think they must have found me and taken me to the police station."

"No." Her mom shook her head. "That can't be it. They would have come in. We put up a reward."

"Wait. I want to know what cabin you were in." Her dad's face was tight. "Where did you find the rabbit and blanket? How come you have them now? Who gave them to you? I need information."

"It doesn't matter."

"YES, IT DOES MATTER!" her dad shouted. "It matters to your mom, and it matters to me. We're your parents. We all went through hell, Alaska. The least you can do is tell us what the hell happened to you."

"Calm down." Her mom reached for her father's arm. "You're frightening her."

"I'm not frightened," Alaska told them. "I just need you to promise something."

"What?" Her mom frowned. Her dad started pacing around the kitchen. Leo looked up from his bed and then went back to sleep.

"That you'll listen to me," she told them. "That you'll actually hear what I have to say and not go crazy or get angry or start blaming people."

"I'll listen," her dad growled. "That's all I can promise."

"Then please, sit down," Alaska said. "Because I think you might need to."

25

Cars were starting to line up in the school parking lot, ready for the formal to finish. A group of parents were milling around the steps leading up to Marshall High, their breath turning to vapor as they shot the breeze with each other. Mason stood at the top of the steps, next to the main doors, the ice cold air wrapping around him as the loud thrum of music echoed from the gym through the school hallways.

He glanced at his watch. Five more minutes. And then another twenty or so to persuade the students to leave and go home. He'd only seen Ty once, when he'd introduced Eloise as they arrived. But the kid looked happy and that was enough for Mason.

"As soon as I get home, I'm gonna open a beer," Bob told him. "How about you?"

"I've made plans with a friend." The thought made Mason smile. Truth be told, tonight hadn't been as bad as he'd feared. He'd helped set up the gym and then headed outside for the first arrivals, with a rolling roster of helpers who'd come out to give him support. Bob was the last volunteer, freed from his spot next to the boys' toilets to help Mason make sure everybody got to their cars safely, and then they'd help dismantle the decorations before they all went home.

"Are you married?" Bob asked.

"Nope. Never have been." Mason shook his head. "It's just me and Ty at our place."

"Ty's your brother, right?"

"Yeah, that's right."

"It's nice you have him living with you. I only put up with my kids because I actually had some role in making them." Bob grinned wryly. "Nah, I'm exaggerating. But teenagers, they test your nerves."

"I'm learning that."

A group of three girls walked through the door, laughing.

"Can I take your names to mark you off my list?" Bob asked them, holding up his clipboard. They told him then walked down the steps to their moms who were waiting.

Mason's phone buzzed in his pocket. Before he had a chance to grab it, another group of kids walked out.

"Is your car here?" Mason asked them.

"That's our limo." They pointed at a white one. Bob ticked off more names while Mason made sure they got into their cars.

Then suddenly there was a deluge of kids. Two more chaperones came out to escort them all to their cars while Mason directed the traffic, making sure the kids didn't step out into the road while the cars moved on. It took almost twenty minutes until the surge of teens softened into a trickle, and the last kids came out, including Ty and his friends.

"You okay?" Mason asked him as he walked down the steps with Eloise.

"All good." Ty grinned at him. "We're taking the girls

home first, then us guys. You might make it home before I do."

"You got your key to the cabin?"

"Yep."

"Okay. I'll probably go over and see Alaska for a while once I'm back."

"Sure." Ty's grin widened. "I thought you might."

"You okay with that?"

Ty glanced at the limo. His friends were climbing in. "I'm good with it. As long as you remember to be safe." He winked at Mason then walked over to join his friends. He had the kind of swagger only a teenage kid could have. It made Mason smile.

His phone began to buzz again and he pulled it out, a smile pulling at his lips when he saw Alaska's name flashing on his screen.

"Hey," he said. "I'm just finishing up here. I should be back in half an hour or so. I'll come right over."

"Mason." Her voice was tight. "Something's happened."

"What?" He didn't like the way she sounded. He liked it even less when she let out a sob.

"My dad knows about the cabin. About you and your dad being there. I'm so sorry."

Mason swallowed. One of the last group of kids came down. He held the phone to his ear as he made sure the car moved away safely once they were all in.

"Are you still there?" Alaska asked. "He's so angry. He made Mom leave with him. He wouldn't listen to my explanations. I'm scared he's on his way to you."

"It's okay," he told her. "Try to calm down. I'm sure it's not as bad as you think."

"I shouldn't have told them. But Mom was saying she was having sleepless nights because of what happened. I thought it would make her feel better." She let out another sob.

"Sweetheart, you need to breathe. It's okay. We'll deal with it. Let me finish up here and I'll come to you."

"I'd come there but I drank a lot and I can't drive."

"No. Just stay where you are. It's going to be okay. *You're* going to be okay."

"But what if he finds you? What if he hurts you?" Her voice rose up.

"How old's your dad?"

"Sixty," she told him.

"Then I think I'll be okay. But can you do me a favor?"

"Of course."

"Keep an eye out for Ty. If he comes home before me make sure he's okay."

"I will," she promised.

Mason squeezed his eyes shut. "He doesn't know anything about this. I'd rather he hear it from me."

"I'll bring him to mine. Bribe him with hot chocolate."

He let out a long breath. "Thank you."

"I'm so sorry," she told him. "This is my fault.

"You don't need to be sorry. Just stay calm and be safe, okay?"

"Okay. Mason..."

"Yes, honey?"

"You be safe, too."

"So he knew all along and let us suffer. That man needs to pay for what he did."

Alaska squeezed her eyes shut and touched her temple. She should never have told them. Not tonight. Maybe not ever.

She should have known her dad would react this way. As soon as she'd recounted the tale of Mason and his dad finding her at the cabin, he'd turned a vibrant shade of puce, shooting out questions to her without waiting for her answers.

And then he'd stormed over to Mason's cabin, storming back when there was no answer.

She hadn't dared tell him where Mason and Ty were. But it wouldn't take him long to figure out if he wanted to.

Her mom was no better. She was crying and telling Alaska she should have told them earlier. That it was their right to know.

That she'd let them be broken for far too long.

And now they were gone. Her dad had given her his parting shot about Mason needing to pay for what he did, then practically dragged her mom to the car and sped off into the distance.

She walked to the living room, pulling the curtain aside to stare out once again. This time, instead of blackness she could see a pair of headlights in the distance. Coming this way.

She pulled on her boots and coat, checking that Leo was still sleeping safely in the kitchen. Grabbing her flashlight she walked down the steps, seeing the limo stop, bathed in yellow from Mason's porch light.

Ty got out and waved goodbye to his friends, walking up the steps to the cabin. And though she couldn't see his face, she could only imagine he was smiling from the easy walk he took to his front door.

"Ty!" she called out, hurrying down the path toward him.

He turned, and yep, there was a smile on his face. "Hey. Everything okay? Mason isn't back yet."

"Everything's fine," she lied. "I just wanted to hear how the formal went."

"It was good. Thanks." He slid his key into the lock.

"Actually, would you like a hot chocolate?" she asked him. "I was just going to make some myself."

"Nah. I'm going to bed. Been a long day you know. But thanks anyway."

"Maybe you should come back to mine anyway," she said hurriedly. "Until Mason gets back."

He side-eyed her. "I think I'll be fine."

Okay, so this wasn't going the way she hoped. "Seriously, it's late and Mason isn't home yet." She bit her lip, desperately trying to think. "And to be honest, I'm feeling a little scared..."

"You? Scared?" He looked like he was going to laugh.

"I watched a scary movie," she said quickly. "Maybe you can keep me company until Mason is back."

"What movie?"

Her mind turned completely blank. "You know that one with the ghost and the werewolf?"

Ty blinked. "No, I don't think I do. Who are the actors?"

"Um, that girl from..." Think, Alaska, think. "The series about that couple who travel somewhere."

Ty grinned. "You're as bad as my mom. She can never remember actors' names either."

"Sorry." She smiled back. And then her smile widened because over his shoulder she could see something in the distance. A pair of headlights coming this way.

"Oh look," she said, relief washing over her. "Mason's coming."

Ty peered over his shoulder. "Maybe he can scare away the ghosts in your house," he said.

The lights were fast approaching. She could see the faint outline of his car against the moonlit sky. A sense of calm washed over her. *Everything was going to be okay.* He was here, Ty was here, and so was she. Together they were strong enough to face anything.

They'd faced worse before.

"You got a weird look on your face," Ty said.

She rolled her eyes at him. "What kind of weird look?"

"I dunno. I'm just saying I can read you like a book." He grinned. "One of those romance books my mom loves."

"Didn't you want to go inside?" she asked him, shaking her head at his smile.

"Didn't you want me to go ghost hunting in your house?"

She mock-frowned at him. "Remind me to put you on dirty sheet duty at the Inn on Saturday."

"Hey, no fair," Ty protested. "You can't use work against me when we're at home."

It was true. And now she felt bad. "Sorry."

He bumped her with his elbow. "S'okay. I was just kidding anyway."

Mason pulled onto the mixture of gravel and grass that formed a driveway in front of the cabin. And then he climbed out. His eyes were soft when he saw the two of them standing there, and for a moment he didn't move. Just looked at her.

And she looked right back.

She was in love with this man. She could feel it in every cell of every bone and muscle she had. He just made sense, that was the thing. It was like she was waiting for that final piece of a code to solve the enigma of life. And here he was in all his tall, muscled, sometimes grumpy glory.

She loved him. Damn, she needed to tell him. It felt like it was about to burst out of her.

"Harlequin," Ty whispered. "Or possibly *Fifty Shades of Gray*. But I'm hoping Harlequin."

"Shut up."

"What's going on?" Mason asked, still smiling as he walked toward her.

"Alaska's living in some kind of strange universe that's a mash up of Steven King and E.L. James and I'm going to bed," Ty told him.

"Don't go to bed yet. I need to talk to you," Mason said.

"About what?"

"I'll tell you when we're in the cabin."

"Just as soon as you've kissed your girlfriend." Ty grimaced. "I get it. See ya later, Alaska. Don't let the ghosts creep you out." He turned the key that was still in the lock and walked inside.

"What's he talking about?" Mason asked her.

"It's complicated. I'll tell you later. I assume my dad didn't turn up at the school?"

"Nope. I figure we'll get a respite until morning. I'm going to talk to Ty now and then tomorrow you and I will work out what to do next."

"Will you call me once you've talked to him?"

"Of course."

"And will you forgive me for messing this up?"

He reached for her, his hand cupping her face. And damn if she didn't let out a contented sigh. She needed this. Him. Needed to feel him touching her all the time.

"You didn't mess anything up. It's good. We're good. Now come here, I've been thinking about you all night. The only thing I'm annoyed about is that I'll be spending the next few hours talking to Ty instead of you."

"Don't let him hear you say that." Her last word was cut off by the press of his lips against hers. She melted into him, her arms circling his neck, his own hands steadying her hips so he could deepen the kiss.

A barrage of lights made her blink. Blue ones, flashing as they made their way up the road.

And that's when she knew she'd messed up worse than she'd imagined.

26

One moment she was like soft cotton in his arms, making him feel hard and tight and every which way but loose. And then she was stiff as a board, pulling away from him, her eyes wide as she stared over his shoulder.

Mason followed her gaze, his stomach twisting when he saw the police car. He felt like he'd been physically punched.

Because it was coming for him.

Just like they'd come for his dad all those years ago. He'd been ten when his dad was first arrested, and he'd cried as he watched them take the only parent he knew away. He'd spent three days with a foster family before his dad had been released on bail. And they'd come up here to try to get away from the reporters and publicity that hounded them everywhere they went.

He'd spent a lifetime watching people come for his family. First for his dad, and then for him when CPS pulled him out of the life he knew and understood and threw him into the lion's den.

And now it was happening again. But this time Ty would be the one to watch him being taken away. His heart was hammering against his chest because he couldn't let him. He couldn't.

"Take Ty to your house," he said to Alaska. "Please don't let him see this."

"But you didn't do anything wrong." Her eyes were glistening with tears. "They can't do anything to you."

"I withheld information. They can arrest me if they have cause. And baby, they do have cause."

He softly cupped her cheek. "You withheld it because I asked you to. You wanted to tell them. Let me tell them it was me. It was all me."

The lights were almost here. Panic washed over him. "Please take him. *Now*." He let out a ragged breath. "Please, Alaska."

"Okay." She nodded, her face crumpled, tears spilling out. "Okay." She took a deep breath and opened the cabin door. "Ty, change of plan again," she called to him. "You're coming with me."

"What? Why?" He walked out of the bathroom. "You're giving me whiplash here." And then he saw the lights, still flashing as they pulled up outside of the cabin. "What's going on?"

"I'll explain at my place," she told him. "You need to come with me. *Now*."

"Mason?" Ty walked into the doorway. "Why are the police here?" He turned back to Alaska. "Why are you crying? What happened? Did he hurt you?"

"No, no." Tears were pouring down her cheeks. "It's not like that."

"They're coming to ask questions," Mason told him. Ty was staring at him like he had no idea who he was. "About something that happened years ago."

"When? Tell me. What happened, Mase?"

The patrol car doors opened and two cops stepped out.

Time was almost up. Mason pulled Ty close and hugged him so damn tight it hurt. "Alaska will explain. Just listen to her, okay. Stay with her. Promise me."

"You'll be back for me, right?" Suddenly Ty sounded like a kid again. "You'll come get me as soon as they're gone?"

"Mason Parker?" one of the cops called out.

"Just give us a minute, Simon," Alaska begged. "Just one, okay?"

"Alaska, I'm just doing my job here. I need to talk to Mr. Parker."

"I get that. Please, for me. Just let me get his brother out of here before you start?"

"They're not taking you, right? They're gonna talk to you here?" Ty's voice was muffled against Mason's coat.

"I don't know. Just go with Alaska now, Ty. Do this for me, okay?"

Ty's lip wobbled. "Okay."

She was standing waiting for Ty. Mason caught her gaze. "Don't let CPS take him," he said softly.

"I won't." She was still crying. "I promise."

He had to look away from her. Because all he wanted to do was wipe away those damn tears. Make everything right.

But he couldn't.

"Go now," he urged them. Then he turned to the officers. "Can you wait until they're inside Alaska's house?"

The older one – Simon – nodded, and he was thankful. They stood silently for a moment, watching as Alaska and Ty walked across the snowy path, their bodies silhouetted by the lights outside her house.

And when they were inside, he took a deep breath and faced them.

"Mason Parker," the younger cop said. "You're under arrest. Turn around and place your hands behind your back."

He did as instructed. Cold metal met his flesh as they

placed handcuffs on him. They were still talking, reading him his rights, but he couldn't quite hear them, their voices muffled by the overwhelming rush of blood through his ears.

Alaska watched from her front door as they handcuffed him. In her heart she'd hoped they'd just ask him a few questions then drive away. But she could see them lead him down the steps of his cabin to their waiting car. And it was agony.

"Okay," she said, pulling the door firmly shut and turning to Ty. "How shall we do this?"

"How about you tell me what the hell is going on?" He looked like he wanted to hit somebody.

She winced at the look on his face.

"Sorry." He squeezed his eyes shut. "I'm just... What's happening, Alaska? Why are they talking to him? What did he do? He said it was years ago, was he telling the truth." Ty shook his head. "Did he do something to somebody at the dance?"

"No, honey." Alaska pointed at the living room. "Let's sit down and I'll try to explain." And when she was done she was going to walk outside with her phone and scream at her parents for putting this kid in a position like this. How could they do this? How could they hurt her all over again?

She hated them.

Ty sat on the easy chair and she took the sofa. "Remember that conversation we had about me disappearing?" she asked him.

"Yeah, I remember." He frowned. "But what about Mason?"

"Mason was there."

"What? How? He couldn't have been. You were both kids."

"I know. As far as I can work out, I wandered a long way from our tent. And I ended up at the cabin. I think I must have crawled underneath and hid there for a long while, but eventually I came out and your dad and Mason found me."

"Did they hurt you?" Ty's lip wobbled. "Tell me they didn't hurt you."

"No they didn't, I promise. But your dad was on bail and Mason was about to go into foster care so they didn't want anybody knowing they'd found me. They let me sleep in the cabin for the night then dropped me off at the police station early in the morning."

"The police station where those cops are from?"

That hadn't occurred to her. "Yeah," she said slowly. "I guess so."

"So why are they here? If nothing happened?"

She took a deep breath. "Because I told my parents and I assume they called the police."

"You did this?" He glared at her. "This is your fault?"

She didn't want to cry again. But maybe her eyes needed to get the memo. "Yes," she whispered. "It is."

"You snitched on him. He's in trouble with the law because of you." Ty jumped up from his seat, his hands pulling at his hair. "I thought you cared about him."

"I do, Ty, I do."

"No you don't. You just got him thrown to the wolves." He walked to her window, yanking back the curtain. "They're gone. Does that mean he's okay?"

"No, sweetheart. They took him."

"They arrested him?" His face crumpled.

She let out a breath. "Yes."

"Well fuck them. Fuck everything. And I don't give a shit that I'm swearing because everything's so fucking messed up." Ty stomped out of the living room. She raced to follow him, catching him as he was yanking open her front door.

"Where are you going?" she asked him.

"To the cabin. I'm not staying here. I want to be there when Mase gets back."

"You can't go there. I promised Mason I'd look after you." Alaska reached for him, fully expecting him to shake her off. But instead he turned to her, tears running down his face.

"Oh Ty." She stepped toward him and he crumpled into her embrace. He was taller than her – probably stronger too – but right now he was a child. He needed security. To know the world was still a good place.

"We're going to sort this out," she whispered to him. "Mason will get a lawyer and they'll get him out and I'll do whatever it takes so everybody knows he's the good guy. That he saved me."

"He saved me, too," Ty sniffled.

"I know he did. That's what he does. And he hates people knowing it." And wasn't that the problem? He didn't show a softer side to the world because he'd learned not to from an early age.

But he was vulnerable when he was with her. That's why she loved him.

"We're going to get through this, honey. I promise."

Ty nodded, his face shiny with tears. "Don't tell anybody that I cried."

"I won't. But you know it's not weak to show emotions, right?"

"I know. But I still gotta show my face at school."

She let him step out of their hug. "So here's what's going to happen. I'm going to make us both a hot chocolate and after, you're going to go to bed and get some sleep."

"But I want to help."

"You'll help by being ready in the morning for Mason to come home."

"Okay." He nodded. "But can Leo sleep with me tonight?"

"Of course he can."

An hour later Alaska opened the door to find her sister standing there. She was still wearing her costume from the theater, her face made up with thick grease paint. She ran toward Alaska and hugged her tight.

"I came straight here as soon as I heard," Everley told her as they stood in the hallway.

Ty had finally fallen asleep in Alaska's guest bed, Leo curled up next to him. She'd hung up his suit and put his shirt in the laundry just to give herself something to do.

"So it's all around town?" Alaska said, resigned. It wasn't every day that somebody got arrested in Winterville.

"Yeah." Everley's eyes were soft. "I'll need you to fill me in on the details but I got the gist. So Mason was there when you disappeared all those years ago?"

"Yeah, he was. But he was a kid and it was nobody's fault. You need to believe that."

"I do, I do." Everley cupped Alaska's face. "How are you holding up?"

"I'm keeping it together for Ty."

"Poor guy. Where is he now?"

"In my guest bed. Asleep, I hope." She was keeping her voice down anyway. At least one of them should get some sleep. "It was Mom and Dad who called the cops. You know that?"

Everley nodded. "Yeah, I heard that too. I haven't gone home to see them yet. I don't trust myself not to throw them out."

"Don't hold yourself back on my account." Alaska almost meant it. Even though the thought of them being out on the streets in the middle of the night did make her chest feel tight.

"Anyway, North and Holly both called," Everley told her. "They wanted to come check on you, but I figured you wouldn't want the company. So I came alone."

"Thank you." Alaska nodded. "You want a drink?"

"Something warm would be good." Everley glanced over at Mason's cabin. "Should we sit on the deck so we don't wake up Ty?"

"Yeah." Alaska nodded. "Grab some blankets from the hallway. I'll be out in a minute."

Everley opened the blanket box that Alaska kept next to the deck, and Alaska stopped at the base of the stairs to listen for Ty and Leo. All she could hear was soft snoring – Leo's – which was a good sign. So she made her sister a hot tea and carried it back outside.

Everley was sitting on the swing chair, a blanket wrapped around her body. Soft clouds of vapor danced from her mouth as she exhaled. She'd always been beautiful but tonight she looked almost unearthly.

"How are you feeling?" Alaska asked her.

"Absolutely fine. Dylan just called, he's on his way back from the airport so I'm going to stay up to see him." She smiled. "He's been away for too long."

"He's a good man," Alaska told her. "What he does is important."

"Yes it is." Everley nodded, taking the hot tea from her. She lifted it to her mouth, sipping at it. "Ooh this is good. Thank you."

"Have you decided what you'll do next year?" Alaska asked her. "Will Dylan go away again once the baby is here?"

Everley tipped her head to the side. "I don't think so. He's so excited and so am I. I'd like to take a year off from the show. Start working with some fresh talent." Everley smiled.

"It's still early but we have a lot of planning to do, I guess." Her gaze turned to Alaska. "But I'm more interested in you right now. Tell me what happened tonight."

Alaska took a deep breath, explaining the discoveries she and Mason had made, from when he realized she was the little girl he and his dad had found outside their cabin, to his finding her rabbit and blanket in the crawl space. When she got to the part about telling their parents, Everley's expression turned thundery.

"I hate the way they make it all about them," Everley said, shaking her head. "You were trying to help and they only made everything worse."

"Dad just wouldn't listen," Alaska told her. "I hate that he's done this to Mason and Ty."

"So what are you going to do now?" Everley asked her.

"I don't know." Alaska sighed, looking at the empty road at the bottom of her driveway. "I promised I'd take care of Ty for as long as he needs it."

"Of course you did." Everley gave her a soft smile. "My sister, carer of every type of animal in the world."

"Ty's not a stray animal."

"I know. But you've taken him in anyway." Putting her cup down on the table, Everley twisted in the swing seat so she was facing her sister. "What about Mason? Are you going to talk to the police?"

"Yes." Alaska nodded. "I'll go over there in the morning. I hate that he's in there for something that's not his fault. He didn't even know the little girl was me until he was back here. His dad told him she'd moved away."

"I guess he wouldn't have brought Ty to live here if he'd known," Everley mused.

"Well I'm glad he did." Even if her heart hurt like crazy right now.

There was a moment of silence. Alaska took a deep

breath, ignoring the tightness in her chest. It was only a few days until Christmas. She needed him home.

Right now.

"Do you love him?" Everley asked her, her eyes scanning Alaska's face.

Alaska nodded. "Yes, I do." Even if it hurt right now.

"And does he love you back?"

Alaska blinked. "I don't know." Her chest tightened even more. She knew he cared. She knew that much. But love? It felt like a big flashing light above her head. What if he didn't love her?

Even worse, what if he hated her for causing all of this?

"I can love him enough for both of us," she said, pushing those thoughts away.

"I'm not sure it works that way, sweetie," Everley said, her voice full of compassion. "He's not a stray animal." She lifted a brow, reminding Alaska of her earlier description of Ty. "You can't love somebody into loving you. And I hate to say it, but even if he gets released, there's a chance he'll leave town. Take Ty and go back to where they came from. I mean that's what I would do." Her sister let out a long breath. "You need to be prepared for that."

A gust of wind scraped Alaska's face, making her eyes sting. She blinked but the tears refused to go away. "He won't leave," she said. "Not when Ty needs to finish school. He'll stay. I'm sure of it."

"Okay." Everley nodded. "You know him better than I do." She reached over and took Alaska's hand. "I just want you to be happy, you know that?"

"I do." Alaska nodded. "And I was happy. Until I messed everything up."

"You didn't mess anything up. You just tried to make everything okay." Everley squeezed her hand tighter. "That's what you do. Take care of everybody. Especially those who need it the most. But maybe you need to let us take care of you now. I know you hate it, but we're your family. We care for each other, honey."

"I know you do." Alaska's voice was tight. There was too much to think about, and too many hours before she could do anything to make things right. She wanted the hours to pass fast, but instead the minutes were creeping by like they were stuck in molasses.

"You should go home," she told her sister. "You have another show tomorrow. I'll be fine."

"I can stay over if you like," Everley offered.

"It's fine. I have Ty and Leo." Alaska gave the smallest of smiles. "And anyway, you'll want to see Dylan as soon as he's home. I just need to get some sleep and be ready for tomorrow."

"Okay." Everley stood, reluctantly unwrapping the blanket from her body. "But if you need me, call me, okay?"

27

Mason looked down at his now-cold half-drunk coffee. It was in a mug whose logo had almost worn off. He could see a C and a G but nothing else. He'd been in the interview room for an hour, ever since he'd been booked and had given over his wallet and phone.

It was cold in the interview room. There were no windows so they must have the heat turned down. He looked up at the wall where there was a bit of peeling paint and he wondered if his father had sat in this same way, staring at a different but similar wall, wondering where the hell it had all gone wrong.

He'd thought he was different. And yet here he was, arrested in front of the kid he was supposed to be taking care of, sitting in a cop shop waiting to be questioned about something he knew he was guilty of.

The apple hadn't fallen far from the tree. Jesus, he was still attached to it. He'd tried to not be like his father. Chosen a career in the law because he wanted to be on the right side of it, unlike his dad.

But maybe it was in the blood. You could fight against your nature but you couldn't defeat it.

He'd never forget the expression on Ty's face. It wasn't just that he was watching Mason being taken away by the police, though that was bad enough.

It was the look of accusation. The way he'd turned to Alaska and asked *'has he hurt you?'*

Did Ty really believe he was capable of that?

The thought twisted his guts.

He'd sat in rooms like this before as a lawyer. At the beginning of his career when he was sent to all the grunt cases. DUIs, robberies, anything the partners didn't want to take. But in the past few years his clients had been blue chip companies. No interview rooms in the local precinct for them. It was all shiny conference rooms and constant deliveries of lattes and americanos.

He'd forgotten how gritty the law could be.

The door to the interview room opened. Mason turned his head to see Simon – the older police officer – shuffling another man in.

"Your attorney is here," Simon told him. "You have ten minutes together. Then we'll start the interview."

Good. Get it over with.

"Hello, Mr. Parker. My name's Eric Cobb." The man held his hand out to Mason. He looked more disheveled than Mason, in a pair of old chinos, a crumpled blue shirt, and a sports jacket that had seen better days. Probably in the eighties.

"Thank you for coming," Mason told him.

"No problem." He sat down in the chair next to Mason's and put some papers on the table in front of him. "Okay then. So I see you were involved in the Winter child abduction."

"I was there when it happened, yes."

Eric looked at him. "How exactly?"

He listened as Mason explained, making scrawling notes on the yellow legal pad he'd brought with him. His face betrayed nothing, no emotion, no surprise. He remained narrow eyed and tight lipped until Mason had finished.

"Well as you know there's no statute of limitations for child abduction," Eric told him.

"I didn't abduct her. She was at our cabin when we came home."

"Yes, well they may say different." He looked carefully at Mason. "You understand that, right? It's a he-said she-said situation. Especially now that the only other witness – your father – is no longer with us."

"I get that. But Alaska remembers nothing."

"You've spoken with her?"

Okay, so he'd left out their relationship when he explained everything to Cobb. It wasn't his secret alone to tell. And if she didn't want people knowing he sure as hell wasn't going to tell them. "We're neighbors. That's how we realized what had happened."

"So she's not the one who came to the police?"

"I don't believe so. I believe it's her parents."

"And they know because..."

"Alaska told them."

"Hmmm." Eric jotted down something else.

"What does hmm mean?" Mason asked. Eric looked up from his notepad, his eyes hooded as they caught Mason's gaze.

"In my experience, once parents get involved the victim will usually testify. She may not want to, but they'll encourage her. So we need to decide how we're going to play this."

"I'm going to tell the truth," Mason told him.

"Which truth? Your truth? Her truth? Her parents' truth? You know there are different versions, right?" He glanced at the printed sheet he had in front of him. "You're a lawyer, you know how this works." He shook his head. "And it's only the truth if somebody believes it. Do you really think anybody's going to believe a little girl walked for miles and just happened to appear on your cabin porch?"

"So what do you want me to do?" Mason asked, feeling angry now. He was tired, he was annoyed, and he wanted to be with Ty. Wanted to be with Alaska.

Wanted to be anywhere but here.

"Say nothing. For now. Refuse to answer their questions. Give me some time to work out what to do next. Who knows, they may just let you go in the morning."

"Then won't it be better if I tell them what I know now?" Mason's head was fuzzy. He was so damn tired. Why couldn't he think properly?

"You're a lawyer, you know it's always better to wait and see before opening your mouth." Eric gave him a knowing look. "Let's buy ourselves some time until morning. Get some damn sleep and then we can work out how we're going to play this."

It made sense. But anything would probably make sense right now. All he knew was he needed to get home. "Will they let me out soon?"

"Not tonight. As for tomorrow, it depends on how they want to swing this. My guess is they don't know at all. It's late and nobody in charge will be getting involved until morning. That's why it's best to say nothing now."

Jesus Christ. How had he gone from chaperoning a school dance to possibly being investigated by the cops? It would be laughable if it wasn't so damn shocking.

Ty would never get over this. The same way he'd never

gotten over his father's conviction. He'd blame Mason forever and Mason couldn't blame him.

"Okay," he said to Eric. "We'll play it your way."

Alaska woke up with a start in the middle of the night. Not that she was certain she'd been asleep. Most of the past few hours had passed in a daze of broken thoughts and panicked awakenings, like she was bobbing on a sea of sleep, only occasionally drifting under.

Everley's words from earlier were still playing on her mind. *It doesn't work like that, sweetie. He's not a stray animal...*

Was that really what her sister thought? That Alaska saw Mason as something broken? A lost animal who needed loving kindness? Because the truth was the opposite. He was the strong one.

She was broken. Or at least she had been.

But not anymore. She felt fierce. She had ever since he'd come to town. And no, she wasn't relying on him to make her complete. But she was finally ready to shake off the shackles of her past.

She glanced at the clock. It was almost three in the morning. Ty was asleep in the guest room next to hers, Leo curled in his arms on top of the blankets. When she'd checked on them both earlier, they'd been snoring softly together. Ty had looked so young and vulnerable.

But he'd be okay. They'd make sure of that. All of them. Not just her and Mason, but all of Winterville. Whether he liked it or not he was one of them now. And the town took care of its own.

And was that really so bad? Wanting to take care of people. Wanting to love them so much it mended whatever was broken?

It was no good, this time she couldn't get back to sleep. It was Everley's fault.

Her sister should never have said those words, dammit. Should never have planted them in her brain.

She grabbed her phone and quickly pressed the screen. A moment later a ringing tone echoed from the earpiece.

"Hello?" Everley's voice was groggy. "Alaska is everything okay?"

"I need to ask you something."

"What?"

"Why did you say Mason might leave?"

"Uh. I dunno. Let me think. Are you sure you're okay?"

"Did you say it because you wanted to prepare me?"

"I... ah... probably. I guess I don't want you to get hurt."

BINGO!

"But I'm going to get hurt. Don't you see that? I'm going to get so damn hurt it'll take my breath away. But isn't that better than not being hurt? Because if you don't hurt you don't feel anything at all. Not the good stuff, not the beautiful stuff. You can't love if you're afraid of being hurt."

It was like the sun had come out in her room despite it being almost black in there. She felt giddy with the realization. It wasn't just North and Gabe and Everley and Holly who'd been protecting her. She'd been protecting herself.

She'd loved animals because they never threw love back in your face. She'd ignored her parents because it hurt too much that they didn't care. And even with Mason she'd held herself back.

She'd known for a long time that she loved him. Maybe from that first stolen kiss. Definitely from the moment he'd let her trace his tattoo and she'd seen that he'd suffered as much as she had.

But she hadn't told him. Hadn't even admitted it to

herself for the longest time. Because she was afraid of not being loved back.

"But that's not how love works."

"No, it isn't," Everley agreed. "It's not. It hurts a little sometimes. But the good stuff makes it worth so much."

"It does. And now I need to figure out what to do next." Alaska felt energized, like she could go fight a dragon. "Thank you."

"For what?" she asked, sounding confused.

"For being you. For caring. But I think I have this."

"I know you do, Alaska. You just have to let us get used to it. We've been worrying about you for twenty years. Old habits die hard."

"Yeah, but they need to die."

"Yes they do. And they will. Give us time."

"I will. Good night, Evie."

"Good night, Lassie."

She smiled at their childhood nicknames. And she was so ready to let hers go. It was the girl she was then, not the woman she was now.

She was Alaska Winter. Kick ass hotel owner. A woman to be reckoned with.

She hung up her phone and looked up, jumping when she saw Ty standing in the doorway.

"I heard voices," he said. "I thought you might have gotten a call from the police."

"It was only my sister," she told him. "Sorry for waking you."

"I couldn't sleep. I just want to do something, you know?" He shifted his feet. They were bare in the moonlight.

She nodded. "I know." She ran her tongue along her bottom lip. "First thing in the morning we'll go into town. Sit outside the police station until he comes out."

"We can do that?"

"I don't have anywhere else to be. Do you?" She lifted a brow and he grinned.

"Nope."

"Okay then. And Ty?"

He was walking away when she called out his name. He glanced over his shoulder. "Yeah?"

"We need to call your mom in the morning."

He wrinkled his nose. "Do we have to?"

"We do. No matter what's happened between you two, she's your mom and she needs to know where you are." She gave him a pointed look. "That you're with me."

"Okay." He nodded. "I'll call her."

Three a.m. The moment of darkness before the dawn. The time when only drunks, shift workers, and screaming babies were awake.

And him. Mason was still awake. Laying on the uncomfortable concrete slab they called a bed, staring at a ceiling that held no answers. Only scrawls from previous occupants and dark patches where insects had gone to die.

Right now he kind of knew how they felt.

This time of day was like an old acquaintance. He remembered being awake for the whole first night he was in foster care. Wondering how long it would take for somebody in his family to take him in. Or maybe the judge would suddenly have a change of heart and lower his dad's sentence.

And then one of the other kids had slowly pushed open the door, and made a grab for Mason's sneakers. The ones with the Nike logo that his dad bought for him right before he was arrested.

Mason had jumped out of bed and tried to stop the kid,

but back then he was too weak. Too afraid. Too unversed in the way of foster kid life.

He'd ended up with a punch in the gut and a warning that if he said anything the next punch would be to the groin. And in the morning he'd had to explain why he had nothing to put on his feet.

Stupid thing was he'd loved those shoes. Been fucking pleased as punch when his dad had bought them for him. Cleaned them off every night so they were still sparkling new.

Losing them had taken his breath away. He'd felt like he'd been punched in the gut a hundred times. But the pain never went away. It was there, reminding him that every time he loved something he lost it.

And that's when he'd learned the most important lesson of his life. If you don't love something it won't hurt when it's gone. Losing his mom, his dad, and those damn sneakers. They were the last time he was gonna let himself get hurt.

So over the years he'd gotten harder. Learned to punch first and ask questions later. Until he'd met Preach at another home. This one for boys who'd gotten into trouble.

It was Preach who'd pointed out that he had a chance for escape, if he studied hard until the day he left foster care. Then he could get a career that meant he'd never have to guard his sneakers again.

"You'll be able to buy as many sneakers as you want," Preach had said. "You could buy the whole damn shop on a lawyer's salary."

"How about you?" Mason had asked him. "You gonna study hard, too?"

But he hadn't. Preach had chosen the other path. The one where he never got out from under the shadows. And yet he was free while Mason was incarcerated and jobless.

It was all such a waste.

He felt a tug at his gut. The punch he'd drunk at the

winter formal was making its way through him. He shouldn't have had so much of it.

Yeah, but you didn't know you were gonna end the night in the cop shop, did you?

Getting up from the most uncomfortable bed in his life, he walked over to the thick metal door with five bars in the window and slammed his palm against it.

"Anybody there?" he shouted.

"What d'ya want?" a voice yelled back.

"I need to p— I mean, the bathroom," Mason told them.

"Use the bucket. That's what it's there for."

Mason looked over his shoulder. Sure enough there was a bucket. Metal, rusty, the white enamel paint mostly peeled off.

Christ, was this where he was now. Pissing in buckets and staring at ceilings.

Yep. Exactly where your genes want you. Somewhere deep inside he'd always known he was like his dad. That's why he'd avoided relationships. Didn't want to mess up someone's life the way his dad had messed his up.

And yet you have.

He squeezed his eyes shut, trying to ignore the voice in his head. He'd done more than mess up. He'd caused so many damn problems he didn't know where to start.

All he knew was he didn't deserve Alaska. He should never have gotten involved with her. Should have stayed away like he'd planned to.

Should have been the island he'd always been.

But he'd let her get under his skin. Let her believe they had a future. But she deserved better than this. She deserved a man who could love her. Who could protect her and take care of her.

A man who made her smile every goddamn day.

And that man wasn't him. He'd tried like hell, but he

couldn't outrun his genes. And he sure as hell wasn't going to ruin her life the way his dad had ruined his.

He rubbed his temples. The voice in his head was driving him crazy. And no, he wasn't about to use the bucket. He'd sleep and hope that the urge would go away.

And by the morning maybe he would work out what the hell to do about Alaska.

28

By seven a.m., Alaska was cooking breakfast. A full on American fry up. Bacon, sausage, biscuits and gravy, and a pan so full of scrambled eggs that they could probably eat it for the next year. She was brewing some coffee when Ty stumbled into the kitchen, rubbing his eyes.

"Any news?" he asked her.

"Nothing. We can eat, then we go into town." Not that she wanted to eat anything. It was the cooking that soothed. She just needed to do something, and right now cooking for Ty fulfilled that need.

Ty looked at the food on the stove and blinked. "How many people are you cooking for?"

"Just us. Hope you're hungry."

"Always." Without being asked, he grabbed the silverware and set two places, then filled them both a glass of orange juice. Before she could even say anything, he was grabbing two plates from the rack and passing them to her.

"Thank you." She smiled at him.

"Anytime."

She'd slid his full plate in front of him right as she heard rapping at her front door. “You eat, I’ll get that,” she told him. Ty nodded, already cutting into the sausage.

When she opened the front door a man she’d never seen before was standing on the other side. He was short and stocky, with dark hair slicked back and a crucifix hanging from his left ear.

“Can I help you?” she asked him.

“Alaska Winter?” he asked. “I’m Alexander Calvin.”

She still had no idea who he was, but she shook his outstretched hand anyway. She opened her mouth to try to find out more but then footsteps barreled down the hallway.

“Preach!” Ty threw himself past Alaska and at the stocky man on her doorstep. “You came.”

“Preach?” Alaska asked.

“That’s what they call me.” Preach shrugged. “Not my choice.”

“Are you a preacher?”

“No, ma’am.” He looked amused at the question. “I’m a friend of Mason’s. Can I come in?”

“Mason hasn’t mentioned you,” she said, looking carefully from Preach to Ty.

“Why does that not surprise me?” Preach shook his head. “I’m his oldest friend. Closest thing he has to a brother after this guy.” He ruffled Ty’s hair and Ty didn’t seem annoyed at it. “Got your message last night, buddy. Got here as quick as I could.”

“You came from Baltimore?” she asked him.

“Yep. And I’m fuc—I mean, I’m tired. Is it possible to come in and sit down before I fall down?”

Damn! Where were her manners? “We were just about to eat breakfast,” she told him, standing aside so he could pass. “Would you like some?”

“Does a bear shit in the woods?” Preach blinked. “I mean does a bear defecate?”

Ty started laughing.

"I think so..." She frowned.

He looked at her dead in the eyes. "In that case, I'll take some breakfast, ma'am."

Five minutes later, he and Ty were shoveling eggs and bacon into their mouths like they hadn't eaten for months. Alaska watched them both, her coffee mug cradled in her hand. She'd managed one mouthful of eggs before her stomach had given her a groaning warning.

Best to stick to the caffeine for now.

"So you're a friend of Mason's?" she asked Preach.

"Yep. Been friends since he was fourteen and I was sixteen." Preach picked up a piece of bacon and shoved it into his mouth. "Damn, this is good. Can't remember the last time I had a cooked breakfast."

"Preach doesn't usually get up until the afternoon," Ty told her.

"Okay." She nodded.

"Business starts when the lights go down." Preach told her, still chewing. "I'd get up earlier if I had this to eat every day."

"Alaska's a good cook. You should try her pot pie," Ty said, scraping up the last of his eggs.

"You make pie?" Preach asked.

"I do." She nodded.

"Will you marry me?"

She laughed for the first time in what seemed like forever. "I don't know. I'll think about it."

"I'm more fun than Mason," he told her. "And not such a grumpy ass bastard either."

So he knew about her and Mason? She parked that thought to ask him later, if he was still here. When Ty wasn't listening.

Speaking of which. "How did you get here so quickly?" she asked him. "It's a long way from Maryland."

"Got a flight." He shrugged. "Any more of those eggs? How the heck do you get them so creamy?" He waited as she scooped some more onto his and Ty's plates. "A friend of a friend had a plane. Then another friend picked me up."

"Preach has a lot of friends," Ty told her.

"I'm getting that impression." She nodded.

"Speaking of friends, what's the plan with Mase?" Preach asked, finally pushing his plate away. He rubbed his stomach like there was something precious growing there.

Ty stood and picked up the plates. Damn, Mason had trained him well. Before she could even tell him to leave it he was loading them into the dishwasher.

"Ty and I are going to Winterville in a minute," she told Preach. "To see what's going on. I know the officers there."

Preach tipped his head to the side. "You done time before?"

Ty unsuccessfully stifled a laugh. "She runs the local inn. She probably feeds them."

"Okay," Preach said. "Just asking."

Alaska started to run the tap to wash the pots and pans, but Preach pushed her gently away. "We got this," he told her. "If you cook you don't wash up the dishes. That's the rules."

Well okay then. Leaving them to it, she walked up the stairs to get herself ready for the trip into Winterville. She was scheduled to work this afternoon and evening, and if she couldn't find anybody to cover her shift she'd still have to do it.

She glanced at herself in the bathroom mirror. There were puffy shadows under her eyes and her face looked almost gray. She did what she could with the bad situation and pulled on a pair of jeans and a cream sweater, letting her blonde hair fall over her shoulders.

When she got back downstairs, Preach and Ty were waiting for her. Preach let out a low whistle. "So that's how we're gonna play it," he said. "You're gonna charm them until they let him go."

"She always looks this nice," Ty said.

She smiled at him. "Thank you."

"C'mon," Preach said. "Let's go spring our boy out of jail."

"You're trouble," she said. "I can tell that."

"Damn right." He winked. "And don't you forget it."

Her stomach felt like it was tied in knots as they climbed out of the car and stepped into the ice cold Winterville air. There was nowhere to park in town, so she'd driven to the Inn and taken her usual spot. Even here the parking lot was heaving. A dusting of snow had fallen overnight and it glistened in the sunlight, making the ground look like it was covered in diamonds.

"I feel like I've woken up in a Hallmark Movie," Preach said, his head turning from left to right as they walked through the town square. "Any minute now a choir is gonna burst into a Christmas song, right?"

"Gotta wait until the afternoon for that," she told him. But she wasn't looking at Preach anymore. She was looking at the older couple hurrying across the square toward the three of them.

"Dear God, not now," she murmured.

"Who's that?" Preach asked, following her gaze.

"My parents."

Ty tensed beside her.

"The ones who threw Mason to the lions?" Preach asked. His voice was so even it sounded ominous.

"Um, yeah. But don't hurt them, okay?"

"Hmm."

"Alaska!" her mom called out. "We're going to the police station. Daddy's going to tell them it's all a mistake."

Her dad said nothing, though his jaw twitched. He looked as tired as she felt.

"Aren't you, darling?" her mom nudged him. Her dad did something that looked like a nod.

"Funny thing," Preach said, eyeing them carefully. "We were just heading there, too."

Her dad's eyes fell on Preach, taking in the man who was almost half his height but twice his width. He blinked when he saw the crucifix in his ear and the curling tattoo around his neck.

"This is Preach," Alaska told them. "Mason's friend."

"His best friend," Preach added. "Blood brother, you might say." Then he put his arm through her dad's, making her father do a double take. "Let's go in together," Preach said. "See what we can do."

The five of them walked over to the tiny police station. Preach pressed the button to let them in.

"Yes?"

"Alexander Calvin to see Mr. Parker," Preach said, any trace of his east coast accent disappearing from his voice.

"I'm sorry," the voice at the end of the speaker said. It sounded like Marie Jonas. Alaska used to go to school with her. "Only Mr. Parker's lawyer is allowed to see him."

"That's me," Preach said. "I'm his lawyer."

Alaska's mouth dropped open. She looked at Ty, who shrugged.

"Do you work for Eric Cobb?" Marie asked.

"Work for him? I own him. Bought his company up fair and square."

Okay, so Preach was definitely a liar. And actually quite a good one.

"I'm afraid only Mr. Cobb can see Mr. Mason."

"Then at least let me in and you can tell me he's okay. I'll report back to Mr. Cobb."

She waited for Marie to tell them to go away, but instead she must have hit the buzzer because the door lock released.

And all five of them walked in.

"Oh no," Marie said, walking around the counter. "No, no no. Alaska you can't be here." She looked up at Alaska's parents. "And you two shouldn't be here either."

"I just want to see him," Alaska told her. "Five minutes, okay?"

"Nahuh. You're the victim. You need to stay away from the perp."

"He's not a perp," Preach said, rolling his eyes. "He's a suspect."

"Whatever." Marie gritted her teeth. "You, leave." She pointed at Alaska. "In fact, all of you leave."

"I need to report back to Mr. Cobb, remember?" Preach said. He looked over her shoulder, his eyes narrowing as he took in the door that divided the reception area from the rest of the small station. "You sure I can't see Mase?"

"Mase?" Marie repeated.

"I mean, Mr. Parker."

"I'm sure you can't see him," Marie told him, deadpan. "Absolutely certain. Now can you please get her out of here before I get in trouble?" She glanced at Alaska again.

Alaska couldn't walk out of here without talking to him. She glanced sideways at Preach who shrugged. Behind them her parents were having some kind of heated whisper debate. And Ty was watching everybody with wide eyes.

"Can you get Ty out of here?" she asked Preach quietly.

"Why? You gonna try to break through that door?" He glanced over at it. "Because it's unbreakable. We gotta think outside of the box. Probably come in through the roof."

She shook her head because Preach was too out of her league to even reply. Then she turned to her parents, because she didn't want them here for this.

"You both need to leave. *Now*."

Her mom blinked. "We're here to support you, Alaska. Your dad's going to pull his complaint."

Her throat felt tight. "You are?" she asked suspiciously. He nodded, looking embarrassed.

"You see?" Alaska said, turning to Marie. "You can release him now. Nobody's complaining about anything." And yes, she still wasn't officially talking to her parents. But if they could help, she was all for it.

Marie lifted a brow. "Doesn't work that way. The wheels of the law are in motion."

"What does that mean?" her dad asked.

"It means we're investigating a complaint. Just because you've been forced into retracting it, doesn't mean we're going to drop the investigation. I'll give you a number for the DA's office, you can talk to somebody there."

Dear God. "Dad, Mom, can you leave now?" she asked them. They were doing no good here and she couldn't stand to be near them.

"Alaska, I..." Her mom reached for her and Alaska shrugged her off. "Seriously, I don't want to see you. Retract your complaint and go home. I'll talk to you when I'm ready. If I'm ever ready. Now go back to Florida and leave me to clean up your mess."

Her mom gave her a baleful glance, then grabbed her husband's arm and they left. Alaska let out a mouthful of air. She turned back to Marie.

"Are you seriously keeping him when nobody is actually complaining about anything?" she asked her.

Marie put up her hands. "It's above my pay grade. I'm just the desk sergeant. I do as I'm told."

Alaska groaned internally. She felt impotent and she hated it. She needed to see him.

Dammit. She ran for the door that separated the desk area from the rest of the small station. "Mason!" she screamed, banging on the door.

"Alaska, I'm gonna arrest your ass if you don't move away." Marie was heading toward her, looking pissed.

"Will you put me in the same cell as Mason?" she asked her.

"Nope." Marie shook her head. "In a different cell. In a different town."

Ah crap. She took a deep breath. "Mason, we're going to get you out of here. Somehow. I don't know how."

"Alaska?"

Her heart almost stopped at his voice. He sounded closer than she'd expected.

"You okay in there?" Preach had joined her. He was as good at taking instructions as she was.

"Preach?" Mason shouted. "What the hell are you doing here?"

"Saving you. As usual."

"I'm here, too," Ty shouted. "You okay, bro?"

"You were supposed to take him outside," Alaska whispered to Preach.

"I know, but he's a little punk who thinks he knows best." Preach looked proud.

Marie went to grab Alaska's arm, but Preach stepped in the way. Marie's mouth dropped open.

"You gonna arrest me, too?" Preach asked. "Because you should know that I'm gonna resist."

"Jesus." Mason sounded pissed. "Go home. All of you. For Christ's sake."

Marie turned back to Alaska. They were on borrowed time.

"I love you, Mason Parker," she shouted. He needed to know it. She should have told him long ago.

There was a pause. She felt everybody's eyes on her face. Her cheeks pinked up but she tried to ride it out.

Then his voice came back. Lower and grittier.

"You shouldn't. You really shouldn't. Just go home, Alaska."

29

"You shouldn't," Preach said, in a passable imitation of Mason's gruff voice as they walked back to the Wintervillc Inn. "Stupid bastard. That's even worse than 'yeah'."

"He says that to you, too?" Ty asked.

"Yeah." Preach wiggled his brows and they both laughed. "I'm telling you, I've never seen a grown man get so stuck on three little words."

Alaska turned to look at him. Her chest had felt tight ever since they'd walked out of the police station. It hadn't helped that her mom started begging for her forgiveness in the middle of the sidewalk. Thankfully one look from Preach had sent both her parents scurrying off. She'd deal with them another day.

Or hopefully she wouldn't.

There was a message on her phone from Martin agreeing to take her shift that night. Another one from Everley asking how she was doing. And a deluge of group messages that she couldn't bring herself to check yet.

"It doesn't matter. I didn't say it to hear it back," she said, pressing the car door open with her key.

Preach put his hand on her arm. "You know he didn't mean it, right?"

"Mean what?" she asked him.

"That *you shouldn't* crap. He doesn't know how to deal with love."

"He's right," Ty said. "If it makes you feel any better he doesn't say it to me either."

"Right? We just say I love you, man and he says, 'yeah'. As if we don't know he loves us too."

"Kind of like Han Solo to Princess Leia in Star Wars," Ty said helpfully.

They were trying to make her feel better. And she appreciated that. But he hadn't replied 'yeah'. Or 'I know'.

He'd told her *she shouldn't.* Like he didn't want her love.

And she had no idea what to do with that.

Traffic was thick coming into Winterville, though the road out was thankfully emptier. It was funny to think there were only three days until Christmas. She should be excited, planning all the fun things they'd be doing with their guests. Dressing up in a stupid elf costume to spread some festive spirit.

Instead, she was driving home realizing that every word Everley had told her last night was true. She couldn't love Mason for the both of them. Love didn't work like that between a man and a woman.

She'd needed to hear it back so much. And he couldn't say it.

Because he didn't feel it.

"Why do they call you Preach?" she asked, changing the subject because it was way too painful to think about this anymore.

Ty coughed out a laugh.

"Because I told all my foster parents that my dead dad used to be a preacher. It made them feel sorry for me. They'd give me the best room and good food and make a fuss."

"I'm guessing he wasn't a preacher then."

"Nope. He was a wise guy."

"A wise guy? As in the Mafia?" She almost hit a bank of snow, swerving the car right in time.

"We don't call it that. But yeah."

"So what do you do?" She wasn't sure she wanted to hear the answer.

"A bit of this. A bit of that. Whatever it takes to pay the bills. I'm not smart like Mason. Not book smart anyway."

"Tell her how you used to sell Mason's assignments for soda money," Ty said, leaning forward from the back seat.

"Ah, but he never knew it. Until he got an answer wrong and got beaten up over it." Preach shrugged. "That was my fault. Mea culpa. I helped him clean up the scrapes."

"You care about him," Alaska said softly.

"Yep." Preach nodded. "He's a good man, really. I mean, he's an idiot. He should never have said that to you. But he's the best kind of friend. There when you need him."

"He likes taking care of other people."

"Yeah, he does." She could feel Preach's gaze on her face. "Talking of taking care, I don't suppose there's any chance of a pot pie for lunch?" he asked.

"Of course." She couldn't help but smile at his enthusiasm for her cooking. It would take her mind off Mason at least.

Preach beamed. "Thank you, darlin'. As I said, you're way too good for that asshole locked up in jail."

"You shouldn't. You really shouldn't."

Those damn words rebounded through his brain like they

were a pinball determined to get a high score. Had he really said them to her?

In front of Ty and Preach and whoever else was listening in? Probably half of the Winterville PD at the very least.

He hadn't meant to say it. He'd opened his mouth to shout the words back, but those three words clung to his tongue like barbed wire. They tasted bad. Painful.

They made him feel like the kid he used to be, alone and unloved.

Why the hell couldn't he say them? Those three little words danced out of everybody's mouths like they meant nothing.

And yet here he was, a prize goddamned asshole because he'd thrown her words back in her face.

She must hate him. *He* hated him. He sat down on the hard concrete bench and lowered his head to his hands.

He was a fuck up. Incapable of love. And she deserved so much more than that. So much more than a man so closed in on himself that he panicked when he heard words of affection.

She deserved the fairytale. And he was her biggest nightmare.

These four walls were driving him crazy. He needed to get out of here. Get back to the cabin.

And then what? Pack up. Get Ty. Get the hell out of this town. Away from the trouble he'd caused.

From the pain he was feeling.

From the love he couldn't give the woman who deserved it.

"Mason Parker, stand back. I'm opening the door. Your lawyer's here," the new cop – Marie – shouted. "Your real lawyer."

"Do I have any other lawyer?"

"That stocky guy who said he worked for them."

Preach. Mason shook his head. He still had no idea what his friend was doing here.

When he walked into the interview room, Eric Cobb was already there. He looked up and smiled. "I have good news."

Mason blinked. "You do?"

"Yep. The DA isn't interested, especially since the parents retracted their statement. And the local PD is happy for you to be released this afternoon pending future interviews. But honestly, I don't think there'll be any future interviews."

"So that's it?" Mason frowned. It couldn't be that easy, could it?

"For now. It's an old case. Alaska was unharmed for the most part. They'll take their time investigating but I'm pretty sure you're off the hook."

"So what, I can go home?"

"That's what I'm planning on doing. We got a couple of days until Christmas. I suggest we both spend those with our families."

"And do I have to stay in town?"

"You're not out on bail, Mason. There are no stipulations you have to stick to. You're free to go where you want, when you want, as long as you keep them informed of your permanent address. If they need you they know where to find you." Eric looked up at him. "I have to say, I thought you'd be happier than you are about this."

"I'm surprised. I thought I'd be here for a few more days."

"Getting used to that concrete bed, huh?" Eric lifted a brow. "So that's it. Some paperwork for us both to fill out which should come through in the next couple of hours. And then we're done."

"Okay." Mason nodded.

"Shall I call somebody to pick you up?"

"No. Don't call anybody."

He didn't need saving. He didn't deserve it. He was a fuck up, a loser. He couldn't even tell Alaska he loved her.

And God, did he love her.

But he didn't deserve her, and he definitely didn't want her coming to pick him up.

"I'll take you back."

"Thank you. Can I call my friend to let him know I'll be coming soon?" He needed to make sure somebody knew. Preach could get Ty out of there and he could talk to Alaska.

Tell her it was over. Because he couldn't give her what she needed. What she deserved. He never should have let her in. Never should have taken advantage.

For her sake, this needed to be done with.

Preach was snoring in the easy chair, his head back, his mouth wide open. Ty was in the spare room talking to his friends by the sounds of things. And Alaska was pacing in the living room, looking out of the window to see if he was there yet.

Truth be told, she was a little hurt he'd texted Preach and not her that he was being released. But maybe he couldn't remember her number.

She tried to push that ache down, because she should be happy. He was coming home. Everything was going to be okay.

She'd wanted to drive into town to pick him up but Preach had made her promise she wouldn't. "If he'd had wanted us there he'd have said so."

"Would he? He never asks for anything."

Preach raised his eyebrow. "Exactly. Maybe he needs to learn to ask. Maybe we shouldn't be anticipating his every need. You can't save him, Alaska. He has to save himself."

It sounded so eerily like Everley's words that she hadn't

protested. Preach had known Mason for years, so she did as he suggested.

Didn't mean she wasn't feeling edgy. Her mom had tried calling about a hundred times, and all her cousins had checked in with her. They were happy that Mason was being released.

And she hadn't told them about his reply to her love declaration.

It was almost four when she saw the car moving steadily toward their houses. "He's here," she said to Preach.

He blinked. "Wha?" Without taking a breath he was on his feet, eyes darting this way and that, his hand patting his pocket.

"Mason's here. Or at least there's a car coming."

Preach peered over her shoulder to see out of the window. "Good. Where's Ty?"

"Upstairs."

"TY!!!!" Preach's roar made her jump two feet off the ground. "Your asshole brother is back."

"You can't swear at Ty," Alaska whispered to Preach.

"Sorry." He grimaced. "Old habits, you know?"

Ty came running down the stairs, his eyes bright. "He's here?"

"Just coming," Preach told him. Ty stared past Preach's head. The three of them watched as the car approached. But instead of making its way to Alaska's house, it stopped short at Mason's cabin.

Preach let out a sigh.

"What?" Ty asked.

"Nothin'." Preach shook his head then muttered something unintelligible under his breath. "Listen you two, I got a favor to ask."

"What?" Ty frowned.

"I need you to stay here for a minute. Let me go talk to Mason by myself."

"But I need to see him," Ty said. "I need to say sorry. I said some stuff..." He looked down. "Some stuff I shouldn't have."

"He knows you didn't mean it," Preach said, patting his arm. "Just ten minutes, okay? Half an hour tops. I need a bit of man to man time."

"Okay." Ty wrinkled his nose. "But only 'cos it's you."

Alaska's eyes met Preach's.

"All right?" he asked softly.

"All right." She nodded, though her chest hurt. "Come on, Ty, let's empty the dishwasher."

"I changed my mind," Ty said, the undercurrent completely passing him by. "I'm going with Preach."

"Shut up," Preach said, ruffling his hair. It looked funny because Preach was at least six inches shorter than Ty. "Go do the dishes, princess."

Climbing out of Eric's car, Mason leaned in to shake his hand. "You know if you're ever thinking of taking up law again, you should give my office a call," Eric told him.

"I'm a corporate lawyer, don't think I'll be much good to you."

"You'd be surprised. And it's hard to find good lawyers out here. They all want to be in the cities where the money is."

"Thank you, anyway," Mason said. "But I think I'll be back in the city soon enough."

"Shame." Eric started the car back up. "Be safe. And keep us informed of your location."

"Yeah, I will."

Eric backed out of the gravel path that served as a

driveway and Mason took a deep breath, grabbing his keys that the desk sergeant had returned to him. From the corner of his eye he could see movement. He turned, expecting to see all three of them walking from Alaska's house.

He had it planned. He'd ask to speak to her. Explain that he couldn't be the man she needed. That he and Ty had to go back and make a new start.

That she'd be better off without him.

Because she would. She deserved a man who could tell her he loved her a hundred times a day. She deserved somebody that her family loved as much as she did. Because he knew how much she adored her family, and how important their opinions were to her.

The fact is, her parents hated him. And he understood that. It was time to let her go.

But instead of the three of them, one lonely figure was walking toward him. Short, squat, with arms that looked like they could lift a thousand pounds without any problem. Preach reached the steps of the cabin and walked up them, then enveloped Mason in the tightest of bear hugs.

"You scared me, man," he said, his voice muffled against Mason's shoulder. "You shouldn't be on that side of the fucking law. That's my job."

Mason nodded. "Not planning on doing it again."

"So that's it? You're free?"

"I get the impression they just want to close the case. They'll interview everybody again at some point, but it's not a priority."

Preach let him go, his eyes narrowing as he took Mason in. "You didn't come to Alaska's even though you knew we'd all be there."

"No. I want her to have somewhere to escape to."

"Escape to?" Preach's brows knit. "You stupid bastard, she doesn't want to escape. She loves you."

Mason's throat felt tight. "I know."

"And you love her, too," Preach told him.

He was finding it hard to breathe. "No," he said thickly. "I can't love. You know that."

"Ah, shit to the heavens." Preach pinched his nose. "Get inside before you fuck everything up."

"Is she okay? And Ty? They both all right?"

"Nope. She's not because some asshole is about to break her heart. Ty's fine though. Because he knows what a chump you are."

"I'm going to do the right thing." For once in his damned life. "She deserves more."

"I know that. But maybe she doesn't want it." Preach followed him in, slamming the door behind him. "Okay, we have half an hour. And I'm not sure I can kick all the stupid out of you in that time, but I'm gonna try."

"You want to kick me?" Mason's lips twitched.

"I want to punch the hell out of you, but I was speaking metaphorically." Preach pulled the curtains shut, casting a gloom over the living area. "You'd better sit down. Tell me why you're about to make the biggest goddamned mistake of your life."

Mason sat down hard on the sofa, because he didn't have the energy to fight with Preach. Not physically, anyway. He had a feeling he didn't have a choice about the other kind of fight.

"It's not a mistake if it's the right thing to do," he told Preach. His friend was sitting on the coffee table to give him some height advantage.

"Why is it the right thing to do?"

"I told you. I can't love her and she deserves love. Deserves better than I can give her."

"Isn't that something she gets to decide?" Preach asked him.

"No. Because her heart is too big. She'll try to accept me as I am. She'll trade her happiness for mine and I'm not letting her do that."

"Ah, you stupid mother fucker." Preach grimaced.

"What now?" Mason asked.

"You're not doing this to make things easier on her. You're doing it for you."

Mason frowned. "That's not true."

"Yeah, it is. You're afraid. Admit it. You're scared because for once in your life you've found something that you love. And don't give me that bullshit that you can't love, because I know you can. You love Ty and you love me. You just think that if you don't say it you won't get hurt."

"When did you become a psychoanalyst?" Mason asked him.

"I've been reading stuff. And stop changing the subject." Preach glared at him. "She's an amazing woman. And she can cook, dammit. Do you know how good her pie is?"

"Stop talking about her pie," Mason rasped. "You know I'll hurt her. I always do. You know I'm right to end this before I do."

"Okay." Preach threw up his hands. "So you end things. Then what?"

"Then Ty and I go back home and she gets back to normal here."

"You'll break her heart."

"Better to do it now than later." He was certain of that.

Preach laughed, but there was no joy in it. "She's a goddamned catch. She'll find somebody else. You get that, right?"

His throat felt tight. "That's what I want for her."

"Is it? You want her to be with another guy? You want her to smile at him the way she smiles at you? You want her to adore him and make him feel like he's the king of the world the same way she does to you?"

His fists curled tightly. "No." Just the thought of it made him want to hit something. Preferably a brick wall that would break his goddamned knuckles. Because he could deal with that kind of pain. He knew what to do with it. That it eventually went away.

But not the other kind. The emotional ones. The ones that broke your heart.

"So then you've got some thinking to do, my friend. And I don't mean the kind of thinking that you do in a police cell. Because we all want to flip the world upside down in those. I mean some deep, hard core what-the-fuck-do-I-want-out-of-life pondering. Before you make the biggest mistake you ever have." Preach stood, still looking pissed. "Do me one thing, okay?"

"What?"

"Don't talk to her until you know for absolutely fucking certain. I'm going to get Ty, and we're going to have some dinner, which you're cooking, by the way, and then you're going to think about things before you talk to her and mess up both of your lives."

"She'll expect to see me now."

"And I'll tell her you can't."

"But she'll know what I'm thinking. She's an intelligent woman. I shouldn't leave her hanging like this."

"Ordinarily, I'd agree with you," Preach told him. "But—"

The door opened and Ty was standing there, and behind him was Alaska. Preach let out a low groan. Then he shot Mason a warning stare.

"I'm sorry, I couldn't wait anymore," Ty said, walking into the room. "Are they going to take you away again?"

"No." Mason stood and Ty hugged him tight. "It's okay. It's all okay."

Over Ty's shoulder, he could see Alaska standing in the doorway. His heart clenched at how beautiful she looked in a soft cream sweater, her hair cascading over her shoulders in golden waves. Her eyes were like pools of blue.

"You're not wearing a coat," he told her, his heart heavy. "You'll freeze."

"I'm sorry, he insisted on coming over."

He wanted her in his arms. Wanted her smiling up at him from his bed. Wanted to touch her soft skin and let himself disappear into her for a while.

"Ty, can you and Preach go get some wood for the stove?" he said, not yet able to pull his eyes from hers.

"But we got some yest—ow! Okay, okay we'll go."

Mason turned to watch them walk out the backdoor. Preach looked at him and shook his head. Ignoring him, Mason grabbed his coat and passed it to Alaska. "Put this on. Let's talk outside."

Ignoring his outstretched hand she walked out and he followed, still holding the coat. "Will you put it on, please?" he asked. "Before you get pneumonia?"

"I'm fine." She looked at him, her chin jutting out. "I'm guessing this isn't going to take long."

Every part of him wanted to hold her. "Alaska, I..."

"Say it." She swallowed. "You can do that, can't you? Be honest with me?"

"I don't want to hurt you," he whispered.

"Why not?" she asked him, her jaw tight. "Because I'm too weak? Too fragile? Don't tell Alaska the truth because she might break in two?" She shook her head. "Come out with it, Mason. I'm a big girl."

He hated the way she was looking at him. Like he was a stranger. "I can't let you love me," he told her, his voice hoarse. "Not when I can't do it back."

She let out a ragged breath. Her teeth were starting to

chatter. "No, you can't. Because I deserve more. Do you know what I thought last night? That I could love you enough for the both of us. But that was wrong because I shouldn't have to do that." Her voice broke. "I just shouldn't."

No she shouldn't. "I'm sorry," he told her. "I should never have let this happen between us."

"I'm not sorry," she said, wrapping her arms around her body. "I'm not sorry at all. Because I now know what I want. A man who's strong enough to fight his fears. A man who doesn't bullshit me about not wanting to hurt me then throws everything back in my face. A man who doesn't lie to me that he's trying to protect me when really he's protecting himself."

"Alaska..." He reached for her despite himself.

"No. You don't get to touch me." She stepped back, her foot almost slipping on the wooden porch. "That tattoo on your arm? The one with the date you got out of foster care? Well you shouldn't have bothered. Because you're still captive. You never let yourself be free."

He opened his mouth but couldn't think of a damn word to say. Nothing that would make it better. Nothing that would make her smile. She whipped around, her body shivering, her hair dancing in the air from the movement. Then she walked down the steps, not looking back.

He was doing the right thing, even if it was killing him. She'd survive the way he would.

They both knew how to do that.

When he walked back into the cabin Preach was standing at the back door, his arms folded tightly across his barrel chest.

"You really are a stupid asshole."

Mason couldn't disagree.

30

She refused to let him see her cry, even though it felt like her world was shattering around her. She walked back to her house along the same path she and Ty had walked. Their footsteps were still molded into the snow. When she made them she still had hope.

And now she knew that there was none.

When she pulled the door open, Leo ran up to her excitedly, jumping around her legs. She was still dazed as she pulled off her boots, walking into the kitchen with Leo following her, and leaned on the kitchen counter, trying to work out what to do next.

He was free. And he didn't want her. That was the truth of it. He wasn't willing to fight for her. Everley had warned her and she hadn't wanted to listen.

Damn, it hurt. So much.

Her phone buzzed. She looked down at the message.

. . .

I hear Mr. Wonderful is free. So happy for you! I'd offer to come over to celebrate but I expect you'll be busy doing other things. ;) – Everley

She looked at her sister's words through dry, dry eyes. Why couldn't she cry? She wanted to let it all out. Wanted to howl, to shout, to scream.

But then he'll hear you.

The thought was like a cold blanket being thrown over her. She was going to have to live next door to him still. She'd have to see him every day, there was no avoiding him.

Unless he leaves town.

But he couldn't, could he? Not until Ty graduated. She started to shake. How was she going to deal with knowing he was so close yet didn't want to be with her?

Maybe she'd have to move. She could stay at the Inn, or at least she could after Christmas when they had some free rooms.

Leo nudged her leg. She reached down to ruffle his hair and he gave the lowest of growls. It was almost a purr. Satisfied and happy.

At least one of them was.

From her kitchen window she could see the cabin, but all she wanted to see was *him*. His smile, his soft eyes, the desire that took over him whenever they came close to each other.

And it felt like her heart was shattering all over again.

She couldn't stay here. Not when he was so close. She needed to get away. Scooping Leo into her arms, she saw something from the corner of her eye.

Mr. Bunny. She picked him up, too, the memories overwhelming her.

Mason realizing she'd been under the cabin all night as a

child. Him not stopping until he'd found the blanket and discovered the truth.

His face when the cops had shown up and he knew he was being arrested.

She inhaled raggedly. All she wanted was to feel his arms around her. But he'd made it clear he didn't want that.

Didn't want her.

And she was too proud to beg.

But if she stayed here, the temptation would be too big.

"Come on, Leo," she whispered. "Let's go to the Inn." She could work her way through the heartache. Pretend that she'd never met Mason, that he'd never made her feel like she was the strongest woman alive.

Because right now she felt weak and she hated it.

"You promised me," Ty shouted. "You promised me you wouldn't hurt her."

Mason pinched the bridge of his nose. He had the worst goddamned headache. "That's what I'm trying to do," he said, wincing at the pain. "I don't want to hurt her anymore and I will if I don't break it off. She deserves better than that."

"She sure does." Ty shook his head. "Preach is right, you're an asshole."

"Yep." Mason nodded. "I am."

Ty stared at him for a moment. "So that's it? You're not going to fight for her? You're just letting her walk away?"

How the hell was he supposed to explain this to a teenager? Everything was so black and white for Ty. He hadn't lived for long enough to see the thousand shades of gray that life threw at you.

"I'm doing what's right for Alaska," Mason told him. "Simple as that."

"She loves you. She shouted it at you. Didn't you hear that?"

Mason winced at the memory. "Yeah, I heard it. And did you hear me? She shouldn't love me. Not when I can't love her back."

"Why can't you love her?" Ty demanded. "Why? She deserves love. She's fucking fabulous. I've never met anybody as kind as she is." Ty rubbed his face with the heels of his hands. "What about me? Do I not get to talk to her either? Do I have to quit my job?"

"Of course not. You can still work for her. If you want to." The thought of it made Mason's stomach feel tight. "Or we could think about going back to Baltimore," he said.

"What?" Ty blinked. "Why would you say that?"

Because he wasn't sure he could live next to her without wanting to touch her. "Because things have improved. Your school might take you back. You always said you wanted to go back."

"You really are an idiot. You dragged me here against my will, then as soon as I make some friends you want me to leave again? Jesus, Mason. You're a bigger asshole than I thought."

"Watch your language."

"Yeah, well you watch yours." Ty shook his head. "I'm going to my room."

Mason reached for his arm. "It'll be all right, I promise," he said, his voice cracking. "Alaska will understand. And you will, too. I'm doing the right thing."

"Sure." Ty shrugged him off. "Lie to yourself all you want, but don't bother lying to me." He stomped across the cabin, yanking his bedroom door open. A moment later, he slammed it closed behind him.

"Happy now?" Preach asked. He was standing in the kitchen, his thick arms crossed over his chest.

"Yeah. Ecstatic," Mason said, shaking his head. Preach raised an eyebrow and walked over to Ty's bedroom, disappearing inside as Mason stood like a statue on the spot.

It was for the best. That's all that mattered.

They'd come around to it. They'd have to.

Alaska walked into the Inn as the carolers started singing around the tree. Sweet voices filled the air, echoing through the lofty, spacious entranceway. People were smiling, children were giddy. A reminder that Christmas was only three days away. Leo was in her arms and she let him down and he excitedly yapped around her feet.

She took a deep breath and walked over to the reception. Martin looked up. "I thought you weren't working tonight."

"Change of plans." Alaska attempted a smile, though she feared it came out as a grimace. "You can go home if you like."

"But we swapped," he protested.

"I know. I'll still cover your other shift. I need something to do."

Martin looked at her carefully. "Is everything okay?"

She swallowed. "Everything's fine. I just need to be busy."

"Is it something to do with what happened at the police station this morning? I heard you were there. Your parents, too. And some guy who looked like he could barrel his way through the walls."

"No," Alaska said, her voice thin. "Nothing to do with that."

"He got out, though? Your neighbor?" Martin smiled. "I assumed that's why you wanted the day off. Figured you'd all be celebrating or something."

Her lip wobbled. She wasn't sure how much longer she

could keep it together. It was a bad idea coming here when people were all so happy and celebrating. But what else was she going to do? Sit in her house knowing he was next door?

No, she couldn't do that. It hurt too much.

He didn't love her. That was the truth. No matter how much she loved him she'd never get it back. She'd thought she knew what heartbreak was.

Turned out she was wrong. She never realized it would feel like a jagged knife stabbing at your chest. Like you couldn't breathe for hours even though your body was desperate for oxygen.

And the worst bit of all were the memories. Every time one flashed in her head it felt like the most painful of explosions. She could see him smiling. At her. In a way he'd never smile again.

She blinked back the tears she hadn't known were forming. Through the shimmery haze of her vision she could see Martin starting to panic.

"Are you okay? Should I call somebody?"

The tears started to fall. And the singing was still going on.

She'd never felt more alone in her life.

"I need..." she gasped, because the pain was visceral. "I should be alone." Without waiting for Martin's reply, she ran into the manager's office, Leo on her heels. Closing the door and collapsing onto her chair.

The tears were pouring down her face now. Even in here she could still hear the singing. "Away In a Manger". A song she'd always loved.

She wanted everything to disappear.

With a ragged breath she pulled open her drawer, ruffling around until she found a pack of tissues. She pulled one from the pack and tried to stem the tears but they kept falling.

And she kept hurting.

She cried through three more songs. When the third – 'Silent Night" – started she felt the smallest sense of relief. This would be the last one. Then the singers would disperse and the guests would either go for dinner or to the theater.

And she'd get some blessed peace.

And then what? She let out a ragged breath, because she had no idea what to do next. All she knew was that she couldn't go home.

Couldn't drive past his cabin knowing he was there.

Couldn't take Leo out and risk seeing him standing on his porch drinking his morning coffee. She loved that house, dammit, and now she didn't want to be there.

They'd have to stay here tonight even though they were completely booked. She'd grab some linens from housekeeping and sleep on the sofa in the corner. Leo could curl up in his bed that she always kept in this room.

Just as she was figuring out how to get some clean clothes for the morning, the door to the office opened. "Alaska?" Her cousin Gabe was framed by the doorway. "Martin called Holly. Said you were upset."

"I'm fine." She wiped away the tears. She didn't want to ruin anybody's holiday. "Just feeling sorry for myself."

"Can we come in?"

"Who's we?"

He stepped inside and she could see Nicole behind him, along with her cousins, North and Holly, and Holly's husband, Josh. And just as she thought that was it, Dylan followed, too, giving her a huge hug.

And suddenly the room was teeming with people.

Leo gave an excited bark and ran around all their legs, while Gabe walked over to her to give her a hug.

"Look at you, sweetheart," he crooned gently. "You're not supposed to cry this close to Christmas. Who do I need to hit?"

"Nobody. I'm fine. Just..." she took a deep breath. "Women's problems."

He jumped back, alarmed.

"She's lying," Holly said. "We're in sync, it was last week."

Alaska sent her an annoyed look. *Traitor*. Holly grimaced, sending her an apologetic look.

"So what is it?" North's jaw was tight. "Who made you cry?"

She couldn't tell them. It was too embarrassing. She'd thrown herself at a man who didn't want her. She could see it now.

She was the one who kissed him first. She'd pretty much thrown herself at him the first time they met. She'd mistaken his kindness for love. Their hook ups for a relationship. And she couldn't tell her cousins because they'd know how damn naïve she was.

"I don't want to talk about it," she told them.

"Yeah, well I can take a pretty good guess," North muttered. "I knew he was trouble. I knew it." He glanced at Gabe. "You wanna do something about this?"

"Hell yeah."

"No," Alaska told them. "You're not doing anything."

They looked surprised at her vehemence.

"I'm serious. This is my problem. I'll sort it out when I'm ready. Not you, not Holly, not Everley. I'm a big girl and I can work this out for myself."

"You sure?" North asked, sounding disappointed.

"Completely." The tears had stopped. She wiped away the last of them with the back of her hand. "I'll be angry if any of you interfere."

Nicole was grinning at her. "Way to go."

North sighed. "Okay then. But if you change your mind..."

"I'll hit him myself."

Holly sniggered, then tried to straighten her face when

North sent her a glare. "Well I guess there's only one thing to do," she said, giving Alaska a wink. "I'm going to get us all a round of drinks."

"You ready, Ty?" Preach hollered, walking out of the bathroom and grabbing his coat.

"Yep." Ty wandered out of his bedroom. "Let's go."

Mason looked at him, frowning. "Where are you going?"

"Into town to get some dinner."

Mason shook his head. "I'm not hungry."

"That's good because you're not invited." Preach lifted a brow. "Only non-idiots are allowed at our table."

"You'd only get punched anyway," Ty said, as though that was some consolation. "Alaska's cousins have probably found out by now. They'll be wanting your blood."

"They can have it."

Preach said something that Mason couldn't really hear. Whatever. His head was too full of thoughts anyway. He'd be better off alone. Maybe he could go chop some more wood. Anything to stop thinking about *her*.

It was only when he heard the engine start up that he realized Preach was taking his car.

Of course he was. Preach didn't have one. He grabbed his phone and tapped out a message.

Bring my car back you asshole. You're not insured. – Mason

I'll bring it back when you pull your head out of your ass. Which I'm guessing is never. – Preach

. . .

Fuck you. – Mason

Fuck you right back. By the way, Alaska left something for you outside the door. Not that you deserve anything. – Preach

Mason swallowed. She'd left him something? His gut twisted. He'd seen her car drive off a couple of hours ago. Hell, he'd spent most of the afternoon staring out of the window at her house.

But he couldn't bring himself to look. Preach was right. He didn't deserve anything.

Dear God, had she left him a Christmas gift? The thought made him want to hurl.

He managed to stop himself from going to the porch for eleven minutes and fifty-five seconds by a sheer force of will. But then he couldn't fight it anymore. His shitty need for some kind of connection with her overrode his good senses.

So he opened the front door, and there it was. The one thing she had to know would kill him.

Mr. Bunny. Still as dirty as when he found it. Sitting on the wooden porch with a piece of paper underneath it, words written neatly across it in blank ink.

I think you need her more than I ever did. – A

. . .

He lifted it up and stared at the grubby, stained fabric. The bunny's ear flopped down, its eyes staring glassily up at him like he held all the answers.

And all he could think about was Alaska. The way she'd carried this rabbit all the way from the Inn at the age of eight and had crawled under the cabin. She was so damn brave. He couldn't even imagine doing something like that at the age of eight.

Sure, he'd dreamed about running away from foster care. But they always found you. He'd seen enough kids brought back to the home to know that.

He let out a slow breath, wondering what that kid would think of him now. He was free, the tattoo on his arm was enough to tell him that.

And yet he was still a prisoner. The thought made him blink. He was a prisoner because he was afraid. Afraid of being honest about his feelings. Afraid of losing the things that meant the most to him.

Afraid of love.

His chest was so tight it was hard to breathe. But the truth of it couldn't be ignored.

Preach's words reverberated around his head.

"You're scared because for once in your life you've found something that you love."

The thought of the word made his heart race. He couldn't love. He couldn't.

He wasn't capable of it.

So why did this hurt so fucking much?

Because you love her.

He blinked. Is this what love was? This overwhelming ache that made you feel like you couldn't breathe? He closed his eyes, seeing her face behind his lids.

Her smile. Her softness. Her everything.

He tried to breathe again but it was almost impossible.

And the fucking bunny was still staring up at him.

He was angry, he was lonely, he was goddamned devastated. But the strongest of them all was the anger. He was furious at himself. For not being the man he wanted to be.

The man she needed.

The one who could tell her he loved her.

He threw the rabbit to the porch, not acknowledging the tears falling down his face, and walked to the nearest tree, punching it as hard as he could. The pain felt good.

But not good enough.

It didn't wipe out the thoughts of her or the ache that tugged at him. It didn't wipe out the emotions he had no idea how to deal with.

It was a temporary fix. Fleeting, really.

A distraction from the fact that he'd caused this all himself.

He'd hurt her and she'd left him a stuffed toy. She couldn't help herself. That was who she was. She tried to make people feel better.

And he adored her for that.

No, fuck it. He loved her.

He loved her, he loved her, *he loved her*.

He opened his mouth to shout the words out, but still they got stuck. He was that kid again. The one without a mom, a dad, or even shoes for his feet.

The one who knew that love meant weakness because it always got you hurt.

And yeah, it did, when you tried to fight it. But it also made you feel alive in a way you'd never felt before. His love for Alaska was like a light in his life, illuminating those dark shadows he never thought he'd get rid of.

But they'd gotten rid of their dark shadows together.

And then he'd pushed her away. Because he couldn't say three damn words. Preach was right, he was an asshole.

He hadn't done it for her own good, he'd done it for his. Because he hated feeling weak. Out of control.

But maybe he needed that. Because God knew he needed her.

More than he'd needed anything in his life.

And maybe she didn't need him. Maybe she shouldn't. Maybe she was realizing right now what a lucky escape she'd had.

But either way he needed to tell her. She was loved. By him.

He tried it again. "I... fuck." He took a deep breath. "I adore you." No, that wasn't good enough.

Those weren't the right words. She deserved more.

He'd force them out, even if it killed him.

He'd wait until she came back. And then he'd tell her. He'd practice until his voice was hoarse.

But what if she's not coming back?

Shit. He grabbed his phone from his pocket, his fingers icy cold.

I need my car back. – Mason

Fuck off. And I'm turning my phone off now. – Preach

Asshole. He knew his friend. He and Ty would be out for hours. And he couldn't wait that long. He stomped back into the house and grabbed his coat and hat, shoving his hands into the gloves he didn't normally wear.

It was a long way to Winterville. It was dark and it was cold.

But it didn't matter. Nothing did. Except her.

31

Alaska was feeling a little drunk. Okay a *lot* drunk.

It was all her cousins' faults. What kind of family uses a breakup as an excuse for an impromptu cocktail session? And yes, they hadn't forced her to drink them, but she figured that if she drank they would too, then there was no chance of North or Gabe deciding it would be a real good idea to mess with Mason at his cabin.

Something licked at her face. It took her a moment to realize it was Leo. And that she was actually laying on the sofa in her office. She blinked, sitting up and looking around.

Where had everybody gone? And then she remembered that Everley had come by after her show and insisted on driving everybody home.

"And then I'll come get you," she'd told Alaska. "You're sleeping at ours."

"No. Mom and Dad are there."

"I'll throw them out." Everley had shrugged.

"Noooo." Alaska's eyes had widened. "Let me sleep it off here."

Everley had eventually acquiesced, leaving Leo because

she didn't want her sister to be alone. "But if you need me you call me."

Alaska had agreed but she knew she wouldn't. She wanted to be alone. Something that was turning out to be real difficult when you lived in a town full of family and friends.

What time was it anyway? It felt like the middle of the night. She looked at her wrist for her watch and saw it was missing.

It took her two minutes to realize she was looking at the wrong wrist.

Okay then. She had to squint and tilt her head to the side but eventually she worked out it was just past ten o'clock. They'd started early. That was the problem. Nobody should drink cocktails before six.

Or before sick. She giggled. Ugh, she really was a little drunkie. She should close her eyes and sleep it off some more. Yes, that was nice... wait...

Ouch! What the heck was that crashing noise in her brain? She squeezed her eyes closed tighter but it wouldn't stop.

"Alaska?"

Was she hearing voices now?

"Alaska?" More banging.

Okay, that didn't sound like the voices in her head. She finally opened her eyes. "Who is it?"

"It's Martin." Oh thank goodness he didn't go home after all. She'd forgotten she'd told him he could go home and she was supposed to be manning reception. "There's somebody here to see you."

"If it's my parents tell them to take a hike." Everley had promised they wouldn't be allowed near the Inn. Ugh, shouting really hurt her head.

"Um, it's not your parents." There was a low voice, followed by Martin's. And then the door opened and a big hulk of a body filled the entranceway, haloed by the light from the lobby.

Mason Parker. In a coat that was wet and covered in snowflakes. Leo gave a yelp and ran to him, yapping around his legs. So much for doggy loyalty.

"What are you doing here?" she asked, really trying to not slur her words.

"I needed to see you." He frowned and she realized she was still splayed out on the sofa bed that she hadn't turned into a bed. She hadn't gotten any linens on it either.

"Here I am. In all my glory. You can go now."

"I'll leave you to it," Martin said, hastily walking away.

"Can you turn off the light?" she asked. "It hurts."

"It's the Inn's main lights. I think the guests might complain," Mason told her, closing the door to block them out.

"Ugh." She rolled over so she was facing away from him. She heard a shuffle and peered back over her shoulder. He'd taken his coat off and hung it on the rack right next to hers. "Put that coat back on. You're not staying."

"Have you been drinking?" he asked, sounding concerned. She didn't like it when he used that soft voice. It made her want all the things she couldn't have.

"What do you care?"

"I care, sweetheart."

"No, you don't." She shook her head then grimaced because that was such a bad idea. "Go away. I don't need you. I don't need anybody."

He was quiet for a minute. She stared at the back of the sofa, refusing to look at him.

Okay, she needed to look. And when she did, she saw he'd taken a bottle of water out of the refrigerator next to her desk and was pouring some into a glass.

"Try to drink all this." He held it out to her.

"I don't want to."

"You need to. Drink this, take a Tylenol, then sleep it off, okay?" Still with that soft voice. It sent a shiver down her aching spine.

"Alaska? Baby?"

"You can't call me that anymore."

"I won't. Please just drink and take some medicine. I promise I'll let you sleep after that."

Finally she let him hold her head, his palms warm as she sipped at the deliciously cool water. Then he popped two Tylenol – he must have gotten them from her emergency drawer – and fed them into her mouth. She swallowed without complaining.

"Good girl."

She hated that she liked that.

"You can go now," she told him.

"Sure. Now go to sleep, okay?"

"Mmm." She closed her eyes again. That felt nice. Was he stroking her hair? That felt nice, too. Wasn't he supposed to be leaving? She opened her mouth to remind him, but sleep over took her before she could. Beautiful, welcome sleep.

When she woke up next it was four in the morning according to her watch. The room was dark but she could hear something.

Soft breathing. And it wasn't hers.

It took her eyes a moment to acclimatize before she realized Mason was laying on the floor next to her, still in his clothes and boots, his coat rolled into a makeshift pillow beneath his head. Leo was curled up next to him, his head nestled against Mason's chest.

Dammit, she didn't need to see that. It made everything hurt all over again.

Mason watched her as she slept. He'd sat up to make sure she was okay, having woken just after five, his neck aching from a bad angle on the ground. She was snoring a little, not too much but it was cute as hell.

How could he ever have believed that he could have lived without her? He needed her. And he hoped she needed him. Not in a weak way, never that. But because together they were stronger.

They always had been. From the moment they met when they were kids.

Her lips started to move. She was dreaming about something, but he had no idea what. Something good, he hoped, because she deserved only good things.

And he wanted to be the man to give them to her.

Part of him knew he wasn't good enough. But there was another part – getting stronger every minute – that told him maybe he could be. If he tried hard and didn't give up. If he learned to show the love she deserved.

Because he felt it. So damn much.

His phone screen flashed on. The volume was muted but he could see Preach was trying to call him. "Yup?" he said softly, accepting the call. He stood and walked across the office, not wanting to wake her.

"You didn't come home. Just checking that you're not doing anything stupid." Preach sounded groggy.

"What are you doing up so early?" Mason asked him.

"Had some business to do. Online."

Fair enough. Mason knew better than to ask him what type of business. "I'm at the Inn. With Alaska."

There was silence for a moment. Then Preach let out a long sigh. "You guys talked things through?"

"Not yet. She was drunk. I stayed with her to make sure she was okay."

"But you're gonna talk, right?"

"Yeah." Mason's stomach clenched. "But I don't know that she'll listen." Not that it would stop him. He loved this woman without a doubt. Wanted to spend the rest of his life showing her.

And telling her. If only he could.

"So what are you going to do?" Preach asked him. "How you gonna make her listen?"

He had no idea. That was the problem. He needed to do something big. Something that told her he'd been a goddamned idiot but he wouldn't be again.

Something that showed her how much he loved her, even if he couldn't say it. Because she needed to know, then she could decide what to do about it.

"I'm still thinking about that."

"Well you'd better think quick," Preach said. "It's nearly morning."

He knew that. And he knew that when she woke up she'd still want him to leave. That was understandable. He hadn't given her a chance. Hadn't been honest with her.

Damn, he'd lied that he was doing this to protect her when he was trying to protect himself.

"I will," he told Preach. "I'd better go and figure it out."

"You do that. I'll be in town later in the morning. I'll come see you then."

"Okay." He nodded, even though his friend couldn't see him. "Thanks, Preach. I appreciate it."

"Just do the right thing."

"I'm planning on it," Mason said.

"Good. Because if you mess up again I'm gonna beat your ass."

For the first time Mason smiled. "Like to see you try."

"I might be smaller than you, but I'm mightier. Now get out of here and win your woman back." Preach let out a long yawn. "I love you, man."

"Yeah."

"We're gonna have to work on that, too," Preach told him. "Now do whatever it takes to win that goddess back."

"What exactly are you doing?" Preach asked Mason later that morning as he walked into the Inn. Mason was next to the tree, trying to make everything perfect. Alaska was still asleep but when she woke up he needed to do this.

For her.

Even if it was the most embarrassing moment of his life.

"What you said I should do. I'm fighting for my woman." Mason stood and tapped the microphone. The three dull thuds echoed through the lobby speakers. A new receptionist had arrived, replacing Martin, but she didn't look at all perturbed by the big man with three days of beard growth setting up a singing booth next to the Winterville Inn's thirty foot Christmas tree.

"And how exactly are you doing that?" Preach asked, shifting his feet. "You're not going to do any more stupid things, are you?"

"Nope. This is the least stupid thing I've ever done." He glanced at Preach. "Where's Ty?"

"Well, I tried to make him go to school but he reminded me that school's out for break." Preach shrugged. "So I dropped him off at the Cold Fingers Café. Dolores was making him a hot chocolate before he was even through the door."

"Thank you for taking care of him." Mason's voice was gruff.

"You're welcome. Did you get a chance to talk things through with Alaska yet?" Preach asked him.

"Nope. She's still asleep."

"So you're gonna talk to her through a microphone?" Preach frowned.

"Nope. Not talk. Sing. I'm gonna sing."

"Oh shiiiit." Preach let the vowel sound slide for a long moment off his tongue. "You can't sing, man."

"I know. But I don't know how else to do this. I need to show her that I care."

"You're fucking crazy."

Yeah, he was. Crazy about her. And when she woke up she'd know how much.

"Can you shut up and help? When the door to her office opens, I want you to press that button on the PA. Just that button. Nothing else. Got it?"

"I think I can press a button," Preach said, rolling his eyes.

"That's good. Because I think she's coming."

The door to the office opened and Alaska tumbled outside. Her face looked healthier than last night, but her clothes were crumpled and her hair looked like she'd put her finger in an electric socket.

It suited her.

"Okay, go," he told Preach.

"Your funeral, man."

The music started. Alaska stopped in the doorway and he saw that she had all the sheets of paper in her hand that he'd left for her. He'd spent half the night writing all over them.

I love you.

I love you.

I love you.

He'd written about a hundred of them. Littered her office with them. Leo had ripped some of them up but that was okay. She'd get the message.

He could write it okay, that was easy. But he needed to do more and this was the first step.

The music started. Preach's eyes widened so big you could fit a dinner plate in there.

"Whitney Houston?" he whispered loudly. "Seriously."

"Shut up," Mason told him as the first bars of "I Will Always Love You" filled the huge room.

Alaska looked over at Mason, confusion in her eyes. His heart was hammering against his chest.

This was so stupid, but he didn't know another way. And he had to tell her. Not just in writing. It had to come out of his mouth. So here he was, about to sing like Whitney in *Bodyguard*.

And somehow he managed to get through the first verse. Mostly because it meant nothing to him. He wasn't going away. He was staying. He wasn't going anywhere that she wasn't.

But then the bridge came and he knew. It was time to say it. Or sing it. Alaska still hadn't moved from the office door.

Then it was here. The chorus. He would always love her. He was pretty much murdering the song, but she didn't look like she noticed. She was staring at him, her brows crunched, her lips tight.

His throat tightened, his breath caught, and for a moment he wasn't sure he could do it.

But he had to. For her. For him. For the life he wanted to have.

So he sang it loudly. He'd always love her. Because every word of it was true.

It was only when he was on the second verse – which frankly he sang even worse than the first, that he realized he'd attracted a crowd.

"The entertainment standards have gone down this year," one of the guests whispered to another.

"What happened to the good singers?"

"You want a punch in the nose?" That was Preach. Mason

wasn't sure whether to laugh or cry. So he sang, noticing that half of Alaska's family had walked into the lobby right as he was asking her not to cry.

It was futile because tears were pouring down her face. He wanted to kiss each one of them away.

Then another group of people walked in. Ty and his friends. He had his hand wrapped around Eloise's waist. Ty grimaced as Mason continued to sing but the girl was smiling widely, elbowing him as Mason got to the next chorus.

It was easier this time. He belted it out. Put her name at the end because he needed everybody to know it was about her. He loved her. He'd always loved her. He always would love her.

And then he got to the end. The music stopped and there was silence in the room.

"Should we clap?" somebody whispered.

"Probably not. Don't want to encourage him." That was Preach again. Mason sent him a death stare. Preach shrugged and pulled the PA system plug out for good measure.

Sliding the microphone back into the stand, Mason walked to where Alaska was, in the doorway to the office that frankly smelled like it was a speakeasy.

She wiped her tears with the back of her hand.

"I don't want to make you cry," he told her. "Not ever."

"These are good tears, stupid." She looked around, as though she'd only just realized they'd attracted a crowd. "Come in here," she told him, grabbing his hand. Then she looked at the morning receptionist. "Can you get everybody out of the lobby?" she asked. "Give them all a free eggnog or something?"

"It's eight in the morning," the receptionist said, frowning.

"Ah, it's Christmas. They'll love it," Alaska said, tugging him into the office. He closed the door behind them, but they could still hear the loud rumble of conversations behind it.

"You're crazy," she told him. "And you can't carry a tune."

"I know. But I can sing those words," he said. "I know they're not enough. And I know I have no right to ask this. But take me back, Alaska. Let me prove to you how much I care. I'm not going to rest until I say them to you. Not sing, not write, but say them."

"You don't have to say them," she said softly. "You have to show it. By not pushing me away when you're scared. You hurt me."

He winced. "I'm so sorry. I hate that I hurt you. I won't do it again." He swallowed. "And if you can't forgive me, I understand. But I'll still be here, caring, watching over you. But I'll let you be free if you don't want me anymore."

She was blinking back tears again. This time he wiped them for her with his thumbs. Her breath hitched at his touch.

He felt the thinnest sliver of hope lighting up in him.

"You didn't trust me with your feelings," Alaska told him. "That stings."

"I didn't trust myself. I've always trusted you. There's nobody I trust more." It was the truth. "You're the strongest, kindest, most reliable person I know. And I hate that I pushed you away. I'm not going to do it again. Please forgive me. I care, baby. I care so much."

Did she know what he was saying, or at least what he was trying to say? He grabbed one of the pieces of paper he'd written on. "These words? They're true. Every single one of them. I know I can't say it yet, but I will. I promise." His eyes met hers. "If you still want that."

She slammed her hand against his chest, sniffing loudly. "Of course I want you, you idiot. Don't start with that crap again."

He laughed because it was so good to hear. "I'm not starting with anything but you."

"Well you can start by driving me home. I smell and I'm supposed to work today," she told him.

"Yeah, about that. Preach has kind of stolen my car and knowing him, he won't be waiting for me when we leave this office."

"Stolen it?"

"Commandeered. Taken it away. Whatever."

She frowned. "So how did you get here last night?"

"I walked."

Alaska blinked. "From your cabin to Winterville? That's crazy. It's the middle of winter."

"I figured if you could do it as a little kid I can do it as a grown up. And I needed to see you." He shrugged.

Her deep blue eyes caught his. "Careful," she told him. "I'm beginning to believe you love me."

"I do, Alaska. I do."

It was late Christmas Eve when he finally managed to say it. He'd been practicing in the mirror, glaring at his reflection until he could form the words without a lump the size of Hawaii forming in his throat.

He was planning to tell her in a few hours time on Christmas morning. It'd have to be early, because they were all expected at the Inn at first light. All the Winter cousins and their partners worked at the Inn on Christmas Day to give the staff a chance to spend time with their families.

He and Ty had offered to help, too.

And so had Preach. Who hadn't yet shown any signs of wanting to go back home. He'd told Mason that somebody needed to protect Ty from the constant displays of affection he was having to witness.

"And this way you get to bone the love of your life in her house without any of us having to wash our brains with bleach."

Yeah, there was that.

Speaking of which, he slid his hand along Alaska's bare thigh. She turned onto her side, naked, and gave him a slow, sexy smile.

"Again?" she whispered, her eyelashes sweeping down as she blinked.

"I need you." He always did. Couldn't get enough of her.

"It's mutual," she breathed as he kissed her slowly and thoroughly. Her body melted into his, soft against hard, and he knew this was his forever.

And when he slid inside of her, he felt it from the tips of his toes to the crown of his head. His desire for this woman. His need for her.

His love.

He twisted onto his back, bringing her with him because he loved to look at her. Loved to watch as she abandoned herself to pleasure, her back arching as she called out his name. And as she exploded around him, dragging him with her into oblivion he called out her name as he spilled inside her.

She crumpled into him, breathless, her hair stuck to her face. He brushed it out of the way and kissed her softly, still surging within her.

"Oh my God, Mason," she gasped, her body boneless in his arms. "I think you killed me."

"I think you're beautiful," he told her. "I love you so much."

Those words. Those painful, heartbreaking words. They'd escaped before he even thought them through.

Her eyes caught his and she started to laugh.

"You just..."

"I did." He laughed to. "Jesus, I did."

He pulled out of her, lifting her over him. "I was supposed to tell you tomorrow. When we were dressed and shit."

She covered her mouth, still laughing. "What if people ask where we were when you first told me you loved me?"

"We'll tell them." He winked. "No shame in that." He felt lighter than he'd ever been. So in love with this woman that he could move mountains.

And he'd do it. For her. Because she deserved the very best.

He glanced at his clock. It had just turned midnight. It was Christmas and the woman he loved was in his arms.

His chest contracted because he had everything he needed right here.

"Merry Christmas, sweetheart."

She blinked. "Is it Christmas?"

"Yep. Just past midnight."

"Our first together," she said softly.

"The first of many. By the way I love you," he had to say those words again, because now that he'd said them once he never wanted to stop. She gave him the biggest, brightest smile.

"That's good. I love you too. And now you can say them out loud promise you'll never sing to me again."

EPILOGUE

Six Months Later...

She was crying and she didn't care, because Ty was walking across the stage wearing his cap and gown, shaking the principal's hand as she passed him his diploma. He took his scroll from her, then turned to look at the audience of parents and friends sitting on the bleachers in the school field, and grinned when he saw them all sitting there.

Mason's jaw was tight as he clapped, his eyes suspiciously glassy. As though he realized she was staring at him, he looked over and his gaze softened. He leaned in closer and wiped away her tears with his thumbs.

A loud sob came from her right. Preach grabbed a handkerchief from his pocket and blew noisily into it.

"Hay fever," he muttered. "Bad at this time of year."

She nodded. "It sure is."

Her cousins were sitting in the row in front, hooting and hollering as Ty left the stage. His cheeks were pink, but he looked pleased as punch, especially when Eloise ran up to him and threw her arms around him.

"So that's it," she whispered to Mason when the final diploma had been handed out. "You did it. You got him through high school."

"He got himself through high school," Mason said. "He did all the work."

Ty's mom was sitting next to Mason. She'd arrived right before the ceremony and Alaska only had time to say hello, but she knew Ty would be delighted to see her. They spoke regularly, and Ty had calmed down toward her.

They all agreed that leaving Baltimore was the best thing he and Mason ever did.

In the fall, Ty would be going to Fairmont State University and Eloise was going to WVU. She didn't know if they'd stay together for the long term, but right now they looked happy.

Mason slid his hand into hers and she squeezed it tightly. "Did you ask Ty's mom to join us at the Inn?" she whispered to him. That was where they were holding Ty's graduation party. Just for family at first, then in the evening all his friends would join them and they'd dance into the night.

Mason nodded. "She'll come for the meal, then she needs to head back."

"Hopefully I'll get to talk to her some." She wanted to make Ty's mom feel welcome because she knew it meant a lot to him. And she loved him to bits.

She'd only spoken to her own parents a couple of times since Christmas. They'd come to see her and Mason before they went back to Florida and apologized again for her dad's actions, but everything was too raw and they'd just nodded. Then a few weeks ago her mom had called to talk and they'd spent an hour on the phone.

They were baby steps, but she was okay with that. She'd

never be close with her parents, but she didn't want to hate them either. Her life was too good to have any bad emotions in it.

While Ty stood around talking to his friends, Mason walked her back to her car. She'd head to the Inn to make sure everything was ready, while Mason was going to let Ty drive him, Preach, and Ty's mom back there once he'd finished here at the school.

Ty bought the car on his eighteenth birthday last month. She and Mason had chipped in because they didn't want him buying something unreliable.

"We want you to come back and visit us for weekends sometimes," she'd told Ty. "So you'll need something reliable." And he'd protested a little but not a lot. And he sure did love his Toyota.

Preach had christened it The Love Machine. Mason didn't think that was funny.

She did though. And she loved Preach, too. He was spending more and more time here. She'd even noticed him talking to Marie, the cop, the last time they were all at the Winterville Tavern.

She hadn't mentioned it to Mason yet, but there was a twinkle in Preach's eye whenever she was around. Opposites definitely attracted there.

They reached her car and Mason looked around, before turning to cup her cheeks and kissing her hard and hot. She felt it right down to the tips of her toes, her cheeks heating up at the sudden response of her body.

They still couldn't get enough of each other. And sometimes it was difficult because Mason was still living at the cabin with Ty, although he spent a lot of time at her place. And Ty spent a lot of time with Eloise.

But once Ty started college, Mason was moving into her house full time while he knocked the cabin down and rebuilt it as a ranch house. He owned the land and had the zoning permit. He just needed to start it, because her house wasn't big enough for the three of them and they always wanted Ty to have a room to come home to.

And maybe one day they'd want children of their own.

"Stop looking at me like that," Mason whispered, a grin playing at his lips.

"Like what?"

"Like I should take you home and throw you on my bed and show you what I like eating best for breakfast."

She laughed. "Can you read minds now?"

"Only yours." He brushed the hair from her face. "Yours is the only one I want to read."

She tried to rearrange her expression. "What am I thinking now?" she asked him.

"You're thinking, 'try not to think about sex,'" he told her, grinning.

Her mouth dropped open. "How the hell did you know?"

"Because I've been trying not to think about it all morning. Which is a challenge when you're wearing that dress." He glanced down at the white and yellow striped cotton, his eyes darkening as he followed the lines of her curves. "Maybe I should just take you home."

"Any other time and I'd take you up on that," she told him, kissing his cheek. "But this is Ty's day."

"Thank God he's staying at the Inn tonight." That had been their gift to him. He and his friends had rooms so they didn't have to rush home. And yes, she'd made sure Mason had the safe sex conversation again, even though Ty was sharing with his guy friends.

"Yeah," he murmured, kissing her jaw softly. "Now go before I change my mind."

She started laughing again. "I'll see you at the Inn."

"You will." He opened her door for her. "And Alaska?"

She looked up at him. "Yes?"

"Thank you for everything. I mean it. Ty's day is amazing because of you."

"It's because of him. And you. That's why I'm doing this. That's why we're all here," she told him. Her cousins had welcomed Mason and Ty into the family on Christmas Day. They all knew how much they meant to her. Even North had slapped Mason on the back and given him kudos for singing in front of the guests at the Inn.

Holly and Josh had both asked him to come work for the family business, too. They'd expanded significantly with the building of the ski resort next to Winterville, and were looking at taking on a legal advisor full time.

Alaska didn't care what he did. She was glad he wanted to stay here. Because if he'd wanted to go back to Baltimore she'd have gone with him.

But she'd miss her family. And she was glad she hadn't had to choose.

"I love you, Alaska," Mason told her, kissing her cheek as he helped her into the car. "So damn much."

She smiled because it came so easy now, but she knew how hard those words once were. "I love you, too." And wasn't that the best thing in the world? To love and be loved.

She definitely thought it was.

Alaska had once asked Mason if he'd go through everything he'd been through all over again if it meant they ended up together.

And he'd said yes. Without a pause and without a doubt. Because every step he'd taken on every difficult road ahead of him had led him to her.

And he never wanted that to change.

"Beer?" North asked, passing him a bottle. From the corner, all the Winter women squealed loudly. Mason took the bottle, thanking North, and watched as North's business partner extended her left hand and showed them the sparkling ring on her finger.

"When did Amber get engaged?" Mason asked, glancing at North. He didn't know Amber very well, but from what Alaska had told him she and North had been best friends for years.

North took a mouthful of beer. "Happened yesterday."

"That's nice," Mason murmured.

"Yeah," North muttered. "Real nice."

Alaska turned to look at them again, and Mason widened his eyes at her. She pressed her lips together and then kissed Amber's cheek before wandering over to where he and North were standing.

"Hey," she said to North. "Isn't Amber's ring pretty?"

"Yep." He nodded. "Sure is." He took another mouthful of beer. "I'm going to drink this and head home."

"You sure?" She frowned. "The party just started."

He shrugged. "I got something to do there. I'll catch you both later."

When he'd left, Alaska turned to Mason. "Did he say something to you?"

"No. Just told me she got engaged yesterday."

"Yeah." Alaska nodded. "She's so happy. If he ruins her vibe I'm gonna kill him."

"Maybe that's why he left," Mason said, shrugging. "I assume the two of them used to date, right?"

Alaska shook her head. "That's the stupid thing. They've only ever been friends. He's being an asshole because she doesn't spend all her time with him anymore." She wrinkled her nose. "I'll talk to him tomorrow. Make sure he makes amends."

"Always keeping everybody happy," he murmured. "But who keeps you happy?"

She tipped her head to the side, tracing the line of his jaw with her fingertip. "You do," she told him.

"Want me to make you happy again?"

Her eyes widened. "What, now?"

"No time like the present," he told her.

"But we can't leave Ty's party. Not until later."

"Who said anything about leaving?" he asked her. "I was thinking we need to have a talk in your office."

"In my office?" she breathed. Her eyes darkened. He loved the way she was so responsive to him. Even after all these months they couldn't get enough of each other. When they finally moved in together it was going to be carnage.

"Mmhmm." He curled his hand around her waist.

She smiled mischievously. "But people might talk."

"Let them." Because he didn't care. He'd lived here for more than six months now. He'd quickly learned how small towns worked. They'd talk about you for a while then move onto the next thing just as fast. He and Alaska were old news. If anyone noticed the two of them had disappeared for a while, that was their problem.

He slid his fingers through hers and pulled her into reception. There was nobody there behind the counter. Alaska pushed the door to her office open, stepping inside.

Just as he was about to follow, she stopped dead. And let out a little squeal. Her whole body went as stiff as a statue.

He tried to peer into the room but the door was at the wrong angle so he couldn't see anything. Alaska clearly could, though.

"Preach?" she shouted. "Oh my God, is that Marie? Oh Jesus, what are you doing to her?"

"Have a guess," Preach shouted. And Alaska groaned and pushed Mason back.

"Change of plan," she told him, slamming the door closed. "I need to go wash my eyes with bleach."

He laughed at the pained expression on her face. "Do I want to know what was happening in there?" he asked her.

"No. Not now. Maybe one day, when we're old and gray."

Weird how much he liked that idea. The two of them getting old together. Sharing stories and laughing as they sat on the porch swing of their house, watching the world go by together.

She made everything better. For the first time in his life he actually looked forward to each day. Loved making her a coffee as she walked out of the bedroom, bleary eyed and wearing the stupidest pajamas.

Everything about her enticed him. She was his and he wasn't planning on letting that change.

"Okay," he agreed. "When we're old and gray."

And yeah, he'd hold her to that.

Thank you for reading! I hope you enjoyed Mason's and Alaska's story. The next book in the *Winterville* series is EVERY SHADE OF WINTER, North and Amber's story.

ALSO BY CARRIE ELKS

THE WINTERVILLE SERIES

A gorgeously wintery small town romance series, featuring six cousins who fight to save the town their grandmother built.

Welcome to Winterville

Hearts In Winter

Leave Me Breathless

Memories Of Mistletoe

Every Shade Of Winter

THE SALINGER BROTHERS SERIES

A swoony romantic comedy series featuring six brothers and the strong and smart women who tame them.

Strictly Business

Strictly Pleasure (available for pre-order)

ANGEL SANDS SERIES

A heartwarming small town beach series, full of best friends, hot guys and happily-ever-afters.

Let Me Burn

She's Like the Wind

Sweet Little Lies

Just A Kiss

Baby I'm Yours

Pieces Of Us

Chasing The Sun

Heart And Soul

Lost In Him

THE HEARTBREAK BROTHERS SERIES

A gorgeous small town series about four brothers and the women who capture their hearts.

Take Me Home

Still The One

A Better Man

Somebody Like You

When We Touch

THE SHAKESPEARE SISTERS SERIES

An epic series about four strong yet vulnerable sisters, and the alpha men who steal their hearts.

Summer's Lease

A Winter's Tale

Absent in the Spring

By Virtue Fall

THE LOVE IN LONDON SERIES

Three books about strong and sassy women finding love in the big city.

Coming Down

Broken Chords

Canada Square

STANDALONE

Fix You

An epic romance that spans the decades. Breathtaking and angsty and all the things in between.

If you'd like to get an email when I release a new book, please sign up here: https://www.subscribepage.com/carrieelksas

ABOUT THE AUTHOR

Carrie Elks writes contemporary romance with a sizzling edge. Her first book, *Fix You*, has been translated into eight languages and made a surprise appearance on *Big Brother* in Brazil. Luckily for her, it wasn't voted out.

Carrie lives with her husband, two lovely children and a larger-than-life black pug called Plato. When she isn't writing or reading, she can be found baking, drinking an occasional (!) glass of wine, or chatting on social media.

You can find Carrie in all these places
www.carrieelks.com
carrie.elks@mail.com

Made in the USA
Monee, IL
20 February 2023